BABY TAL

Judith Jones

Constable · London

First published in Great Britain 1998
by Constable & Company Limited
3 The Lanchesters, 162 Fulham Palace Road
London W6 9ER

Copyright © 1998 by Judith Jones

The right of Judith Jones to be identified
as the author of this work has been asserted
by her in accordance with the Copyright,
Designs and Patents Act 1988

ISBN 0 09 479130 9

Set in Palatino by Pure Tech India Ltd, Pondicherry

Printed and bound in Great Britain by MPG Books Ltd, Bodmin

A CIP catalogue record for this book
is available from The British Library

I'd like to acknowledge guidance on the background to this book from several publications. If I have strayed anywhere from what I learned the fault is mine and covered by novelist's licence, I hope.

The publications are:

Identifying, Recruiting and Handling Informants, Phil Hanvey, Home Office Police Research Group, 1995.

'Green Grasses', an article by John Weeks in the magazine *Police*, March 1997.

Intelligence, Surveillance and Informants: Integrated Approaches, Mike Maguire and Timothy John, Home Office Police Research Group, 1995.

Alas for the love of women! – Byron

1

When she listened to this child she heard all sorts, some of it lies, but she did listen and remembered what she could. No note-taking, no recorder. That was agreed. This child set precise conditions. This child finger-searched her for a mike before they spoke. He worked swiftly, little lingering. If he was excited, it did not show. Just the same, the first time and the second and third she had resented this handling and froze up slightly, really struggled not to, but revulsion won. To be groped like that by anybody would be bad enough, but to be groped by a kid was eerie. Now, though, she could let it happen more or less without the trauma. In any case, occasionally he would skip the search or forget about it. The body prowl did not seem major with him, however creepy it was to her. His chat drifted every-where, as you would expect from someone of thirteen. She let it drift. Keep him comfortable. Give him control. What amazed her was how his tone remained cheerful. The words he spoke often showed fear, but his voice stayed bright, full of the future.

And, obviously, Kerry would try to make sure he *had* a future. About the same age, her youngest brother was already talking about college and a career. This lad, Christopher, talked about a career too. They both deserved their chance. Christopher's chance depended on her, perhaps too much on her. She chose very carefully the places where they met. The information he provided she used sparingly, not just because some of it was flaky or deliberately false, but because the wrong kind of court case would highlight him and maybe finish him. When you came into this job you accepted risks: risks to yourself and to others. That troubled her and excited her. It was what had made her join.

'I save nearly all this money from you,' he said. 'One day I'll have a stack. Start a shop. A pet shop – animals in cages, so bloody kids can't walk in and pinch them like chocolate.'

'Save it where?'

'In a box.'

'Where?'

'I found a tree, hollow at the bottom.'

'Is that safe?' she said. Oh, God, sometimes she hated children, or *this* child: the stupidity, the carelessness. It was like talking to fog.

'This is a proper box and I make it waterproof,' he said.

'Someone might discover it.'

'Might. So, do I keep it in the house? Dad find something like that, he'd kill me. I mean really fucking kill me. Taking from police. Do you know what he's like when he's mad? Mad.'

'Oh, look, it could be money from a burglary,' she said.

'I wouldn't save that sort of money. I'd spend it. I'd give him a share. He would know where this was from. He'd kill me.'

'Chris, you've never told me anything that could hurt him.'

'Don't matter. It's grassing. He'd kill me. He'd have to, in case it was found out. He couldn't face the street. He's big in the street. He's like the Lord of Daniel Street.'

'And is your mother the Lady?'

'She don't care about all that sort of thing, but she'd agree with him. Got to be.'

'Or you could put the money into the Post Office Savings Bank,' Kerry said.

'They might write me a letter about it. He'd see that. He'd know.'

'Or in some places the police set up a trust fund for children who help and are paid.'

'What's that – a trust fund?'

'You could get the money when you're grown up.'

'No, now,' he said.

'Or clothes. We buy some children clothes, instead.'

'So I go home in a new pair of super trainers. How do I say where I got the fuckers?' he asked.

'Stole them.'

'Money's best. Money now.' Folding the notes he pushed them into the back pocket of his jeans. She would have liked to put an arm around his bony shoulders for a moment, maybe even kiss his skinny neck: give him the big sister warmth, this foolish, invaluable talking child. But she thought he would not

8

care for that. 'A shop, yes,' he said. 'OK, I like the money but that's not why I do it.'

'I know.'

'I'm hunting someone.'

'I know.'

'I want you to get him. I want to get him for you.'

'I know.' Of course she knew. That was why she played him along and led him into terrifying risk. That was why she agonised now and then about this risk.

'Will they bring back hanging for the bastards?' he asked.

'I don't think so.'

'Life. They're out in eight or ten.'

'Some.'

'Dad said nobody can get Coventry Tom anyway. He's too big. He knows people who are too big. He's got stuff on people who are too big. I mean world-wide people, people with fur collars. Keep on his right side.' He scratched a chin spot.

'People do keep on his right side. Yes, he's big. I'll get him.' It sounded arrogant. She knew she probably *was* arrogant and didn't mind, but best not sound like it. 'Well, *we'll* get him.'

'Who?'

'You and me, Chris. And my colleagues, naturally.'

'Oh, *them*.'

'We can't do it alone, you and I,' she said.

'Can't we?'

'Almost,' she replied.

'Coventry Tom's like in high society, you know. A chauffeur and what's called a celebrity suite at the football, TV for action replays.'

'Yes, I do know. I'll most likely see him tomorrow night at a charity ball.'

'What's that – a charity ball?' he asked.

'To raise money for heart research.'

'He gives plenty – hearts, kidneys, lifeboats. That's his way. That's how he gets into society and with big friends who look after him.'

'I know.'

'My dad – people like that, they wouldn't go to this ball, would they?'

9

'They could. Anyone can go. It's more money for the Heart Institute.'

'How much?' he asked.

'Ninety-nine pounds each, dinner and wine included.'

'And dressing up? Bow ties and everything. Shiny black shoes?'

'Evening clothes, yes.'

'That's what I mean. My mum and dad couldn't go somewhere like that. They wouldn't look right. My mum might look all right, if she had the clothes. Once when she was small she had pony lessons, all that. You seen my dad's hands? How do *you* get into society then?' he asked. 'Are the police in society?'

She would have liked to answer that she could go where she liked and that people should be pleased to see her, whoever they were: some piffling provincial social scene wouldn't keep her out. It hurt her to give the true answer, but she did: 'I've got a boyfriend.'

'He's important somewhere? Not police?'

'No, not police,' she said.

'What? With a title? A doctor? Something like that? A media baron?'

'None of those. His firm does the catering – for free. This is large-scale catering.' She did not want him thinking Mark worked for Pizza In Your Porch Home Delivery. 'Businesses contribute like that. It brings helpful publicity.'

'And free tickets.'

'They pay for the tickets.'

'To eat their own food?'

'It's for charity.'

'They pay out of the firm's cash?'

'Probably,' she said.

'This would be the same way Coventry Tom gives, out of his dirty company money. Charity don't care where it comes from as long as they get it. This seems funny – you might be dancing with him.'

'I don't think so.'

'But it could be, if he asked you.'

'He doesn't know me. I'll be there with a party.'

'The top lot from your boyfriend's firm.'

'Yes,' she said.

'But Coventry Tom *could* ask you for a dance, couldn't he? He comes over in his bow tie and says how great the free sausage rolls are to your boyfriend and the business team and he might look at you and say, "Feel like a dance at all, Kerry?" when he been introduced. For charity.'

'I suppose so,' she said.

'He killed a mate of mine.'

'I know.'

'For no reason.'

'I know.'

'So?' he asked. 'If you know.'

'Not enough evidence.'

'They're always saying that. That black boy killed in London. Everyone knows who done it, but not enough evidence.'

'Really, not enough here. We're still trying.'

'I'm looking,' he said.

'Be careful how you look,' she replied.

'Maybe you could keep it in your bank for me and then give it back when I got enough to buy a shop and I'm older.'

'I don't know about that.'

'I'd trust you – would that be a trust fund?'

'Thanks. But I don't think so.' This might put the risk a bit too close to her, not him.

He seemed to understand. He could be child-dim. He could be child-sharp: 'You mean if they got a look at your money in the bank and saw this extra going in and not coming out they'd say, "Hello, what we got here?" Like pinching the grassing money? Do cops look at cops' bank money?'

'Sometimes.'

'They look at everything. I'm on that list, aren't I?'

'What list?' she said.

'Like the register in school.'

'What would you know about school?'

'Bound to be on a list,' he said. 'You ask them for a hundred, two hundred, to pay out to a voice for info, you got to say where it's going. Or you could be on the fiddle.'

'Not your real name. I've told you, Chris. The code name – Duke, like John Wayne.'

11

'Yes. In old films you said. That the one?' he asked. She had proposed the cover name herself, thinking Chris would be flattered, but Kerry had found *she* could be stupid, too. Age arrogant. She had forgotten John Wayne died before Chris was born, and not even TV repeats kept him fresh for boys of this age. 'Baby talk' was how disapproving police colleagues dubbed tips from child informants. And it was almost true. Several of these grasses were not far out of infancy. 'Somewhere they got my real name wrote down,' he said. 'Somewhere a list says Duke is not this John Wayne but Chris Mallard, him who Kerry Lake talks to and buys. Bound to be. For when people from the Home Office look at where the money's supposed to be going.'

'Your real name is locked up. Only myself and one other officer, a very senior officer, are allowed to know that.'

'That's what I mean. A list.'

'Locked up in a real safe, not a box in a tree,' she replied.

'What very senior officer?'

'A really very senior officer,' she said. 'Secure.'

'Who wrote it down? Some secretary, I bet. That's what they all have to do their writing for them, secretaries. Is my name on a computer? Kids hack into that. And I bet you have to write a report or something every time you talk to me. My name in it?'

'It would be your code name, anyway. But I dodge doing a report.' She did put her arm around him now and he didn't pull away, not at all. 'We're going to look after you,' Kerry said. She meant it. She couldn't bear to lose him as a source. And it was more than that. Of course it was. She had a life in her charge.

'Which we?' he asked. 'I don't like it when it's "we", except you and me.'

2

Royalty turned up in person at the Heart Institute ball. The story Kerry heard said that Thomas Ingle-Blake – Coventry Tom as he was so crudely known by some – had personally persuaded the

12

Institute's patron to appear tonight and say a bit before the raffle. Although she was the nominal head, she obviously could not attend every function. Ingle-Blake had done some benign intriguing. This was the talk and most folk Kerry spoke to believed it. Ingle-Blake had all kinds of connections.

After the patron's little speech she drew the first ticket and then stood with him at the side of the stage and shook hands with every winner. Ingle-Blake shook hands with them, too. Kerry found herself wanting to think well of him. She had had some drinks and wanted to think well of everyone tonight. Couldn't law and order and the chase take a small rest? Actually, the law had nothing on Ingle-Blake. There were no convictions, despite some ancient blood-soaked episode in Coventry Street, Soho, London, where he earned his nickname.

When all the prizes had been handed out, their guest danced with Coventry for a couple of numbers, a very slim pale girl in the simple, superb turquoise silk gown, partnered by the tall, hefty, honourable-looking man in elegant tails. He appeared discreetly protective of this brassy wisp of distinction as they slow foxtrotted first to 'Stardust' in the Golden Oldies session. Cameras flashed. Somebody high in the Buck House brigade must surely have checked out Tom before they'd let him get so close to one of their best second string performers. But, as Christopher said, Coventry knew big people, perhaps some of them high in the Buck House brigade. Put it another way, though: would people high in the Buck House brigade let Tom know them if there was a shadow on him? They were into a quickstep now, some inane tune Kerry did not recognise. A vocalist did her best. The song was about scurrying raindrops. Coventry held his partner very respectfully, like a wine waiter fetching something top rate. Watching the royal, Kerry felt part of her self-belief ebb. That could happen now and then. As targets went, wasn't Ingle-Blake a mile or two beyond Kerry's range and rank? It might be much easier to feel well about him than to stalk him. Easier and perhaps safer for Christoper Mallard. No perhaps. Safer. Why not sink into the slick jolly comfort of the evening and of things as they were generally? She went out on to the floor with Mark.

'Well, Tom Ingle-Blake certainly has style,' Mark said.

13

16.00

'Yes.' Coventry Tom was racy, roguish, gaudy, wasn't he? Wouldn't those nice, mild boyo labels do, at least for tonight, and possibly for more than tonight? Probably he was never going to get knighted, no matter how much heart and lifeboat philanthropy he did, but he would have an interesting scrapbook to show his grandchildren, full of distinguished faces. White collar crime did not excite too much police interest these days. Fraud was terribly difficult to nail: fifty failed cases proved it in the last couple of years. Drug dealing at tycoon level was also terribly difficult to nail. All the new law legislation seemed aimed against a different kind of offence – repeated rapes, repeated burglaries. Where the votes lay. Nobody cared about company scams, except business folk who missed out on them. Drugs? They were built into the scene now, accepted.

Another story said Tom had supplied half the raffle prizes tonight but did not want this known. Everybody Kerry spoke to believed this, too, and all of them had heard of the secret generosity. Many said the openhandedness and attempt at concealment were typical of Ingle-Blake. He had bought a raft of raffle tickets himself and won a pair of Leica binoculars and a case of Krug. Of course he put both items back into the draw, but with nearly no fanfare.

The patron and her attendants left before the dinner. Coventry came over to apologise to Mark's chief, Stephen Comble, at his company's table. 'She would have loved to stay, sincerely, but other duties,' he said. 'That girl's a real asset to the Windsors, not like some, regrettably. Wonderful food and wines, Stephen. I know she would have enjoyed herself, and she knew it herself, but time pressed, as can happen with the mighty. Nobody knows that better than yourself.'

'Thank you, Tom,' Stephen, long-time head of the firm said. 'Do you know everyone?' He did the introductions. Almost all of them at the table seemed to have met Ingle-Blake. Kerry, no, though she had often seen him. Whenever it was necessary, more senior officers talked to Coventry, and especially about something as major as slaughter of a child: what she meant about range and rank. 'And this is our newest director, Mark Taber, and his friend, Kerry Lake,' Comble said. Tom shook hands with her and Mark, then drew up a chair and sat at

14

their table, between Peter, the younger Comble, and his wife Alex. Old Comble poured Ingle-Blake a port. In the long hall the music began again, some more whiskery tunes with dud lyrics about roses and farewells. Whiskery people had the money and backed charities.

'I felt really proud we could show her such a grand crowd for the cause,' Ingle-Blake said. 'You and your firm must take a lot of the credit, Stephen. Everyone knew they would feed well. I have to say that charitable work is its own reward, and a wonderfully satisfying reward, yes, but when one can see the delight in the face of such a gracious young woman at what has been achieved here by so much corporate effort, this is a fine bonus.'

'For the success of it all you deserve another dance,' Kerry replied. She liked the notion of equalling with royalty. She felt almost destined to dance with Coventry because of what Chris had said.

'A second gracious young woman!' he cried. 'My, but this is delightful. Will you excuse us, folk – Stephen, Mark?' They were playing 'Georgia' as a slow waltz. He held Kerry with the same gentle respect, his hand wide and uncommunicative across her bare back, his body distant.

'I always wonder what kind of small talk people like that make at these social events,' Kerry said. 'Interesting? Interested?'

Ingle-Blake smiled patiently. 'Is this just opportunism or were you sent to chat to me, sweetie?' he replied. There was something pleasant on his breath – myrrh? Liquorice? It angered her. Crazy? Why shouldn't he smell decent? Ingle-Blake said: 'You're the raw fuzz, aren't you?'

'Well, I'm a police officer, yes, Mr Ingle-Blake. But I still wonder about the royal small talk.'

'You're a fast track girl, I gather. High constabulary prospects. Bramshill College.'

Yes, she was all that. She might be able to prove to him how good she was, given time. 'Gather from where, Mr Ingle-Blake?' she replied.

'That's fame. He's a lucky lad, young Mark – linked to a star and in what could easily be a continuing good job with old Stephen. I must take very good care to return you to Mark completely undamaged.'

15

'Mark would expect that,' she said, laughing.

'I trust so. You know, talking to you, I realise you will bring clear-minded fairness and balance to all aspects of detective work in our city,' he replied. 'It's grand to see someone of your aptitude, and may one say gender, getting recognition. A person with your freshness of vision is essential when such a large part of investigative work is the assessing of dubious information. I think of informants' information, for example. I don't know whether you deal with an informant, Kerry, or grass or nark as the drab terminology goes, but if so I am confident you would see the perils – the perils of error, I mean, of course.'

He spun her suddenly in an unwaltz-like movement, as though to escape a threat. She had felt for a second a hand on her shoulder and assumed someone wanted to intercept and dance with him. But then she heard a woman scream close and above the noise of the band: 'I tried to sneak in earlier when you were with the Highness, you fucking kid killer, but such security. I longed to get to you then, tell her what's what. So who's this piece with the grin, a paid piece?'

Kerry turned and saw she was in street clothes, black slacks and a black leather blouson jacket. The woman was pointing at Kerry, laughing and weeping, her skin drained. 'You ought to know me,' Kerry said.

The woman stretched forward and stared at her. She was about forty, tall, beaky, her brown hair chopped short, tears on her sharp chin, hate right through.

'You don't recognise me in my ball finery,' Kerry said.

She squinted and then gasped. 'Yes, by God, I know you. A cop – came with all the rest of the cops when my son...you came with all the rest of the cops.'

'That's right, Mrs Denton,' Kerry replied.

The music had continued. Dancers kept going but steered wide of them, watched but did not really want to know. Somebody piloted Julia Ingle-Blake, Coventry's wife, past, but they did not stop. Kerry saw two nimble men in evening dress who would be Coventry's walking towards them through the moving crowd, eyes on the woman.

'He killed my boy,' Mrs Denton said. 'So what's a cop doing dancing with the shit?'

'Come along now, dear,' Coventry Tom said with sad amiability. 'Kerry doesn't want to hear all this. These are monstrous, unforgivable words. This is a decent, positive occasion, you know.'

3

True, absolutely, Kerry was a hot-shot cop – picked to rise fast, expecting to rise fast, deserving to rise fast – but she found there were some biggish ugly things still to learn. *Oh, Christ, am I just a very bright unknowing child, not much ahead of Christopher?* The thought came to her at home lying alongside Mark in bed just before dawn. She liked to sleep more or less immediately after good love-making, and the love-making tonight had been so full and fine. Although now and then Kerry might wonder whether she and Mark were spot on for each other, one of these wonderful spells of rightness would suddenly come along and she would feel content. Could anyone do better than that in a relationship? This contentment stayed until half an hour ago, and not just on account of Heart Institute booze, she had been sure of that: no blurring or daft frenzy, just love, a grand rightness.

According to sex manuals, she and Mark ran contrary to the usual post-coital urges of woman and man. She liked to sleep, get those sweet moments into the subconscious for dreams or possible future nourishment. Mark would often want to talk. Mostly it was a mistake to let him. She had discovered this long ago, and rediscovered it now: tried to head it off, but no hope. Mark could slowly drift away from the bonding moment – the fierce blissful closeness – and get chilly and analytical about their lives. Sex put a pruning edge on his generally genial mind. 'Lord, that scene with the woman tonight, Kerry.'

'Awful.'

'How the dickens did she get in?'

'And the way they dealt with her – those chic apes of Coventry Tom. I'm glad I was dancing with him. They'd have known I was a police officer. He knew. I wonder how those thugs would have treated her otherwise.'

'Stephen didn't like it.' There was a boardroom weight to his voice. These days and nights there was often a boardroom weight to his voice. Perhaps she should learn to accept it. After all, he *was* boardroom.

'Well, no, nobody *liked* it, Mark. Safe to say that. Upsetting.'

'This was a decent occasion, but perhaps tainted rather by that outburst.'

'Same words as Coventry's, as a matter of fact. He told Mrs Denton it was a decent occasion, just before those men got to her.'

'I don't really know what Stephen made of it. Nor Peter.'

'Darling, how do you mean, "made of it"?' she asked, but afraid that she might know what he meant.

'Oh, Stephen seemed sympathetic, of course.'

'Who to?'

'You, naturally – the unpleasantness, the unfortunate way you were landed in it.'

She turned away, closed her eyes. 'It would have been worse if – '

'Was that what was intended?' he asked.

She stayed quiet, trying to read this.

'I think Stephen believed this was what was intended,' he said.

She opened her eyes and after a while turned back. 'I don't get you, love. Intended who by?'

'*I'm* not saying it, Kerry. Well, would I, for heaven's sake? It's something Stephen asked, and I think Peter probably thought the same.'

'I'm baffled.'

'Don't want to sound . . . well . . . subservient, Kerry, but I do have to give some attention to how they think,' Mark replied. 'At this stage in things.'

'But what *do* they think?'

'Oh, Kerry, love, from the beginning of the whole episode I picked up little signs. I could see Stephen considered it odd the way you asked Ingle-Blake to dance. You know, just like that. Or seeming to be just like that. That's what Stephen wondered, I

18

could tell. He doesn't know you very well. Perhaps he's taken a bit aback by your impulsiveness, if that's truly what it was. Myself, I love it, if that's what it was. Impulsiveness is your essence. Never lose it.' He turned a little and kissed her briefly on the temple.

'But look, does he really consider it impulsiveness? You're saying he thinks it was set up. A police scheme.' She felt astonished, tried to formulate what he meant. She spoke hesitantly, disbelievingly: 'It would go like this, would it: get Coventry Tom on to the dance floor and stage a confrontation with the mother of a child he's killed? The aim would be to unbalance him by the shock of it, perhaps jolt him into saying something unguarded at last or do something give-away. Even a confession. Mark, is that what Stephen thought?'

Mark yawned noisily, then kissed her again in the same spot, forgivingly. 'Now, you know that's putting it altogether too harshly, love,' he said. 'Ingle-Blake hasn't ever been charged, Kerry, let alone tried and convicted. He runs successful businesses.'

'One of which might be fronting a crack cocaine et cetera trade. Have to say it, Mark.'

'Might. Might. Sure he runs businesses in his own rough and tumble way – something Stephen certainly does not approve of, I can assure you – yes, some corner cutting, no doubt, but that's quite different from what you're suggesting. And what that poor woman suggested.'

'No, he hasn't been charged. We can't get him, Mark. We try, we do. So Stephen wonders if we're forced to lay on some tricks, does he?' She sat up in bed, needing a bit of altitude and dominance. 'Look, Mark, did Stephen actually say any of this?'

'Stephen's genuinely kindly – as I know to my considerable advantage, Kerry – directorships for outsiders in a family firm don't happen all that much – he's genuinely kindly but at the same time very shrewd,' Mark replied. 'Well, he's built a fine business, hasn't he?'

'And is good buddies with other fine businessmen, like Coventry Tom. I hadn't really thought about that, Mark.' *Oh, Christ, am I just a bright unknowing child?*

'Stephen would regard the running of the ball as in part his responsibility. I don't mean just the catering. The whole ambience. He's like that – responsible.'

'Of course.'

'I know he would feel that incident as unfortunate. And, Kerry, I believe you would to, if – '

'Yes, unfortunate,' she said, 'a woman beside herself screaming hate and pain in the middle of a dance floor.'

'And then the royal aspect,' Mark replied. 'Without making too much of that in a silly, sycophantic way, but she caused the disturbance only minutes after a very distinguished ... Anyway, Stephen thinks it might not make the media. Most of the Press party had gone. They were only present to cover the patron bit, thank God. And there would be blatant libel dangers if they reported what the woman screamed. As we've said, nothing against Ingle-Blake but rumour.'

'Stephen *has* spoken about it all to you, then. Spoken a lot. Was he embarrassed to have us – me – at his table?'

'Look, Kerry, I don't necessarily go along with Stephen's view. I know you'd ask someone like Ingle-Blake to dance as ... oh, pretty much as a joke, really.'

'No, I suppose I wanted to see what kind of creature he was.' At Bramshill on the accelerated promotion course they had been warned in seminars against 'demonising': it was wrong to pick out one big villain from the rest and attribute to him/her all the disorder and decay in sight. This, they were told, was not how policing operated, not how crime operated. It simplified matters into symbolism, was the equivalent of making an image of some devil figure and sticking pins in it. This notion stayed with her and not long ago Kerry had made a small voodoo image of Coventry Tom wearing one of his fine suits and stuck those big-style darning needles into it most evenings. Naturally this was private from Mark. She had kept her version of Coventry behind hardback copies of *Alice in Wonderland* and *Through the Looking Glass* in the bookcase. Mark did not go much on *Alice*. Kerry had decided for a while that Bramshill could have things wrong. Maybe there *were* massively evil, massively influential people who did change the state of things, if they were allowed to. There was Hitler, wasn't there, and Pol Pot and – since a

20

child's death was involved – Herod? Now and then Kerry craved the great simplicities. Demons were symbols, demons were real.

Then she wavered. Perhaps it was juvenile to think like this. Yes, juvenile. In police work you chipped away at the small stuff and eventually undermined the big people at the top. So, she had destroyed the Coventry Tom doll – quite a ritualistic destruction, slowly done with scissors and knife. It did not mean Coventry dropped dead in the street, though, did it? Symbolism only, yes.

On the other hand, it did not mean either that she had abandoned the urge to finish him.

Mark said: 'I thought Ingle-Blake took it all pretty well, didn't you?'

She felt weary, hurt, blocked out. 'I do. He's a credit to the Heart Institute. It was Mrs Denton who didn't take things well at all. The grief. The loathing. And then bawling and shouting even more when she was manhandled out.'

'Believe me, Stephen's very aware you have sensitive work to do. It was simply that in the context of – '

She folded back down into the bed and and turned away. 'Oh, well, perhaps Stephen is right. Can we sleep now, though?'

In the morning she regretted this terse cut-off. It was natural for Mark to worry about what the boss thought. She had bosses and worried about what *they* thought: if you were in the police you knew pretty well all there was to know about hierarchy and the frequent requirement to kow-tow. He was sleeping on his side, his face towards her, and she kissed him lightly on the lips. He half awoke, tried for a smile then slid away into unconsciousness. She turned on to her back for a five minutes' think before getting up. Possibly it was natural for Stephen Comble to fret more about ensuring the ball's success than he did over Mrs Denton's state of mind. Possibly it was natural that Mark saw things at least in part as Stephen saw them. It was not just that Stephen employed him. Mark admired him, thought well of his judgement. And Stephen's judgement, plus his son's, said that the regrettable disturbance on the dance floor was certainly that – a regrettable disturbance – and perhaps more. On this last bit they were wrong, but she could understand their thinking. Everyone knew that even the middle classes suspected the

21

police these days. Mark reached out slowly under the bedclothes and put his palm on her stomach. She kissed him briefly once more on the mouth and eased herself out of bed. Just before leaving the flat she looked in on him and said: 'See you tonight, you executive drone.' He opened one eye and waved then slept again. He looked attractive asleep.

4

It was difficult to get hold of Christopher for an unscheduled emergency meeting. She could not telephone. And Chris went to school so rarely that she had next to no chance of spotting him on his way there or when lessons finished. She had often tried to work out some procedure with Chris, but he was never interested enough to make a proper suggestion. Always he said that all she should do was hang about Rush Street or the Square for a while, near the Welcome caff, and he'd probably see her, get to her. Invariably he'd finish with a warning that she must not come close, because he'd probably be 'with people'. If he saw her he'd leave his friends and make for Holt's Corner, where she could pick him up in the car.

So, she dawdled today. Rush Street had record shops and a kind of old-fashioned milk bar called Veronica's, though Veronica herself moved on twenty years ago. The Square sported more music shops, the caff and a couple of bistro-style restaurants with tables and chairs outside in good weather. The area was teenage gangland. All day and late into the evening the kid crowds swarmed, talking, planning, smoking, laughing, fighting, maybe occasionally buying something in a record shop or one of the eateries. Kerry was still young enough to be excited by the scene herself. It had a fine noisy zing and she could feel its superiority to school. Of course, of course, school was better if you wanted to move on in a few years to a job. This kind of pavement society made it easier for the kids who did stick at school: reduced competition. She had stuck at school herself. Now look at her – in a job that gave some pleasure and some money and some prospects and a range of anxieties, especially this morning. Who could say for sure that this chattering young careless mob didn't have things right? Well, didn't she know who could say they didn't: some of the kids' parents, most of Kerry's police colleagues, all teachers, all dole clerks? And she'd say herself they didn't have things right, wouldn't she?

She walked around for a while but could not see Chris. God, it might be one of his school days. Perhaps there was a free trip to Stratford-upon-Avon or London. It was too chilly yet for eating outside and she found a window seat in one of the restaurants on the Square and had some late breakfast. At the flat earlier it had seemed better to leave quickly. Mark might have got out of bed if he'd heard her making coffee, and she wanted no more talk about what happened at the ball. She had managed to settle with herself that his attitude was all right, hadn't she? And that *he* was all right, hadn't she? There had been no basic shift. She did need to dodge more discussion in case things went rancid again, though. She hated those downturns in their relationship, was frightened by them. They had a grand, loving long-time understanding, she and Mark, and you took care of something like that up to a point.

She saw Christopher with a couple of other boys – 'people', as he'd call them – watched them come strutting free along the street and go into the Welcome. They were dressed the same: black school trousers, white shirt, navy tie, no jackets. One had a satchel. As far as the parents knew, they went to their classes, mopped up the State education to make them one day more useful to the State. She was not sure whether Chris had seen her. The three boys were tied up in talk with one another, as if they hadn't met for a term, though most likely they had entered the Welcome together at just about the same time yesterday and the day before, a neat timetable of dodging off. She finished her coffee and toast, paid the bill but sat on watching the door of the Welcome. In a while, Chris came out alone, glanced at her without any sign, then turned and walked towards Holt's Corner. She left and hurried to the car. He was waiting when she arrived at the Corner, looked around anxiously once, then climbed into the back and lay down along the seat. 'What?' he

23

said. 'God, Kerry, it's only a day since I saw you. I haven't had time to get no more on Coventry yet.'

She did not answer but drove to the other side of the town and found a space in a Sainsbury's car-park they sometimes used for meetings. He stayed stretched. 'I think you should take special care, Chris,' she said.

'So you come showing yourself, sitting in windows.'

'It's a bit pressing.'

'Anyway, I do take special care. Bet you hardly knew if I'd seen you just now.'

'Special special care, Chris,' she replied. 'And no contact at all between you and me for a while.'

'This fuss about using kids as grasses? I seen it on TV. You scared? Someone says – someone in the government or social services – something like that – someone on about not using kids as grasses without the parents' permission. Oh, God! They fucking stupid, you reckon, Kerry? Have they heard what it's like in this sort of place?'

'I'm not sure if you're known about,' she replied.

'Of course I'm known about. I'm on the list, my name in the safe – so you say.'

'No, I mean *known* about,' she replied.

He went silent. Then he said: 'Known about outside? Like street people?'

'It's possible.'

'Who?'

'Chris, I don't want you digging around Coventry Tom. Not for a while.' He was a source, but he was a youngster to be looked after. The second was more important for now.

He sat up and leaned over the passenger seat to talk to her, his face bright with fright and anger. 'What – some cop brass told you cool it? Coventry been putting the screws on one of your bosses – that Harry Bell, chief of detectives? Or someone big that Coventry knows been putting the screws on. I hear he knows even royalty. That's what I heard.'

'Yes, he knows royalty.'

'Well, you see what I mean?' Chris replied. 'He gets the Queen Mum or some lady of the bedchamber to ring up one of your chiefs and say, "Pray, leave our dear fucking Thomas alone on

24

account of work for famous charities and we're going to make him a Lord or OBE soon."'

'I talked to him. He warned me about grasses.'

He gasped. 'You talked to him personal? At that ball? The bastard *did* ask you to dance then, did he?'

'Sort of. He might know about our arrangement, Chris.'

He lay back again. 'A police officer dancing with rubbish like Coventry Tom!'

'Go low profile for a while. Stay among crowds as much as you can, will you, please, Chris? The Welcome's probably all right. Or even go to school.'

'If he knows, it's too late.' The terror was into his voice, turning it high and squeaky. 'This is Coventry Tom we're talking about.'

'I'm not totally sure he knows. The talk was vague. No names.'

'He didn't whisper to you while you was dancing that Duke equals Chris Mallard, did he? Someone high been filling him in?' he asked.

'He was talking about informants in general, that's all.'

'He got you worried, though.'

'Let's be careful for a while.'

She started the car but did not move off at once.

'I'm on my own – that what you mean?' he said. '"Thank you Chris and goodbye."'

'Of course not.'

'I can't tell my dad, ask him to help, can I?'

'Would you recognise any of the people who work for Coventry?' she replied. 'Just so you can keep an eye. I'm going to keep an eye, too.'

He groaned. 'What's that mean? Don't you start hanging around near me,' he said. 'Sorry, Kerry, but – '

'This won't be noticeable.'

'Now, please, Kerry. Not like doing it in neon.'

'There's a dark-haired quite fat lad, thick lips, thick nose, about thirty-eight, who operates for Tom. And another, shorter, heavier, older – fiftyish – pretty bald but with some fair strands. Both quick on their feet. I don't know how they'd normally dress. I've only seen them in evening gear. But they're probably on file. I'll try to let you know who they are.'

'Raymond Nide and Jack Sonntag,' he said.

'Met them?'

'Seen,' he said. 'They're in my Filofax.'

She had a giggle. 'These are the sort of folk to be looking out for. It might not be Coventry himself.'

She started to drive him back towards the Welcome. 'Listen,' he said, 'I want to tell you where the hollow tree is. The box. You could have that, keep it, couldn't you? This is money that's supposed to be gone a while ago. Nobody could come back at you for it. This is nearly a thousand.'

'It's your money,' she said.

'Yes, but what if suddenly I can't...'

'It's yours.'

'Yes, but if – Look, I really want you to have it. Buy something nice. Like, you know, sort of a memorial.'

'Don't be so bloody silly, Chris. We're going to look after you.'

He told her where the tree was, all the same, spelled out landmarks. 'I don't want none of that money going to my dad, mind. Some to my mother, if you like, but as a secret, or he'd have it, and not too much. I would rather it was all for you. Buy like a really good brooch with genuine stones, something you could wear to charity balls now while you're still quite youngish but which you could wear on older dresses when you get elderly, not flash but quality.'

She put him down near the Square. Normally, he would walk away from the car immediately, no looking back, as though disowning her, or more as if she did not exist. That was all right. She didn't need some child to tell her she existed. Today he paused, the passenger door still open. She saw he wanted her to say how they could keep contact: first time the initiative had come from him. She was ashamed to realise she would like it better if he had simply gone, disappeared, freighting her responsibility for his life and safety away with him. Yes, *Thank you Chris and goodbye.* She said: 'I'll drive past Holt's Corner every Monday at noon. You'd never go to school on a Monday morning right after the weekend, would you? And by noon you should be out of bed.' He nodded, slammed the door and walked away towards the Square, looking from the back as jaunty as ever.

Kerry went to headquarters for an update meeting on the Timothy Denton case. There was a big turn-out, including all the brass up to Martin Mainse, Assistant Chief, Operations, Harry Bell, head of CID, and his sidekick, Douglas Quinn. She sat next to Claire Bater, another young sergeant, who had done a lot of basic work with Kerry at the start of the inquiries. After they had been listening for twenty minutes, Claire whispered: 'They talk too loud about eventual success. It sounds like defeat. The inquiry's being wound down.'

'We'll see about that,' Kerry whispered back.

'Good for you.'

In the afternoon Mark rang her from his office. 'Look, Kerry, Stephen is still quite a bit concerned about what happened at the ball. Peter too, but especially Stephen. Possibly you'll see it as interfering, even naïve. Stephen is aware of that. Nonetheless, he'll – '

'What is it, darling?'

'It distresses him to think of these undercurrents of hatred flowing hidden in the city, leading to such a terrible outburst. Stephen was born and brought up here, you know, and fancied himself at understanding the community, but this really rocked him. "Undercurrents of hatred" is his own phrase, and, honestly, I don't think it's an exaggeration, not after what we saw at the ball.'

'No, not an exaggeration. The hate was genuine.'

'He's had time now to consider matters more fully and I don't believe he thinks any longer that you and your colleagues and that sad woman set up the encounter, Kerry. I was able to persuade him there's been no plot – explained it was entirely in character for you to make a spontaneous social move towards Thomas Ingle-Blake.'

'Thanks, Mark.'

'It could have been anyone. But what Stephen would like to do, in his constructive responsible way – his "interfering" way, as he might well term it himself – what he has in mind is to clear the air by setting up a meeting in his own home between Mrs Denton – plus Mr Denton if there is a Mr Denton – and Tom Ingle-Blake.'

'No Mr Denton. Not now.'

'Right. Stephen and Peter really feel for that woman. She, too, is of this city and represents something that Stephen sees as most depressing. You, of course, are also invited. And myself. He's already spoken to Tom, who readily agreed, absolutely readily, Stephen said. Ingle-Blake is as sickened by rumour as is Stephen himself. Tom would be glad of the chance to show some slides which apparently demonstrate he was actually away in London when this lad was killed. You know how business people like presentations with visual aids. Both Stephen and Ingle-Blake – and Peter, too – they all feel that for this kind of ill-will to fester is potentially destructive of the whole local social fabric. Additionally, Stephen does not like the idea of being associated with someone targeted by the police – I mean, in his own – Stephen's – interest. A taint can spread. He yearns for clarification, for, yes, truth. Stephen says that Tom really "leapt" at this opportunity to have matters expressed openly and openly discussed in what one might call a neutral setting and with a police officer in the room, among others.'

'I don't think the – '

'The thing is, Kerry, Stephen has no access to Mrs Denton and suggested I ask whether you would be prepared to approach the lady and invite her to such a meeting, stressing all the safe-guards I've mentioned. Stephen thinks confidentiality might be wise at least at this stage. That is, he would prefer it if you did not actually advise colleagues or your superior officers of the arrangement. Could it be treated as a social occasion only, in a private residence? At this stage. Perhaps I shouldn't be saying such things by phone.'

'This is a direct line. You're OK.'

There was a pause. Then Mark said: 'Tell me, Kerry, do I sound like a complete company-man creep, doing my master's bidding – in a sense taking sides against you? I hate that notion, love. Really, it's not like that.'

Thank God he could come up with these harsh glimpses of himself. They were his salvation. Yes, almost. 'When does he want to do this?' she asked.

'Soonest. Within a week or so? It's the festering aspect that troubles him.'

'Bit of a rush?'

'It's a measure of his sincerity,' Mark replied. 'Perhaps it would be useful to you. That's you personally. Haven't they been keeping you at the edge of this case? You could sidestep them. This will be face-to-face with Ingle-Blake in far more convenient circumstances than a dance floor.'

'I'll think about it,' she said.

'And you'll call me back? Stephen would like to know and alert Ingle-Blake if in principle it's on. Obviously, we still have to find what Mrs Denton thinks.'

'I'll call you back,' she said.

She did about half an hour later. 'I'll try it,' she said. She had not really given it much thought but had spent the half- hour worrying about Chris Mallard, still harrowed by guilt that she would have ditched him so easily. There was a duty to compensate and she would start keeping a guardian eye on him from this evening. It had also occurred to her that next week Coventry Tom could have the most unassailable alibi ever if something rough happened to Chris while Coventry was in peace discussions at the home of a commercial eminence, a police officer in attendance.

'Fine,' Mark said. 'See you later, darling.'

'It might be a good bit later.'

In the evening she went back to Rush Street and the Square. Kerry did not know much about disguise, but she kept a long old top coat in the office and a dark soft hat that she could pull down over her ears. She had worn this coat when she first went out with Mark, one reason for not junking it. Sometimes when she had it on, Kerry could think herself back to the certainties of those early days and nights: certainly the coat worked pretty well as disguise. It had a good deep collar which she turned up. Chris would probably still recognise her, but that did not matter too much. What she did not want was to be noted around here twice in a day by anyone else. There might be people who knew who and what she really was, the way Coventry had known who and what she really was. And even those who did not know might make a guess at it if they saw her patrolling and re-patrolling. The police were always expected on these liberated streets. That's what liberated meant.

She did not come across Chris, nor either of the friends he had been with earlier. The evening crowd seemed slightly older.

There were leather boys with their bikes, and some girls in expensive casual gear, maybe too expensive for kids dodging off school. Her coat would not rate much. Perhaps Chris was at home. That did not comfort her. She drove to his street, parked about a hundred yards from the house and watched. A light burned downstairs. The curtains were drawn, and she could see nothing. Although Kerry realised the vigil might be useless, she decided to wait at least a couple of hours. It made her feel better – more *responsible*, to pick up Mark's word about Stephen – less arrogantly ruthless and selfish with Chris's life. At the headquarters meeting earlier the ACC had referred briefly to protests by MPs about the use of children as informants: their vulnerability.

After half an hour someone abruptly pulled open the passenger door, climbed in and sat beside her. 'Dozy,' he said. 'You lock the doors when on surveillance.'

Even in the dark, she had the impression of silver upon silver: silver hair, silver moustache, a gleaming lightweight silver grey suit, a silver tie backed by a white shirt. Not silver shoes, black lace-ups: but they had been polished so ardently they shone more than the rest of him. Vic Othen was an ancient, active, nice-smelling dandy, and probably the oldest detective constable in the force, perhaps the world. Vic was someone who knew everything, except how to pass promotion exams. Or possibly he considered them beneath him. He should have retired an age ago, but by some wangle they kept finding special role names for the work he did, and pushed his money up enough to make him stay. As some told it, he earned more than an inspector. As all admitted, he was worth it. He was called Community Role Co-ordinator at present, a title deftly fashionable and giving away no clue to what he actually did. 'What goes, Kerry?' he asked. 'This is one of my bits of *terre*, you know. When there are ops here I'm supposed to be told. If they put an accelerated promotion girl in it must be serious. And all muffled up like . . . like a detective.'

'Just a personal thing,' she said. 'You're not being cut out, Vic.' Who cut out Vic?

'You did some work on the Coventry margins, didn't you? It's about that?'

'Personal,' she replied. She did not answer to this lad, old and venerable as this lad might be.

'Ah, someone's been teaching you interrogation resistance,' he said, 'even if they didn't teach you not to sit in an unlocked car. People being surveyed can survey you, you know. Think what happened to Jamie Dove.' He stared at her for half a minute or so. She outranked him already, and would probably outrank him a bit more before he retired, but he looked at her as if she hardly counted. 'Must I work out for myself why you're alone at night in Daniel Street, dressed like the flower girl in *Pygmalion*?'

'I knew you'd like it, Vic.'

He was slight, small-featured, only just up to police height, somehow still powerfully attractive. Kerry was not the only one who thought so. She had heard Claire talk wistfully about him, and Jane Nove-Young. It might be the combination of gloss, cheek and indestructibility. His voice was gentle, maybe fashioned to make him seem a pushover in a fight or in court. People discovered this was wrong, even QCs, and especially QCs. She would have preferred he was not in the car with her now, but if it had to be anyone she would have picked Vic, in case she slipped towards self-doubt again. Somehow Vic made those he worked with believe that things would always be manageable and that nothing too grave would ever occur to mess up one of his great suits or his brave silver coiffure. Vic would continue and continue in the job and eventually delight fellow inmates in a lucky old people's home with his stories of London tailoring and discovery of the perfect deodorant.

'And then I hear you're twice around the Square and Rush Street today,' he said. 'Some mission?'

'Just general observing.'

'Helping out the school attendance officer, I expect,' he replied. There was a No Smoking sticker at the side of her windscreen. He lit up now and burned away about half the cigarette with his first draw. 'You won't mind if I share this personal observation stint, will you, Kerry? Fascinated. But I wonder sometimes – it's probably age, unkind wear and tear – I wonder whether someone like Coventry can ever be got.'

'I've come across that idea from others,' she said.

'Commonplace among small-time villains. Tom they see as impregnable now. That's folk wisdom, Kerry. Well, normally I listen to it.'

'He's only – '

'That's why I love this – you turning out against him on a personal whim. You're a tonic, kid.'

She turned to look at him in case he was laughing. But Vic had gone deep into another mighty pull at the cigarette.

'I can believe in you,' he said, reluctantly freeing the smoke from his body. 'You know fuck all – if you'll excuse me, Sergeant Kerry – but you've got that lovely, inimitable committed burn and egomania. Guard them. I mean, dancing with the sod in the Heart ball! Did you set it up with Mrs Denton? This is lively, so fucking lively! This is creative. And then all the rest of it.' He waved at Daniel Street, the cigarette stub doing a glowing return trip in his hand. He lit another from it. 'A lesson.'

'I don't really know whether this is to do with Coventry,' she replied.

'Everything worthwhile's to do with Coventry, isn't it?'

'So, you know about this lad, do you, Vic?' She pointed with her thumb towards the Mallard house.

'Your bony pal called Duke and/or Chris?' he replied. 'The Holt's Corner pick-ups? Yes, I'd say he's in genuine peril. I don't think it's out of proportion for you to be here late and fretting. I like the human side. As you say, personal. They're not going to worry very much about him on the top floor, are they, Kerry, because Duke/Chris never comes up with anything of substance.'

'It's a slow job, Vic.'

'That's what I said, everything worthwhile's to do with Coventry. Your lad's been working at it in his gradual little way. He does hear gossip.'

She winced. 'Does he talk to you as well?' she asked.

'He's another one with a mission,' Vic replied.

'Anyway, I make some of my good low league arrests look as if they started with a tip from Chris. They keep letting me buy him. But he's never going to grass on mates or his father or small-timers.'

'I believe it,' Vic replied.

'He makes his father sound like a savage. I don't swallow it.'

'Mallard? Dimmish. Dangerous temper. Occasionally works with guns – carrying them, not using them. So far. Chicken-

32

feed burglaries, mostly. Leads a little troupe. A decent streak here and there. Hello.'

A woman came out of the Mallard house and walked to the front gate. She did not seem to look their way but stared in the opposite direction, as though waiting for someone.

'His mother's spotted us?' Kerry asked.

'I'd say so. What did you expect? Very sensitive people live in these streets. Folk here outblip radar.'

The woman returned to the house and shut the door.

Vic said: 'Back at the buildings I hear some do ask what young Duke provides for his hundreds. Eight going on ten, is it now? He keeps it in a tree, you know. Of course you do. He'd trust you all the way. And quite right.'

'Can you . . .'

'Keep Coventry off him?'

'You're gun-trained, aren't you, Vic?'

'It's something no detective ever outgrows, you know,' Vic said.

'What?'

'Caring for the tipster. They give us their soul and being, along with the rumour and facts. That's very binding.'

'Can you help me look after him?' she replied.

'I'll try. You deserve that. You're a girl who'll get a grip on tomorrow. That kind of push and confidence.'

'I wondered if Coventry might do it just by breathing a word to Chris's dad,' she said.

'So you *do* think Will could be wild.'

'Could he?'

Vic gestured with his cigarette hand again, another red meteor flight, this time indicating the Denton house more precisely. 'If so, curtains.'

5

Ingle-Blake said: 'Mrs Mallard, it's very kind of you to come over and see me.'

'One of your people calls at my house and says it's something urgent about Christopher, of course I'm going to come, aren't I?' Helen Mallard had never seen Coventry Tom before, though, of course, she'd heard of him. It surprised her how kindly he looked, a frown of sympathy like the best sort of ambulanceman, his eyes rich with the desire to help.

'Well, yes, it *is* urgent,' he said.

'Is he here? Is he all right?'

Ingle-Blake moved a hand in the air and chuckled. 'Here? No, no. All right? I expect he's all right. I should think he'll be where he usually is at this time of day – with his mates around the Welcome – wouldn't you, Mrs Mallard? Or at school, of course – mustn't slander him. No. When I asked Raymond to tell you it was urgent I didn't mean there had been an accident to Christopher, or anything of that sort. God forbid. Sorry if I've perturbed you unnecessarily. But urgent in the sense of – I think there *is* a problem, Mrs Mallard. And I wanted to see whether you and I could tackle it without troubling Will or Christopher himself, at this stage. I'm a great admirer of your hubbie. It would give me real pleasure if I thought I could help him – and help you and the boy as well, naturally. Oh, I knew Will would be out when I sent Ray around. I worry about Will. He's so exposed in some of the work he chooses. Unnecessary.'

She tried not to let the cheery flow of talk and the setting put her off balance. Coventry lived outside the city in a done-up super-kitchened couple of farm cottages banged together, with proper slaughterable sheep in sight through the window of this room, and what looked to her like pretty good old furniture all around, genuine dark wood, well polished up. It would piss her off to have that sort of stuff at home now, but he would not do his own cleaning, nor his wife. Helen could have named most of the pieces in the room and put a date to them: mainly Regency or a bit earlier. There had been spells in her childhood and youth when she and the family lived in attractive conversions like this and with accessories like this, including sheep. Her father had had periods of tearaway success with the range of businesses he ran between the 1960s and the 1980s, and when on an up he had tended towards this kind of restored rural property. When he was down they had lived more or less anywhere.

34

From those good days, Helen recognised now all the quality signs of Ingle-Blake's place: no artex ceilings, no bike in the passage. Of course, it would never be called a passage here but hall, with flowers on an oblong table probably not just because she was coming but routine, and changed every day for freshness. There were pictures that could be pictures not just prints and in the main room more tiptop timber on show in the floors, and more polish and more work. Many people like Coventry thought carpets were unsuitable among farm animals. Her father had been that way, too. 'Expose the handsome boards,' he used to cry. In some of the poorer houses there had been no carpets either, nor polished boards, only linoleum or mats. She thought she might even have a memory of newspapers. Helen had glimpsed the Ingle-Blake kitchen through an open door and seen a grey flagstone floor there around the gorgeous units. 'My wife's upstairs,' he said. 'She'll join us shortly. I know she's keen to meet you. You'll see I've made some tea. Does that suit?'

The cups were china, no question. He put Helen's near her on a little card table. She was sitting in a heavy beigish armchair. He was opposite on a beigish sofa. He had on a real country-style check sports coat and beigish cord trousers. He said: 'Well, I've often wondered whether I could find Will a spot in one of my concerns, and now I think there might soon be an opening that would really suit. Prospects.'

'Will does his own thing. He's had a lot of practice.'

'I know it. His dash is a quality that appeals.'

'Oh, yes? What problem with Chris, Mr Ingle-Blake?' she replied. 'What's urgent?'

'I'd like you to talk to him, that's all. In private. No need for Will to be involved. He might turn hasty, and I wouldn't wish that.'

Yes, Will *could* turn hasty, if that was the word. Will was good and full of hope and half full of weakness and liable now and then to be unthinking. 'Look,' she said, 'is this about...If it's about the boy Timothy...Well, I've got to tell you, Mr Ingle-Blake, Chris has a real down on you. I'm pretty sure of that. I believe he thinks you – '

'Mrs Mallard, one evening soon, very soon, I hope to meet up with the mother of Timothy Denton – the boy who died so sadly and violently – and I'm going to convince her – well, I certainly hope I'm going to convince her – that these gross rumours are entirely that, rumour. They mislead lads like your boy, and many others who are older and should be more careful in separating tales from truth. This meeting will be in the home of a celebrated local businessman of unimpeachable reputation, and in the presence of a police officer who knows something of the case.'

The words scared her. They were flip, unfamiliar kinds of words to her these days: *gross* and *celebrated* and *unimpeachable*. She knew what they meant pretty well, but they still unnerved her. These were not the sort of words she heard in the house with Will or Chris. She hadn't even heard talk like that when married to Duncan. This was how people spoke in some other sort of life where they put on a style. She thought she might be able to manage that kind of life after a bit of a refresher, but she was not sure about Will and certainly not about Chris. Was she supposed to help push them in that direction? Was that why she was here? Ingle-Blake spoke the words of big power and probably big double cross. Lately, she was only used to small power and small double cross. She did not know whether she was ready to move on and up. Will often told her he had potential and merely needed openings, but she would never have bet much on it. She thought he might be joking when he said it, anyway. Chris she would try to stop moving on and up, if Coventry Tom was on and up. Will was into miniature lawlessness and could more or less handle it, and if he could more or less handle it so could she. What marriage had come to mean. Chris she would have liked to keep out of lawlessness altogether, although she knew it might be a bit late. She looked at Coventry's face and saw there sorrow at being wrongly judged and the longing to care for others. She knew she must try to look deeper.

'Are you afraid of a thirteen-year-old boy, Mr Ingle-Blake?' she said.

'I'm sure he's a good lad and will sort himself out eventually.'

'Do you know Chris?'

'This is a boy who's built a personal way of life for himself,' he replied. 'I certainly don't object to that. Rush Street, the Square and the Welcome – in a way one wishes one were young enough oneself for it. Comradeship. Plus he does branch out. He's got other friends. Or one, at any rate.'

36

He stood up suddenly and went and locked both doors to the room.

'Don't get anxious,' he said. 'I won't ambush you. I want us to watch something that it's best few people know about. I think you'll agree.' From a drawer in one of the old cabinets he brought out what looked at first like a rolled piece of bed sheet. Then she saw it was a small screen. He hung it from a picture rail. He opened another cabinet and produced a projector which he plugged in before setting it on the dining-table pointed towards the screen. He drew the curtains then switched on the projector and prepared to drop in a slide. 'I'm sure you're the kind of mother who would warn her son against getting into a car with a stranger. Well, it's all right. This is not a stranger.'

On the screen she saw Christopher standing at a spot she recognised as Holt's Corner. He looked persecuted, angry, more like Will than she had ever seen him before, eyes big with pity for himself.

'This is quite a regular rendezvous point,' Ingle-Blake said. He replaced the slide with another. 'I don't know if you recognise this car, Mrs Mallard, or the driver for that matter.'

Yes, she recognised the car. It had remained parked and occupied not far from the house for so long the other night that she had gone out to check whether it was some sort of trouble for Will, police or other worse trouble. Parked vehicles with people in them often equalled menace – basic wisdom. She had not been able to see much, except that the vehicle was an orange Cavalier and that there was certainly one person in it, maybe more. She had watched a lighted cigarette move in slow arcs about the passenger side. It would have been stupid to go closer. Not many in their street would come out to help if they heard bumps or screaming. '*Should* I recognise them?' she asked.

'I'd have thought the vehicle might dawdle down your street now and then, keeping an eye.'

'On what?' she said. 'On who?'

The slide showed only the car and a young woman driver. He changed it again. The next caught Christopher seeming to step out towards the Cavalier. In the next the rear door of the car was open and Chris bent to enter. The last slide showed another side shot of the Cavalier, obviously moving. The door was shut and the driver appeared to be still alone in it. 'Oh, he's there,' Coventry said, 'flat on the back seat. Security, you know.'

'Is she the police?' Coventry Tom had been sharp to mention the shock of seeing Chris get into a car with some unknown driver. Helen felt he was being shipped away from her care, as if for ever. That was stupid, stupid, wasn't it?

'I can't let you take these slides, I'm afraid. You see the risk to your boy, I'm sure.'

He switched off and opened the curtains, then put the projector and screen away and unlocked the doors. He sat down opposite her again.

'I hope the shock has not upset you. Would you like a brandy?' he asked.

'Who took those pictures and made the slides?' she said.

'Good private people. No worry on that score, believe me, Mrs Mallard.' He became silent. She was aware of him watching her with old-fashioned concern.

'He's bought?' she asked.

'Oh, yes. He's quite a profitable little company. Anyone would understand why he can't be bothered with school.'

'How do you know this, how? I've never seen any cash. Chris doesn't spend big.'

'There *is* money, Mrs Mallard. That's how these things work. A stash. I've given my folk instructions that they are not to touch it. It's so important to be fair to the lad. Whatever happens now, those hundreds have been won by him and he's entitled to enjoy them.'

'Hundreds? You're sure?'

'They value him. He's got potential as long as . . .'

'You said "whatever happens". What's it mean?'

'Always there are uncertainties,' he replied.

She had that feeling again: that sense of being squashed by things around her – the nice-looking bits of historical furniture and the pictures mixed in with this horrible fucking gear, the projector and screen. Her voice would not do much for her. Her mouth had dried up. She would not even be able to spit as far as his friendly face.

'One thing you can be sure of, Mrs Mallard,' he said, 'I'm not going to put on picture shows here for all the rag-tag. Why, not even my wife knows about these slides, which was why I locked the doors. Likewise the cabinet is kept locked. Your little lad is safe with me. I've no kiddies myself, but I can understand something of what a mother might feel, I think. Well, one reason I so want to see Mrs Denton and clear her mind of these awful suspicions.'

'Did *her* boy grass?' she replied.

'Well, who knows, who knows, Mrs Mallard – except the police, of course?'

'Is that why they hang back?' she asked.

'*Do* they hang back?'

'Would they want it known they put a child in such raw peril?'

'Well, who knows what they would want?' he said. 'I agree with you that they have not been efficient in seeking the killer. They promulgate disgraceful scuttlebutt, certainly. Their limit.'

He stopped and seemed to be waiting for her. 'And if I talk to Chris?' she asked.

'In your own terms, absolutely, Mrs Mallard. This is mother to son. Am I going to lay down what's to be said in such conversations? Would I be capable of it even if I wished?'

'I tell him to pull back? Not to go sniffing around your life and businesses and reporting to this girl cop?'

He nodded slightly and then said: 'One way of putting it. My feeling is that such a worldly-wise boy – I meant that in the very best sense, obviously – a boy like your Christopher would not wish to blacken business concerns where his own father might be engaged, and profitably engaged, Mrs Mallard. Perhaps you know about the quite dire uncertainties of business, and I can't see that you any more than Chris would want him to aim at that kind of negativism and damage either. Certainly Will himself would disapprove. That's what I meant when I said he might turn hasty. If Will heard there were prospects for him in a good company and then discovered that his own son was seeking to undermine that company – foolishly seeking to undermine it, but nonetheless devoting himself to that – well, I don't know how Will might react, I'm afraid. Will's very much a man of his culture, although, as you say, there is definitely this fine streak of independence to him, also.'

'And when I'm talking to Chris I should mention what happened to Timothy Denton?' she said. 'No need. He never stops thinking of that.'

'They have a wonderful sense of loyalty and friendship, lads of that age.'

'It frightens him, I expect,' she said. 'But maybe not enough. Perhaps he thinks whoever killed his pal could not risk killing him as well because then the police would really have to get workish. The media would chase them.'

'It would worry me if I believed he thought like that, Mrs Mallard, and probably worries you, too. A child could miscalculate. What I mean is that the great danger to Christopher might not come from whoever it was who killed Timothy, but from a whole range of folk with very inflexible prejudices against grassing – should information about his link with this woman officer somehow become general, which, obviously, I say again, God forbid. Will is certainly not the only one who could be hasty in those circumstances.'

'Listen, Coventry, if Will or any other sod and I mean *any* other sod ever gets shown those slides or told about – '

'But I want to view this whole thing positively,' he replied. 'I see a family with such interesting opportunities. *Your* family, Mrs Mallard. The kind of post I have in mind for Will would be responsible and paid as responsible, naturally, but safe – not what one might call front line. He should be taken away from the unnecessary risk I mentioned. I don't know whether you're happy with the place in Daniel Street. Perhaps you regard that sort of area, that sort of local school, as one reason that Christopher has become a ... I certainly would not see it as too late for this gifted boy to be taken out of that environment and set down elsewhere – encouraged by the surroundings and good education towards the kind of academic and career achievement he is patently capable of. I do like people working for me to live in helpful neighbourhoods. It's a plus for the businesses, you see, as well as for them. My companies have a policy of assisting folk towards purchase of sound properties in favourable spots. I'm sure you and Will would also want – Why here's Julia now. Yes, come in, darling. Mrs Mallard and I were just talking about her son's future – the wonderful possibilities. He's thirteen.'

40

'Oh, yes,' Julia Ingle-Blake said, slowly entering the room. 'Exciting. How one envies you, Mrs Mallard – to be able to watch a boy growing like that into the fascinating promise of the next millennium.'

She might be a bit older than Coventry, say forty-three or four. Coventry could still be late thirties. She was tall and big-nosed, with a long olive-skinned face and short dark hair. Helen Mallard was reminded of an actor she'd seen playing a Spanish bullfighter in a Movie Channel picture not long ago. She wore a pale suede belted jacket and cream skirt made of some imitation skin, maybe shark. It was all right for her age more or less. She came and sat in an armchair near Helen.

'Do you have a picture of your son, Mrs Mallard?' Julia Ingle-Blake asked.

Helen almost replied that Coventry had at least three, but then wondered whether she really knew nothing of the slides. Helen wanted to believe this sad, dignified woman was not tied into all the major muck of her husband's life. A possibility. 'Not on me,' she replied.

Julia seemed to get herself together before she spoke again, settled her big unhappy face. 'I miscarried with a boy, you know. I can't have any more. He'd be around your son's age. So I quite like looking at pictures. Long, long time ago and it doesn't bother me much now. I can find pleasure in parents' pleasure. I'm sure your lad will take the world by storm. We thought of adopting, but I'm not sure they would let us.'

'Mrs Mallard and I were talking just before you came in, dear, about the destructive power of rumour.'

'They do have to be careful, Tommy,' Julia Ingle-Blake replied.

6

When Helen reached home she found that Will had a couple of his friends in and the house was full of good noisy laughter and excitement. They were sprawled shirt-sleeved around the living-

41

room on the 1970s suite, some sketches and an AA road map strewn across the floor between them. The three shouted a greeting to Helen and Jake Lowe jumped up and danced a couple of steps with her on his skinny long legs, humming 'Always'. Will and Oscar Knight joined in with the words.

'So where've you been, Helen?' Oscar asked. 'Somewhere fascinating? Afternoon aerobics?'

She felt relieved to see them, restored to her ordinary life with Will. Although there had been not a thing about the meeting with Coventry Tom that Helen could definitely have identified as sexual, she felt uneasy afterwards, as if she had been mauled. Oh, he had made his ambush joke when locking the doors, but that's what it was, a joke, a joke with no follow-up. Of course, he had been charming and considerate, too damn charming and considerate. A performance. Or maybe she'd been troubled by the invitation to share secrets with him and exclude Will – exclude Coventry's wife, also. *Just the two of us.* And yet those secrets were to do with motherhood and the safety of Helen's son, surely, not lech pressure. He had actually invited his wife to join them and talk children and no children, which would be unlikely if he were trying something on, wouldn't it, would it?

What she hated were the hints that Will might be a bit of a hasty idiot and needed the protection of brighter people, such as herself and Coventry in a smart secret alliance. She hated it because it could be true. Coventry spoke as if she and he were of course familiar with the ways of business life. Had he ordered someone to research her? Why? At one of the better schools she attended during her father's switchback career she remembered studying an Irish play called *Juno and the Paycock* where women carried nearly all the family load while the men were bluster and and daft ambition, full of Dublin shit. Sometimes, even before seeing Coventry today, Helen had caught herself feeling like one of those women. Maybe it was the surprise of seeing Coventry guessed this that troubled Helen now. She was ashamed she had ever thought it about her and Will, and more ashamed Coventry could spot it. An insulting invasion – that's how it had seemed.

Now, at home, she was back with things she understood. Usually the kind of jollity on display today meant Will and his pals were hatching a job and already planning how to spend the take. Sometimes the jobs happened. Sometimes they withered as plans only, because too many obstructions were found, or too many dangers, or because Will or one of the others lost belief in it or lost nerve or lost energy – especially those two, failure of nerve and/or energy.

'Information – the heart of all fine work of our type, Helen,' Oscar said. 'Eisenhower for D-Day – tide tables, weather forecast. The Great Train Robbers – departure time and route. Perfect information. And perfect information is what we bloody have this time.'

'Get that, get that, get that, Helen,' Jake yelled, with a mighty giggle. '*This* time.' The dancing was over but she and Jake still stood near each other in front of the fireplace. He had a long, pointed blanched face always ready to fold up into a laugh. 'That's this sod giving me a kick in the you-know-where – well, maybe deserved – yes, a slip-up last outing, I got to say.'

'And the outing before,' Oscar replied.

'All right, and the outing before,' Jake said. 'What he's telling you, Helen, is my info on them occasions before a job was a bit off.'

'Was rubbish,' Oscar said.

'Yes, a bit off,' Jake replied. 'Well, no real need to tell Helen. She knows it. When was the last time she saw some good profits for the housekeeping? Months? Yes, I was a bit off. But nothing fatal, for God's sake. We're all still here, I think.' He made a crazy show of counting the three of them by pointing: Will first, then Oscar, then himself. 'No deads. Nobody over the wall. All still available for a great new project.'

There were beer cans around the room and a smell of ale though the three men were not drunk. Elation – each with a happy helping. Although Helen would always have her spiky pessimistic doubts, she also adored it when they tried to arrange something. The three became like thrilled kids, delighted by their own cleverness in finding a target, whatever it might be, and gloriously sure the operation would work: they would locate unmatchable treasure and bring it home, without getting caught or hurt. The three throbbed with such certainty she could almost believe in them. She found it a treat after the sly stateliness and threats of Coventry's place. They did not mind what Helen knew – altogether trusted her.

Jake turned towards Helen, his body tense with pleasure. 'We got a sweet project here. Most of the information from Will. A bit from Oscar.'

'Not just information,' Oscar said. 'Will's landed us inside help. Crucial.'

'You live with a magician, Helen,' Jake said.

She knew from old times that their newest scheme would be real and fragile, ambitious and most likely unworkable, bright with life and possibly doomed from the start. Helen went to sit down. She took a can of beer from an open six-pack on the table. One thick-cut cheese sandwich made by Will and an apple stood on a serving plate and she helped herself to these, too. She drank and ate while they talked. They wanted her approval. They thought she had a grand mind and they'd let her use it. In this company she *did* have a grand mind.

'Will's always good on information when he wants to make the effort,' Jake said.

She was glad of their total belief in her. Always she kept her cynicism about their plans hidden, and they never seemed to detect it. But *total* belief in her? She had her worries.

'This time a furniture depository, love,' Will told her.

Everybody stopped talking for a moment. Someone was moving at the back of the house. After a moment the door to the living-room was pushed open and Christopher looked in.

'Chris,' Jake said, 'school out already? Them teachers got a doddle of a job.'

'How was it, darling?' Helen asked.

'As usual,' the boy replied. 'You got another prayer meeting on, have you?'

'Not for long,' Will replied.

'I'll play some music upstairs,' he said, leaving.

'Not too loud,' Helen called. In her mind was a glimpse of him climbing into that Cavalier at Holt's Corner. Hadn't she heard that some police called tips from a child grass 'baby talk'? God, would this baby ever talk about his own dad?

'If – a big, big if – if he went to school at all today,' Will said. 'Does it matter? What can that dump give him?'

'I think school is . . . is crucial,' Jake replied. His long face grew suddenly longer from this slab of seriousness and his dark eyes were grave.

'You never went,' Will said.

'Look what happened to me.'

'A bit of education never did anybody much harm,' Helen said.

'It didn't do *you* no harm,' Jake said.

'You really think the one he goes to, or doesn't, you think this school will get him somewhere?' Will asked. He leaned forward and picked up one of the sheets of paper from the floor. 'This depository's a class place, Helen. It costs to keep stuff there. This is a place where the wealthy put their valuables – that's pictures and ornaments as well as furniture – they store it here for a while if they're doing up some grand new house or if they're moving from one property to another and the dates don't come together, so they have to stay in an hotel a week or two.'

She thought it sounded big-time for Will and the others. There would be guards, there would be alarms. Occasionally lately she had wondered whether they would tell her if they planned to carry guns on an outing. They trusted her, yes, but that much? Guns put the risk right up. Police rapid response crews responded rapidly and shot straight. Will might decide she need not be bothered with such knowledge, and such extra anxiety. He was like that – considerate except when shoved into sudden mad rage. Was Coventry Tom hinting at gun perils when he said Will might be 'exposed' now, but need not be if he worked for him?

Will spread a sheet of lined paper on the floor. It was a simple two-dimensional drawing of a big rectangular hall or room, with doors labelled A and B at each end and windows shown as barred squares. 'This is the area where they keep the most valuable pieces,' Will said. 'People don't leave things in here very long – sometimes only a few days or a week, while they're sorting themselves out.'

'Why the information is critical, Helen,' Oscar said. 'We've got to hit when it's at max.'

Will pointed to a portion shaded with close pencil lines along about two-thirds of one wall. This section was labelled *18th century and earlier furniture.* 'They're well stocked up on this just now,' Will said. 'We reckon we've got three, possibly four, days to move. After that, a lot could be gone.' He put this sketch aside and found another piece of paper. 'Here's a list of what's available, love. Some sketches. All this from our friend who works there.' He turned to the other two. 'The thing about Helen is she's really bright about furniture.'

'She's bright about a lot of things,' Jake replied.

'This is on account of her childhood – famous old styles all around.'

'So how come she finishes up with you?' Jake asked.

'Oh, she knew I was fond of old furniture, naturally,' Will replied.

'All top class fucking plastic and glue here,' Jake said.

Almost all of it *was*, but for a second Helen thought Will would turn wild at that. This meeting place – *his* place, shoddy or not – turned him into a sort of convener, gave him a prized bit of eminence. He did not look at Jake. That was the way with Will in a rage. She read the tremor of hate in his face. Quickly, Helen took the sheet of paper from his fingers and read it slowly, smiling with appreciation, giving an occasional grunt of pleased surprise. After a while this began to work. Will's anger seemed to slip away. It came and went with Will, sometimes as fast as that, sometimes not. Oscar looked at the list over her shoulder. 'I like this,' he said, ' "eighteenth century or earlier". It's a place that doesn't bother with Victorian or Edwardian junk.'

Four late 16th century oak armchairs, with panels and scrolled cresting. Value about £3000 each. There was a drawing, with the decorated back panel of the chair nicely coloured in crayon, yellow, pink, turquoise, gold.

'God, sixteenth century! Where are they from – a stately home?' Helen asked.

'Will's checked it all out,' Jake replied. Although these three usually acted like equals, obviously someone had the last word, and she knew it was Will. Perhaps there had even been some sincerity in Coventry Tom's praise of him. Will did have qualities. Would she have married him if not, for God's sake? She was not a kid then – had been divorced a year and knew what living with someone long term could be like. Of course, she had

46

realised Will talked big. Most men did. Her father had talked big, especially when he was fucked up. They needed that, poor lads. They lived by a myth. Helen had seen Will loved her and would go on loving her. On that she had been right. She had known she would go on loving him, too. After Duncan she had decided this was what mattered. The rest would sort itself out, most probably. The money would usually come from somewhere. Love was more difficult. But not as difficult as luck.

Georgian mahogany bottle rack, value £2500 she read. There was a sketch of that, and another of a Regency mahogany pedestal sideboard, *value around £12,000*. Briefly she felt a little educated lust for them, these quality things. The solidity of that repeated word 'mahogany' thrilled her. She could recall the pleasure of seeing nice furniture around as a child. 'You've got someone who'll buy this kind of stuff, Will?' she asked. 'Very traceable.'

Oscar said: 'He'll take them, for a price.'

'Meaning value around twelve thousand pounds turns out to be around five thousand?' she asked.

'We pay receivers for the risk,' Oscar said. 'But we shift the pieces in bulk, so the money piles up, even if the price per item looks down.'

'A van?' she said.

'Oscar's fixing that,' Jake replied. 'Vans are in and out of there all the time and it will look natural.'

Lead-framed mirror, probably Italian, late 17th century or early 18th century. Value £12,000.

'Plus art and ornaments stacked here, look, Helen,' Will said. He pointed to a different shaded area on the first sketch, then read a list of painters from another sheet. 'The pictures are more modern but still worth a bit: Hockney, Pollock, Tissot, Steer, Sickert, Ford Madox Brown.'

'And then ornaments and that,' Jake said. He gave a whoop of delight. 'Tell her about them swans, Will.'

'Staffordshire saltglaze polychrome. 18th century. A pair of swans with cygnets looking out from under them,' Will read. *'About £70,000.* That's seven zero, zero, zero, zero.'

Jake said: 'Swans – cygnets. That's something I *do* remember from school. We did a lesson called The Young Of. Like horse – foal, frog – tadpole.'

47

'Didn't I see you win the *Mastermind* vase on TV once, Jake?' Oscar asked. He wore glasses and parted his dark hair in the middle, keeping it very flat. Like Jake he was pretty bony and had long hands with lumpy knuckles. He could have played a goofy shopkeeper in one of those thirties Hollywood comedies that padded out the Movie Channel.

'All items are insured up to the limit,' Will told her. 'We're not really taking from anyone.'

'No?' she replied. Often there came these half-baked moments of conscience from Will.

'And now it got to be one of our terrific before-the-job parties, yes?' Jake asked, beaming.

'Absolutely,' Will said.

'First pick up the girls?' Jake asked.

'Absolutely,' Will replied.

'We'll give them a ring, say to smarten up, ready,' Oscar said. 'They're on alert.'

This was one of their procedures. After a planning meeting they liked to celebrate with dinner out somewhere. It signalled the general happiness and hope: morale off the leash. Will always said it was stupid to celebrate *after* a job, because the police watched for people doing a fat spend.

Another reason for going out together early, though, was that the plans might not come to anything. Or they might never come to anything very much. Of course, Helen would not speak these doubts to Will or the others. Heartless. But she thought they were in everyone's mind and mixed a little sadness with the high spirits.

Helen went upstairs and dressed then looked in on Chris. He was playing a video game. Would she talk to him soon, as Coventry wanted? It would be like surrendering herself to him – that smelly alliance. Now, she wanted to think only about Will, share the evening's brilliant fragile buzz. At these times, Will achieved style, and she loved him for it, adored being part of it. Will was not born to crookedness, but crookedness could give him a great little glow. When she first met him he was in a marketing job and starting to get very good promotion. The firm folded and he found another job, not such a brilliant one, but all right. That firm folded, too. By then, Chris had arrived and Will

48

wanted her to be at home with him, not out working. She thought this was when the drift towards small-time crime must have started – those other kinds of jobs, and that other kind of thinking which came with them. She had not liked it, and perhaps she should have tried to end it then, early. But she had seen Will's anger when crossed and was afraid. Also, they had needed the money, such as it was.

And they still did, of course. Coventry deduced that. So would anybody with one eye open. Just the same, when meetings were in this house, Will would lay on booze and food and the other two took it, never offering to split costs because they thought Will big enough to look after those himself. If you hosted you picked up the bill, this was routine in their game – the privilege of status. Although Will was younger than both the other two, they gave him the leadership without question. Helen knew that when things turned out well after such a meeting people were grateful and expected the convener to take a slice extra as special reward – hazard fee. Now and then, things *did* turn out well. Then there would be good cash around. Will always talked as if those times were the norm. No. He still did not want her to work, though. It was part of the dim culture he had gradually moved into, especially part of leadership culture: a top man's woman did not go out hairdressing or selling in a store or cleaning. That helped prove he *was* top, even if his results seemed to prove something else.

'I'm going to send a taxi for Gran to come and sit with you,' she told Chris.

Once in a while they might leave him unattended in the house at night, with orders to open to nobody. Suddenly, today, she knew this was impossible.

'Mum, I'll be OK,' he said.

'But I'll get Gran, all the same.' Gran could not do much, but at least she would dial 999 if things went rough. Chris probably would not. Helen feared he was already into a code which said you never called the police for help, even though you baby-talked to one of them. When the four left she looked up the street to where the Cavalier had waited, but it was not there now. Why should it be? Threats came and went.

49

They were in two cars, Will's and Oscar's. Oscar would go to his place and Jake's and pick up Lesley and Petra, then bring them on to Will's favourite French restaurant, the Bordeaux. In the car he was still loud with satisfaction. 'This comes from keeping old mates happy, love,' he said. 'This voice inside I've helped along now and then.'

As he was parking near the Bordeaux, Helen saw the orange Cavalier saunter past. Perhaps it had been behind them from the start. The later part of the watch could have been kept from a side street. There were two people in it. The driver was the girl she'd seen on Coventry's slides. Alongside her sat a man with radiantly silver hair and silver moustache. Neither of them seemed to look at her and Will. Of course not.

She enjoyed the meal. Helen always got on well with Lesley, and Petra seemed more or less all right, clever and coarse, neglectful of her teeth but pretty enough. She'd suit Jake. Helen felt edgy, all the same. Sight of the Cavalier disturbed her, and she was troubled that the car contained not just Chris's contact but the passenger. She thought this might have been Vic Othen, an eternal detective constable, who they said knew everything and was known by everyone, or known of by description – the hair and and moustache and tailoring. How did Vic the Potential figure in things?

When Helen and Will drove home, the Cavalier was where it had been the first time she spotted it. Will seemed to take no notice. The car moved off slowly as he and Helen went into the house. Abruptly, Helen found their vehicle less alarming: it was as if the baby-talker had been getting some extra baby-sitting. But since when did Vic Othen worry about the kids of small-time villains?

Always Helen and Will made love after one of these evenings. This was part of the procedure, too. And yet it was not like that, not routine, programmed. Her love for him soared when he looked so positive and so much in peril. Duncan had slumped into timidity, almost despair, when years younger than Will now. Will was a man who still managed lightness of heart and optimism off and on, and at thirty-seven. She wanted to be a part of all that, and she wanted to help and sustain him, if it could be done. In bed for say half an hour or less it could be

50

done. She felt warm, wet, secure, hopeful. And her son was asleep safe in the next room, perhaps a lot safer than she could have hoped, a grass but in a decent cause, a necessary cause. Surely.

7

Kerry Lake decided that after all she would not, could not, ask the mother of the dead boy to attend any private meeting with Coventry Tom. It would be a disappointment for Mark, and she was sorry about that. It would be a disappointment for Stephen Comble, and she was sorry about that, too. She thought Mark might understand. Mark lived with all those tough business pressures, excelled among them, but he could be wonderfully sensitive and quickly spot when she was seriously troubled. Perhaps Stephen would understand as well.

Or did you need to be a woman to see the objection? Kerry disliked this idea, had always suspected all that gender stuff as simple and limiting. It couldn't be, could it, that only a woman would feel Sonia Denton now deserved all the tenderness around? And, although Stephen probably did mean well, Kerry could not believe this meeting would have had much to do with tenderness. For a start, there would be the set-up of it, in a big businessman's big fine house – all the bits and pieces of wealth and normality to soften Sonia: could that be right, or even half right? She felt sure Coventry would try to browbeat Sonia or fool her, in surroundings also shaped to browbeat her. Christ, it could turn out so heartless, just a slide into opportunism. Kerry knew about opportunism, of course: a lot of good police work was opportunism. All the same, she would prefer not to exercise it on Sonia Denton. Kerry felt she must switch off for a while her usual fierce and narrow commitment. The chase was important and so was a career, but other things had to count, too. She might have been able to manoeuvre Coventry into some kind of indiscretion at Stephen's place, but there

51

would be different ways to do this to Tom, wouldn't there: cleaner ways, more humane ways – cleaner and more humane as far as Mrs Denton was concerned, that is? She did not mind how dirty she played to shaft Coventry. In any case, who said she should regard Coventry as her special prey? None of her superiors. They wanted him for themselves, if he was to be done at all. Yes, if. He knew the royals.

She told Vic Othen about the proposed meeting and her rejection of the idea. He was appalled. 'Do it, kid,' he said at once. 'This is a chance. They're rare with Coventry.'

'Yes, they're rare.'

'Do it, Kerry,' he said. 'Please. This could be Coventry turned inside out. It's only a minor amendment of the rules. He might say something we can use. Shall I come with you to see Mrs Denton, if you're troubled?'

He talked on and she listened. When he finished she immediately drove out alone to invite Sonia Denton to the confrontation. Naturally alone. She did not want her to feel crowded. Kerry was grateful for Vic's offer to go with her, but turned him down. She did not need him, did not need support, never needed support. Well, hardly ever. He had magicked her volte-face, hadn't he, and that should satisfy him.

As soon as Kerry knocked on the door, Mrs Denton opened it and said: 'Ah, news for me! You've arrested Coventry?' It was as if she'd had a tip it was done and had been waiting for confirmation. She sounded ecstatic, the words bright and chubby with triumph, but there was no joy in her big-boned face. Her eyes seemed dulled by hopelessness. There had been so much more fight in them at the ball. Kerry saw she did not really believe the police had moved. It was sarcasm, agonised sarcasm. What Sonia Denton meant was: *If you haven't arrested him why the fuck show your cop face here again?* Sonia left the door open, turned and walked back slowly into the house – a theatrical do-what-you-like walk: get lost, come in, stay where you are. She had on what might be the same black slacks as at the ball and a cream roll-neck sweater. She wore governess-style black boots which made her look undangerous. *Please, Sonia, get back your vitriol and righteousness.* Kerry closed the door quietly and followed her.

52

Just after Tim Denton's death she had spent a lot of time here, asking questions, comforting, asking questions, asking questions. Or trying to comfort. Sonia Denton did not take easily to comforting. The small house had been unnervingly neat then and still was, a prim place. Kerry could see why a kid would rather be out on the streets. She wanted to be back out on the street herself. Kerry longed to help Sonia Denton in her grief yet always felt held off: shelved like one of her pretty vases. The only help this woman would recognise was harsh, triumphant hounding to the end of Tom Ingle-Blake. Kerry did sympathise, could not deliver.

'Well, I'm glad you've turned up, anyway,' Sonia said. 'I can give you the stages of it now.'

'Of?'

'Tim's death,' she replied.

'Sonia, I'm here to ask – '

'I couldn't have put on this show for you before. It was not complete. Well, it still isn't complete. *Have* you arrested the sod? No, of course not. But it's almost complete now. Maybe as complete as it's ever going to be.'

'Which show is it?'

'This is to get your memory going?' Sonia replied. She had that sing-song style of speaking which could turn a statement into a question. 'Not *my* memory. I don't need it. Yours. Yours and your colleagues'. I'm always scared Timothy will slip from police minds. Has he? I know you've got a lot on – traffic, lost dogs, football, charity dances. Where's a dead kid in all that?' It was spoken with a terrible dry off-handedness.

'Sonia, we want whoever did it.'

'Yes?'

'Why I'm here,' Kerry replied. She longed to get hold of Sonia Denton, throw her against a wall, shake her doubts out of her, and scream in her face: *I'm hunting him for you, non-stop, teeth ready to tear him. I've speared him on a table, cut him to fragments with scissors and a knife. I'm not, not, not, indifferent or intimidated or asleep.* Would even that get through to her? She had her ideas in shape – the wrong shape, but who was going to change them?

Sonia looked out of the window for a while, vigilant. 'I think I'm personally fairly safe. Is he going to fear someone like me?

53

All right, I gave him some aggro at the ball. But a one-off thing like that won't turn him mad, will it? I'm insignificant. All right, so was Timmy insignificant – more insignificant, you could say, just a kid. But this was a kid who frightened him some way. You know how? People say all sorts, some of it nasty. I'm investigating.' She rolled this police word, mocking again. '*I* don't scare Coventry. He thinks I'm helpless. Perhaps. All I know is my boy's dead and he did it. But you know that, too, and all your chiefs – '

'No, we don't *know* it, not in the way the police have to know things. I'm not allowed to go on feelings.'

'You *do* feel Coventry did it?' she asked. There was something like a rush of joy in her voice.

'If we *knew* it believe me we'd – '

'Believe you?' Her tone went back to where it had been. 'And nobody does anything, so why should he fret about me, or send people for me? Can I work changes? Is that why you're here – to check up, see I'm OK, give some protection? Queer job you've got. Last time I see you you're in his arms, and next thing you're here to find out if he's left me in one piece so far.'

'He's keen to talk to you,' Kerry replied.

'Oh, is *that* why you're here? Ah.' She nodded slowly. 'Talk to me? Put it all right with me? He sent you? An understanding?' She smiled at Kerry, as though having unearthed some sweet little secret romance.

It enraged Kerry, but she kept things civil. This woman saw only conspiracies and could not be blamed for it. 'No, not like that,' Kerry said.

No, not at all like that. She was here because of Vic Othen, wasn't she? Didn't she owe him that much, at least that much? Vic wanted her to win, seemed to believe she *could* win. This was approval from a sterling silver, far-seeing detective who took no bullshit, and it thrilled Kerry. Like Stephen Comble, Vic thought she had staged the Heart ball scene, but unlike Stephen, Vic loved the audacity of it, saw a whole brilliant campaign against Coventry starting from there. Vic was wrong about the ball incident, but she did not mind that. He made sacrifices for her so she might win the campaign, even neglected his arrest score. Watching from her car the other night, they had spotted two men come jubilantly out of the Mallards' house in Daniel Street, and then she and Vic tailed Chris's parents to the Bordeaux restaurant. Not long afterwards the two men turned up again, with their women now. Vic knew all of them. Of course he knew all of them. 'Will Mallard's setting up a job,' he had said. 'This is ritual – meeting at his house, big spendthrift dinner to celebrate in advance. Will's half idiot, half automaton, can't change the run-up. Normally, Sergeant Kerry, I'd start digging into that. There'd be a possible trap, arrests and moderate *gloire*. But if I do, and Will gets an early whiff of me, how's he going to think I know about it?'

'Because you're you? A famous genius.'

He had ignored that, growled at her for dimness: 'We know Chris was in the house while they're planning, don't we?'

'Oh, God – he'd think Chris grassed?'

'It's a risk,' Vic said. 'Too big a risk. So, obviously, I blind-eye their meeting and dinner. Give up the chance of nailing them. You've got something much bigger on, kid. I do believe you might be able to take Coventry somehow – probably with the boy's help, though maybe not. Madness to disturb the pool now by netting three tiddlers, and put the lad in peril. Priorities. In my old age, Kerry, I long to see someone hard and sharp and young and giftedly pushy – i.e., you – catch a bastard who's defeated the rest of us for centuries. Police are supposed to believe in what's learned at Nellie's knee – the old wisdom. I *don't* any more. Christ, I *am* Nellie, and Nellie doesn't get people like Ingle-Blake. Nellie says he's ungettable. But Kerry might get him and tell Nellie to sod off. You can smash him.'

This was when she had mentioned the plan for Coventry and Sonia Denton to meet. 'I decided not to go through with it, Vic,' she'd said. 'See, I *do* give a shit. Can't help it. To get her there would be cold, exploitive. And it's probably totally wrong police procedure.'

'Of course it's wrong procedure. Yes, exploitive. Yes, a bit cold. Do it, kid,' he replied. 'This is a chance. They're rare with Coventry.'

'Yes, they're rare.'

'Please,' he said. 'This could be Coventry turned inside out. It's only a minor amendment of the rules. He might say

55

something we can use. Shall I come with you to see Mrs Denton, if you're troubled?'

He had talked on and she listened, then drove here. You had to humour your disciples, especially when they were sexy and warm and a hundred times more experienced and knowledge-able: humour them and justify their gambles, if you could. The fast track had obligations.

'Sit on this chair, would you?' Sonia Denton said. 'If you could look at that bit of plain white wall. Like a screen.' Kerry saw she was in for a picture show. Hadn't Mark said Ingle-Blake liked to make points through slides, too? For a moment, this similarity, this sense of pattern, dazed her. It was like two companies bidding with rival presentations. Coventry would presumably be touting his innocence. Sonia would presumably be touting his guilt. Now, on the wall appeared a colour snapshot of the two boys, her son, Tim, and Chris Mallard looking as lively and innocent as . . . as children. 'Taken last year. Do you know this other boy?' Sonia asked.

'Yes, I've run across him.'

'They were friends. I believe Chris thought a lot of my lad. Tim tried to persuade him to go to school more. Some chance.' The boys were in green and white striped football gear, and there was a set of goal posts in the background. Tim had a streak of mud across his brow and his hair looked soiled, as if from a lot of heading. They stood each with an arm around the other's shoulders, both grinning. You could have believed them capable of no worse than mischief. 'Now and then if the school had a match Chris would turn up, just to play in the game. And here's another field.'

Kerry recognised it at once, a sloping rough meadow dotted with small bramble bushes. Tim Denton's body had been found here, tucked under a hedge with three stab wounds, any one of which would have killed according to the post-mortem. Sonia had four slides of this field, showing it from various angles. The hedge was in every shot, but no people. 'I went up there myself not long ago to take this one,' she said. 'I wanted to see what it was like before all this – before they dumped him there, and before the police cars and ambu-lance.'

56

The police cars and ambulance almost filled the next three slides. They must have been made from Press photographs. Kerry saw herself in one of the shots, wearing white wellingtons and overalls and bent down to peer into the small tent they had put over the boy's body. She could still recall pretty well what she saw. That was private and too memorable.

'They wouldn't let me do that,' Mrs Denton said. 'See him there.'

Kerry heard herself muttering something about a sealed area and special clothing.

'I'm not going to ask you what he looked like. I never asked you that, did I?' Sonia's voice went to near a shriek and seemed wrong in this trim room, with its tiny china ornaments and pale water-colours: too raw. But, then, police investigating the death of a child killed by knife wounds had seemed wrong in here, too.

Kerry said: 'I think you've behaved with remarkable – '

'Yes, I have, haven't I? Now, how about these?' She displayed the next eight slides in a very slow succession, leaving each picture on the wall for up to a couple of minutes. All showed Ingle-Blake with their royal patron at the ball. In some the two were dancing. In one she was handing out a raffle prize while he beamed a congratulation in the background and applauded. In two he was chatting with her, looking handsome, solid, at ease, oh, such a social distance from a bloody spat in Soho. These slides, too, must have come from Press photographs bought at the newspaper office. It was a collection. Kerry felt hammered. For a few moments she wished she had let Vic come with her to share the talk and deflect the contempt. Sonia said: 'I like the way she left early surrounded by entourage et cetera. That has to mean he didn't get to fuck her. Not that night. Of course, when he's mingling up in London who knows? This is a thought, isn't it, Coventry Tom giving it to a royal as well as killing a child. I'd say this would be a comment on the world, and as a comment just right. Is he fucking *you*? Power an attraction? I've heard of that. For instance, women fancied that funny-looking Beaverbrook.' She stared at the latest picture on the wall, Coventry radiating graciousness as he waved the patron off. 'You know that word aplomb, at all?' Sonia asked. 'Is that a word around in police matters? Aplomb is what Coventry can really turn on when he's not butchering kids. See the aplomb in that lovely shirt front and the strong yet friendly chin? I should think he'll do aplomb at this meeting you mentioned. And you carry his messages? All right, so what meeting? Do you want to see the slides of the funeral? You weren't there, were you?'

'Senior officers attended.'

'There was room for you. They wouldn't allow me to do pictures inside the church. But here's the arrival of Tim. Here's the departure. Is this boring you? Poor dear, you come to do a go-between job for your pal, Coventry, and you get the whole mourning Mummykins dossier. Here's the grave, before and after he was in it. I keep it neat. Well, as you would expect, I know. I see you looking around, amused by the tidiness. I've always been like that. I'm a pain. I wanted him brought up with a sense of order, you know.' She blared the words, as though afraid she might break down if she spoke normally. 'Some single parents get neglectful, unkempt. I would have hated that. It can set a child even further back. But, you're right – silly to talk about this now. Silly to talk as if he ever had prospects. We know differently, don't we? Here's a side shot of the grave. I think the headstone and strip of lawn tasteful. I do try to tend it once every couple of weeks. Exactly what kind of meeting? Yes, I'll come. Why not? It's an outing. I might give them this show, or maybe a different one. I've got other information, you know. Disgusting information, really.'

'What information?'

'Yes, I'll meet Coventry,' Sonia replied. 'You've done a damn good job for him. I hope he sees you right. I'll put in a word for you with him. It might be good for promotion.'

8

'That your boyfriend who answered – the sausage rolls king?'

'Chris? It's you?' Kerry replied.

Mark had handed her the receiver saying only: 'Someone who won't give his name. Not to me.'

Chris said: 'Sorry to phone on a Saturday. Could you pick me up at the Corner, Kerry?'

'Now?'

'It's important. Can you come and get us?'

' "Us" '?

'I've found somebody. This is to do with ... well, you know.'

'Chris, I asked you to drop that. For now.'

'This is important. She got some real info or would I ring? You know I don't hardly ever although you gave me the phone card. And never when he's not in work, like today, I mean. But it's important.'

'Who's "us" '? Kerry replied.

'This is a contact.'

Kerry had used the word with him once or twice about people she listened to, and Chris liked it. He appreciated jargon, perhaps thought it gave him weight. Well, didn't ten million adults hope it would do the same for them? 'This is a girl who knew Timmy. She's all right, don't worry. She got some facts. These are facts you ought to hear. Genuine facts. She won't tell me, but I know they're genuine facts, Kerry. She's that kind – genuine. I couldn't wait till the next time we arranged. It's important.'

'Yes, you said.' Then she regretted sounding distant. 'You do stick at it, Chris, regardless.' In fact, she was relieved by what he had told her. For a couple of seconds at the beginning she had thought he was ringing to alert her about his father – that project Vic the Potential believed was hatching, and which Chris might know about. She had feared the boy was so upset at being cut adrift by her for a while that he would do anything to hang on. Informants could get like this: an almost sick dependence on their detective. And to keep the link they would continually up the ante, ultimately offering betrayals of even those closest to them, people they normally shielded, friends or relatives. Many detectives worked hard to bring their tipsters to this state. Information came in cataracts then. Kerry would have loathed to receive tips from a boy about his father. Poisoning a family would be vile, crook family or not.

'What'll he think?' Chris asked.

59

'Who?'

'The sausage rolls man. About this call.'

'All right. In an hour,' she said. 'Do you want it to be somewhere else?'

'Why?'

'Oh, I don't know. Habit, sameness – I worry.'

'No, the Corner's all right. Lots of traffic. Safe as ever. Nobody'll spot us.'

When she put the phone down, Mark said: 'That sounds like one of those calls I don't ask about.' He had stayed in the room while she spoke, reading the *Independent* or pretending to, crouched in his armchair like an autistic child. He meant he was excluded. It hurt her when he behaved like this. There were corners of the job that had to stay confidential. They were no real bar between them, surely, unless he wanted to make them a bar.

Kerry crossed the room and kissed him on top of the head, then sat on the floor, her brow against his legs. He was in the purple track suit that he would pull on in the mornings most weekends and wear until they went out. He'd had the suit since he played rugby at school, and you could see its age. Once or twice she had considered buying a replacement for Christmas or his birthday, but never did. He liked this scruffy line to his past, and so did she. It seemed humanising: he had not always been a sausage roll king. On the other hand, the suit did show that if you kept at it in school and played the school's game you could still end up with a directorship in your early thirties. 'Oh, Mark,' she said, 'drop the self-pity. Of course you can ask about the call.'

'I'm asking,' he said. 'It sounded like a child.' He did a piping voice. '*Hello, hello, I got to speak to Detective Sergeant Lake, please. A matter of urgency, please. She'll know who it is, oh, yes. Private business, thank you.*'

'A lot of people don't like talking through the headquarters switchboard. They're jumpy.'

'*Is* Chris a child?'

'This applies to young and old,' she said. 'They want to talk direct or not at all. Some of them would ring off at once because you picked up the phone.'

'I only ask if it was a child . . .' He let that fade out, seemed to go back to his newspaper.

'Oh, because of the boy Timothy Denton,' she replied. 'That's a different – '

'Is this dangerous stuff, Detective Sergeant Lake?' He put the *Independent* aside and reached down and stroked her cheek slowly. She thought that anyone who could see them now – *only* see them, and hear the tone of their conversation not the words – anyone would have assumed it was a relaxed and friendly talk between lovers. It *was* friendly, not relaxed. These days they had more conversations that were not relaxed than were, but she would work on it. She could believe it might be more her fault than his, or the job's fault.

'I don't suppose what he has to say will add up to much,' Kerry replied. 'A kind of panic call, possibly.'

'But you have to go out?'

'They get really nervous, some of these folk, Mark. They need reassuring, that's all. It's duty.'

'Which folk? These are grasses? Kid grasses? There was something anxious in the Press about them. I don't pry, love, and know I mustn't whatever you say, but – oh, I don't know . . . well, doesn't it seem illogical?' He went for that word pretty carefully, spoke it gently, one of his favourites and an all-powerful one, in Mark's view. Hers, too, come to that. He said: 'Here we are arranging something like this promising meeting between Mrs Denton and Thomas Ingle-Blake – and all credit to you for persuading her, Kerry – Stephen is damn grateful, I know, and Peter – we have this more or less in the bag, and yet at the same time there's something else going on, isn't there, actually run by you, perhaps, and, on the face of it at least, possibly at variance with this attempt at reconciliation. I have to believe that a child phoning like that – it has to be about the dead boy?' He pointed with grief at the phone. 'I honestly don't know what Stephen would make of this apparent, well, contradiction.'

So, poor old Stephen. It chilled her to hear Mark refer to Coventry as Thomas Ingle-Blake, like the headline to someone spotless in a *Daily Telegraph* obituary – though she would settle for an obit of him under any name.

61

'Contradiction?' she said, also gently. 'It might not be that. Look, I'll see this contact and it'll be over in half an hour.'

'I thought it was more than one. "Us". A gang of kids? You give them our private number, Kerry? We get calls from the Welcome caff troupe? Might they visit?'

'Darling, now and then they're in need, that's all,' she said.

'*A matter of urgency, please,*' he replied, giggling.

'That's it, Mark.' She put her hand over his on her cheek. She had told herself at the beginning of this talk that she must not turn unpleasant, had no right to. They might not be relaxed but nor did they need to fight. There was too much to lose. They had something, she and Mark, and it must be looked after. She could understand it might be disturbing for him to see her called out by a demanding kid voice on a Saturday morning. Perhaps hers was a ridiculous job to be in. But it was a proper job, too, and she was in it, and not doing too badly. Yes, and she was in a good, lasting relationship, as well, and it was wisest to tread considerately. Mark certainly tried to, most of the time. Could a couple go on treading considerately for ever? Why not? What was wrong with a touch of restraint, a touch of delicacy?

'You'd told him to drop it, because of our meeting with Mrs Denton, had you, love?' Mark asked. 'Wise – if I may say.'

'And for other reasons. It's unnecessary for him to be involved at present, that's all.'

'But he still rings up. Well, the police never sleep. If it's hazard for him it's hazard for you, isn't it?'

'I wouldn't think so. We've got a nice safe procedure worked out.'

'But you asked him if he'd like to change it.'

'I always offer that. Routine.'

'And Chris says it's all right as it is, and you don't argue.'

She wished he would not use the name. Perhaps she had been careless calling him Chris on the phone. 'They're the ones who take the risk, Mark. First thing we're taught. Informants feel most easy with a routine. They dread change.'

'But this is a kid. Shouldn't you do some thinking for him? And I don't believe there's no risk to you as well.'

'I expect I'll discuss a new rendezvous spot with him, yes,' she replied.

'After you've been back to the old one.'

'Only this once.'

' "Only this once," ' he said. 'Isn't that . . . oh, I don't know . . . slack? I don't understand how a child can help you, anyway,' Mark said. 'They're so unreliable, so . . . so childish.'

Child, childish – somehow the way Mark harped on this notion made her think of her youngest brother, Simon. He was about Chris's age and, yes, a child and childish now and then. How would she feel if she heard a detective tried to use him as a grass, exposing him to God knew what? How would her mum and dad feel? She made herself ignore these tremors and turned teacher. 'From most informants, any age, you get one good bit in a hundred,' she replied. 'It's like buying a gold mine – mostly mud. I have to sort it out. The good bits go alongside other people's good bits. Occasionally they build something.'

'And using the same car always,' he replied.

'So now you're a security expert,' she said, but laughed.

'Have we got time to go back to bed, darling?' he said.

'Always.' She saw he had to assure himself he was still her priority. Of course he was. Did he think she preferred meeting lawless kids at Holt's Corner to being with him? In the bedroom she undressed slowly. There had better be no hint of rush. He wanted to give her his love and she longed to give him hers. Yes, always. This was one of those good reaffirmations that every couple needed now and then or oftener. They could not have meant more. They held things together. Naked, she helped him with the zip of his track suit top. It would get jammed where threads had come loose in the tattered cloth. She enjoyed picking at them, did it patiently, to show she always had time for him. With luck this could take the place of talk afterwards.

She liked to stand against him naked, as she did now, her chin on his shoulder, their feet and legs meshing and jostling so that occasionally they would go off balance and stagger a bit like fighting drunks, still holding on to each other. Then they would get back to steadiness and they'd stay still and quiet for a while, just enjoying the body-length sense of their flesh in touch, warm and dry, not sweaty yet, though that would be all right, too. She loved his body, loved the way the nice width of his chest was somehow OK for the leanness of the rest of him. To her his body seemed as it had always been since she knew him: the body of a man, yes, but youthful, too. The rest of Mark – his mind, his work clothes, his language – these didn't have all that much to do with youthfulness any longer.

He cradled his hands under her behind and lifted her a little. Her feet were off the ground and she opened her legs around his hips. It was what they called their *Last Tango In Paris* way to make love. *One* of their *Last Tango* ways to make love. The physical effort of it always thrilled Kerry – the tug on her arms as she held herself to him, the rough smack of her jaw or cheek bone against his when they staggered again, but this time staggered joined, not like fighting drunks now. Occasionally she got face bruising, but it could have been an awkward prisoner. She could sail in and out on the swing-seat of Mark's hands, working herself on him as much as he did on, in, her. How it ought to be.

They lurched, stumble-tangoed to the bedroom and eased down with skill on to the duvet, no uncoupling. She had decided just now that if he came out it would signify bad luck for at least a week, so she did not let him, and he seemed to sense the importance of staying put and kept beautifully sunk.

Although she had savoured the drag on her muscles when they were upright in the other room, there was something to be said for horizontalness, too, at a certain stage. This stage. She appreciated the cool, soft, downy lumpiness under her and the weight of Mark above. She missed that, the comfort of his devoted body weight, when they were on their feet, or on *his* feet. Her breasts got more consistent contact with him now, and she needed this at some stage. This stage. She lifted her legs high, like masts. They should have had bunting on to proclaim a carnival.

Kerry was twenty-five minutes late at Holt's Corner, and almost hoped Chris Mallard had gone. Was he starting to cling? That overwhelming dependence could hit informants of any age. For some, it was partly about the money handouts, yet not wholly this. They seemed to need the personal intimacy, as if it were a friendship, or more. Possibly it *was* a friendship, or as close to one as some of these folk would ever get. Now and then Kerry found the involvements in such relationships trouble-

64

some, especially with a child, a child she would want to big-sister off and on, but a child who ran his hand over her body from time to time in the pursuit of . . . of reassurance?

Chris had waited and was at the Corner with a fattish girl in big-frame spectacles. She was as tall as Chris, had frizzed dark hair and wore white shorts and a navy shirt. She might have been a year older than Christopher and Tim and looked bright and tough. 'We thought you was dead,' he said, as they climbed in.

'I had another call right after yours,' Kerry said.

'Yes? Your boyfriend must think he lives with the rapid response unit. We got to lie down, Liz.'

'Get lost,' the girl said.

'Only till we're out of the centre. It's all right, isn't it, Kerry?'

'Best you're not seen,' Kerry replied.

'I told you,' Chris said. 'It's peril. This is not messing about.'

The girl lay out alongside Chris. She said: 'If you're police and a true sergeant why can't they give you a better car? We wouldn't even nick a car like this, would we, Chris?'

'It's my own,' Kerry said.

'Why can't they give you a better one if you're a true sergeant?' Liz replied. 'Like perks.'

'Of course she's a true sergeant,' Chris said. 'Just because she don't wear stripes like the Enforcer up the Square it don't mean she's not. This is plain clothes, I told you.'

'Like fading into the background, this car – so ordinary?' Liz asked.

'Plus your sort are too snobby to pinch it,' Kerry said.

'Liz got his last movements and other matters,' Chris said.

'Oh?' Kerry replied.

'Ah, you mean so why haven't you seen no statements from her? Well, Liz is one of them who don't talk to the police. Do you know about culture? That's her culture.'

'Oh?'

'Or only police I can persuade her are all right. It takes time.'

'You tell them one thing and they turn it into something else,' Liz said. 'They ask you how you know it, anyway. You could be trying to help them and then suddenly you've got the problems

65

yourself. They don't care as long as they catch *someone*. Everybody knows this.'

'Kerry's not like that.'

'Well, I'm going to be an architect,' Liz said. 'This is better than art itself.' Her voice sang. 'Have you seen some of those buildings on TV, Kerry? Barcelona. San Francisco. The Rainbow Triangle in London. Lines. Such beauty. I've found out all about this in a great careers book down the library. They won't let you take it out, obviously, because it's got good pictures in, but there's a reading room. I'll be out of Rush Street and the Welcome. If the police let you drive a car like this I'd never be a cop, although I'll be big enough, but there's also eyesight. But don't tell me the twenty-first century won't need plenty of buildings. Are you telling me that?'

'I should think it will,' Kerry said.

'Bound to. The thing is, Kerry, if we're in Europe with the same money for all countries known as the Euro note instead of pounds people will be coming here from all over – Holland, Denmark, everywhere – to buy stuff, so who's going to get all the shops built? This is the architects. People think shops are just open the door and people come in and spend. But these shops have to look smart outside so people from all over will say in Dutch or German or any language to their family, "Here's a really beautiful store. Let's hurry in and purchase many items." I'm going to save for college. My mother doesn't know much about architects and when I say college she says, "What for?" and things like that, like "What college?" and "Have you got to buy your own books, I bet?" Chris is saving somewhere for his own shop, a pet shop, but I'm thinking of bigger shops than that where these Europeans will come to buy fashions. Don't take us out to that field where he was found. His mother goes up there, talking to herself, taking pictures. I expect I would. That's deep, losing a son. Well, probably none of us will ever be what we want to be – architect, pet shop owner, nothing – what chance? – we might be stuck here for ever low-lifing, but all the same Tim was her son. Sometimes I think I ought to go and see her, but then I hear about her up at the field and going odd a bit. I wouldn't like it.'

'Nor me,' Chris said. 'Do you go and see her, Kerry?'

66

'And you were with him right up till nearly the end, Liz?' Kerry replied.

She punched the back of the passenger seat. 'There you are. What I mean. Police,' Liz said. ' "Right up till nearly the end." Next you'll be asking did I do it, then. Or did I lead him to where it could be done.'

'Chris said you – '

'Of course Kerry won't be like that,' Chris said.

'I've been around, you know,' Liz said, 'I'm fourteen and three-quarters. Where you taking us?' She sat up. Chris did, too. Kerry had driven them out of the town and into the hills. She pulled off the road at the edge of some steep moorland. They could stay in the car or walk. Liz stared around. 'What people does this one know, Chris? Has she got people up here?' She pushed the door open and for a couple of seconds seemed about to run, her plump face red with anger or fear.

'What you talking about, Liz?' Chris said.

'Remote. Two of us out of the way at once,' Liz replied.

'Don't be stupid,' Chris said. He leaned across her and pulled the door shut.

'Who's her friends?' Liz said.

'We are,' Chris replied. 'We'll help her get Coventry.'

'Well, Coventry might *be* her friend,' Liz said, still looking everywhere. 'And his people.'

'She dances with him but she's not his friend,' Chris said. 'I told you she danced with him at a famous charity ball, but that's like politeness, because of her boyfriend. Business. She hated it when his hands were touching her body, didn't you, Kerry?'

'Me and my body, we're fussy,' Kerry replied.

'Of course you are,' he said. 'She got a boyfriend and that's as far as it goes, isn't it?'

She disliked this talk. 'I don't think we'll get spotted out here, that's all,' Kerry replied. 'Look, we can place Tim up till about 3.10 on the Thursday afternoon, possibly 3.20. He was on a stolen mountain bike in Marsh Street, possibly going to Rush Street and the Square. Two witnesses, one the Baptist minister.'

'Tim could do the lock on the chained bikes outside Hobb's Cycle Centre,' Liz said. 'Kerry, it was only borrowing. He'd always leave it somewhere, so most likely they'd get it back, unless someone else pinched it, which wasn't really his fault, was it, not really?'

'We found the bike. You were with him later than that, Liz, later than 3.20? When his body was discovered next morning he'd been dead twelve hours. Say from 7 p.m. What's between 3.20 and then?' Kerry did not turn around to speak but off and on watched Liz in the mirror. Keep it casual, not face to face, not an interrogation, a chat. 'Nobody saw him in the Welcome after 3.20. Or nobody will say they saw him. Were you in the Welcome at 3.20 or afterwards, Liz? Did he have the bike with him when you saw him?'

'I got to frisk you, Kerry,' Chris said.

'That's a line from *The Godfather*,' Liz said. 'The rotten police chief says it to Al Pacino, "I got to frisk you, Mike," but it's all right because Mike's got a gun hidden in the restaurant toilet.'

'Can you turn and kneel on the seat?' Chris said.

He seemed to be especially thorough to impress the girl. Kerry let it happen.

'What's this other car?' Liz said. A silver Mondeo passed and stopped off the road a few hundred yards ahead.

Kerry turned and studied it. 'People come up here to walk and sight-see and picnic,' she said.

'It's a man on his own,' Liz said. 'Solo picnic? Know him, Chris?'

'He got his back to us and a hat on.'

'Do *you* know him?' she asked Kerry.

'Don't think so. Should we move?'

'Coventry's got a hell of a lot of people,' Liz said.

'I'll walk down there, if you like – have a real look at him,' Kerry replied.

'What? No, no, don't leave us here,' Liz said. Suddenly, for a couple of moments, she was all child: all the suspicions of a child, this kind of child, and all the longing of a child to be looked after, any kind of child.

'He's shoving off, anyway,' Chris said.

The Mondeo disappeared. As far as Kerry could recall, the driver had not looked around at them once. It was not a car she recognised, nor a hat or back of the neck she recognised.

68

'Yes, let's have a walk,' Liz said. It was as though she had decided Kerry's car might be known, even targeted, and wanted to be out of it. They picked their way up the side of the mountain on a sheep path between ferns. Liz was fitter than she looked and went ahead. For the first time today Kerry felt almost comfortable with the two of them. It was like giving kids a country outing. After about half an hour they came to a clearing and sat on the grass looking down. What might have been the same Mondeo and the same driver returned slowly from the other direction but did not stop. Liz watched. The driver was head-on for a time and side-on for a time, but distance gave no hope of identification.

'So, that's what I'm into, Kerry,' she said.

'What? Architecture?' Kerry asked.

'Like an education fund,' Liz replied.

'I told her nothing up front, she got to provide first,' Chris said.

'While he's really piling it up,' Liz replied.

'This been a long time,' Chris said. 'This been a lot of info when you think about the time.' He wagged his head slowly a bit to suggest history.

'You're going to pay *him* for bringing me, is that right,' she asked Kerry, 'like talent spotting?'

'I haven't heard what's being offered,' Kerry replied.

'And once you *have* heard you know it and don't need me any more, and then you give a roll of notes to Chris for his pet shop for finding me?'

Chris said: 'Kerry will be thinking about you being an architect and the college for it, don't worry, if you can come across. She believes in education. She had some herself and her boyfriend, I should think, leading to a career. That's all you got to do, Liz, is come across, same for anyone.'

'Tim was scared,' Liz replied.

'Well, we know that,' Chris said.

'*You* know it. It doesn't mean *she* knows it,' Liz replied. Her high voice battered him.

'Of Coventry Tom?' Kerry asked.

'Who else is there to be scared of except your crew, and Tim wasn't scared of the police,' Liz said.

69

On the hunt a buzzard rose brown and big from somewhere near and glided down like a nature lesson towards the road. Chris said: 'You don't want to let them shit on you. They eat meat and you'd never get it out. I heard Tim gave Coventry some cheek. That's what Tim told me.'

'Oh, cheek,' Liz replied. 'Don't talk like a babe, Chris. Cheek! This is more than cheek.'

'She acts *so* deep,' Chris said.

'Maybe,' Liz replied. 'If I had told it all to Chris, where would I be, Kerry? He's your voice, yes? So he tells you, and I get nothing. I'm nearly fifteen. I'm somebody in my own right, you know, I'm not just a fucking voice to another fucking voice.'

'I'd square you, anyway, you know that,' Chris said.

'In my own right,' Liz replied.

'Did you see him after 3.20?' Kerry asked.

'Two things I need to worry about,' Liz replied. 'One is if you're a pal of Coventry, taking from him, maybe, asking his questions, passing it all back. That Mondeo. It's part of it all? He sends that to follow wherever you are and you know about it but pretend no. Or ... Or ... Well, you're pretty, not too old yet, you could be – '

'Shove it, Liz, you dirty-mouthed bitch,' Chris said. He was sitting hugging his knees, head hanging forward on that long thin neck, like someone spare to this meeting. 'We don't want your filthy ideas in such a beautiful place.' He unhooked one arm and pointed at ferns.

'Well, I say she could be,' Liz replied.

'I've been asked before,' Kerry said.

'You wouldn't, never,' Chris said. 'I know that.'

'Oh, you know it. How do you know it?' Liz grunted. 'You think she's Saint Bernadette or someone. He can pull all sorts, that Coventry. He's got the money and everything. And, listen, his wife's ... Well, anyway, Coventry probably likes looking around. Or he's got to.'

Chris stood quickly, his breath loud, and seemed about to attack her. Kerry reached up and held his arm. 'It's all right,' she said. 'She's nervous.'

'Yes, I am, I'm nervous,' Liz replied. 'So, I tell you what I know, Kerry, and you murmur it to Coventry one night and

70

where am I? You and your crew going to give me protection? I don't think so. What sense would it make if you're with Coventry, one way or the other, or both?'

'What's the other worry?' Kerry said.

'Well, the money, that's obvious.' She frowned then leaned forward like someone at a board meeting about to whack the rest with a tough argument. 'Listen, let's say you're not with Coventry, yes, just say – so, what about the money? I mean, how much? Chris, he says there's money, but he'll never say how much.'

'Confidential business matter,' Chris replied. He sat down again between Kerry and Liz on the grass.

'He says it's a lot but, well, he's ... I'm nearly fifteen, Kerry, and I'm thinking about looking after myself and the costs. Like I explained. What Chris thinks is a lot I –'

'Did you see him on the day after 3.20?' Kerry replied. 'With the bike, without the bike. At the Welcome, somewhere else?'

'Of course I saw him,' she said.

'Of course she saw him or I would not of brought you out on a Saturday, I swear to God,' Chris said. 'I know when she's telling the truth.'

'Where was it?' Kerry asked.

Liz stood up. 'Look, we need to talk about the money *first*,' she said, 'I've told you.'

'That's not how it is,' Chris replied. 'You tell her something, something good, and you got to trust her. It will be all right.'

'I don't like it like that,' Liz said.

'Was he alone? Where was he going?' Kerry asked. 'Did you actually talk?'

'Yes, we *actually* talked,' Liz replied.

'Don't be so fucking rude,' Chris said.

Liz moved away towards the path down.

'I can't just hand out money or promise money,' Kerry said. 'It comes from a special account. It has to be approved.'

'You'll get a code name,' Chris said.

Liz stopped. 'Approved who by? Do *they* know Coventry as well? I don't like it.' She began to run down towards the car.

Chris and Kerry followed. 'It will be all right,' Chris said. 'I'll persuade her. What I'm paid for.'

71

Will Mallard said: 'We're getting close, Helen, love. On the right. They've got a flag over it, the firm's sort of ensign with S.W. in red, Sidney Waters.'

He sounded good, she thought: unhysterical, on top of the facts, graphic. Even casual: the 'love' made it sound like chit-chat. *Oh, keep it like this, Will, keep it like this.* Helen had done such final reconnaissance drives often before and knew the procedure. She would let the speed of the car fall now, but not so much that they became noticeable. Then, as they slowly passed the target, she would manage a look. There would be another on the way back, and she might get out of the car and do a stroll as well.

Jake said: 'There, Helen.'

She saw the flag and watched a furniture van looking weighty pull into the yard.

Jake's girl Petra was with them, wearing trainers and ankle socks with her long off-white cotton skirt and scarlet striped blouse. 'It looks really stuffed with goodies, doesn't it, Helen?' she asked.

'I counted three security people, two in the yard, one on a kind of balcony,' Helen said.

'That's about it,' Will said. 'I've got information on the whole patrol staff – know their profiles in detail. We can manage them. We know which will be working on the night. These are family lads. They're not going to look for bother. Unarmed, except for sticks, obviously.'

'So thorough,' Petra replied, clapping her hands almost soundlessly five or six times just under her chin. 'I never realised it was done like this – the preparation and everything.'

'Vital,' Jake said. 'Thoroughness. That's Will.'

'Absolutely,' Will said. His voice was still without brashness, shaped for a gentle lesson in robbery to Petra. This trip was another of his rituals. As well as the policy meeting in Daniel

Street followed by dinner at the Bordeaux, he would usually ask Helen to drive him to the target very near the date so he and perhaps Jake or Oscar could have one concluding look at the layout: buildings, security, escape streets, traffic. Will and Oscar had already done a night-time survey on the depository, so perhaps this final daylight check was worthwhile. Will reckoned a car driven by a woman would be less memorable on these journeys than one with a couple of men in it: just an outing.

Helen had the idea there was more to it. Will liked to involve her direct. This seemed to comfort him, steady him. 'Park anywhere you can find now,' he said. 'Jake and I will walk back separate from each other and give it another eyeing. This has to be right. We move the night after tomorrow. I'll see what things are like there from right alongside, and if it's OK maybe you could have a walk past, too, Helen.'

'Oh, and me, and me,' Petra cried. 'I do want to be part of this.'

'Yes, and you, obviously,' Will said, the tone kindly.

In some ways Helen was pleased to help and, in any case, would never have let him see she was not. With Duncan she had been kept on the edge of his life: undoubtedly valued but valued as a fine acquisition. Perhaps he couldn't let anybody really near. There were people like that, men and women, sealed off somehow. Will put her at the middle of everything, or nearly the middle. He needed her there. She loved that. It was *her* need as well. Sometimes – today – she felt like a moll, but a moll who matched him for status. In this there was a real buzz: fun, fear, guts. Some challenge, too. She knew one reason he liked her to come was so she could size up their chances, foresee possible difficulties, even suggest improvements to the detail of their scheme. He listened to her. Jake and Oscar listened to her.

She pulled on to a 'Waiting 20 minutes in any hour' spot, and Jake prepared to leave the car first. 'Just get the feel of it again,' Will said. 'Breathe it. Next time we breathe it, wham!' His voice grew strained then, a little unbelievable. 'And anything that's changed, obviously – possible obstructions, that kind of thing. Don't make notes, not in sight of the place, anyway.' They had plenty of sketches of the store inside and out, supplied by Will's contact in the firm. She fretted about these whispers. If the raid did come off police would trawl for anyone who might have given private briefings.

'You'll be great, darling,' Petra said as Jake went from the car. She kissed him, a long off-to-war sort of kiss, right hand plainly dick-fingering through his jeans, perhaps for a memory print for a week or two in case things went wrong. They watched him amble towards the depository, a film extra doing casualness.

'Me in a minute,' Will said. 'I'll see what kind of stuff they bring from the latest van. We might find even more good gear than in the tip-off.'

All this participation probably made her an accessory, Helen realised that – oh, sure it made her an accessory – and at times she found the notion grim. It was not what she had married Will for. But then, she had not married him to become a crook's wife in any shape, active or passive. That had developed bit by undramatic bit. These car duties were only a small addition to her knowledge of what went on, weren't they? She hadn't suddenly turned into half of Bonnie and Clyde. Will had tried to live straight but conditions would not let him. That was genuine. It had happened while she watched and grieved and raged. She had to back him in living how he could, hadn't she? He needed more than dole, not just for the money but his selfhood. She understood that. Besides, Chris and she enjoyed the gains, when there were any. Always she came back to that argument. They owed him. In the Press a year or two ago she read how some famed woman detective novelist said on radio that inner city poverty might cut people's power to make moral choices. She was accused of snootiness, but Helen thought it could be spot on.

Will left the car. There was no more kissing. He just suddenly, offhandedly, opened the passenger door, closed it behind him and began to walk. Petra said: 'They're so – oh, I don't know . . . so brave. So brave and so methodical, so cool.'

Up to now. It took little to walk past a furniture den and do nothing except gaze. 'They know each other so well, Petra,' she said. 'It brings them confidence.'

'And pluck,' she replied.

God! Did she read boys' annuals from the 1930s? Of course, if Helen ever got Will working for Coventry there would not be any more dicey chauffeur roles for her, because Coventry had plenty of his own people, and Will would not be involved in this kind of risk work, anyway. Coventry's scheme for Will had nudged her mind once or twice lately. She tried to kill it but it would edge back. Now it edged back. Although she thrilled to see Will bucked up by the planning and responsibility in this kind of operation, she dreaded the possible disaster he might fall into, or the possible humiliation if he called off. Oscar was away somewhere negotiating for use of a furniture van. Did he know how to do that without starting gossip? Could anyone do it without starting gossip?

Petra said: 'You must be really proud, Helen – Will running this little team, with everybody's respect. I know Jake worships him.'

'Will's a good man.'

'He certainly is,' Petra replied. 'Who'd say different?'

Of course, before Will could be given a job by Coventry she would have to talk to Chris. The deal. Her orders were to stop him making trouble over Tim's death, stop him looking for information. Helen was not sure she wanted to do that – or even whether she could make herself do it. Perhaps she did have moral choices after all. And possibly there were others: for instance, would she really like to see Will on the staff of Coventry Tom? He was a man who talked terrible oblique menace and who might have killed a child, though he somehow stayed this side of the wall. Then, that other question: would Coventry scent sex if she agreed to talk to Chris and Will were taken on to the payroll? There would be no whiff of promise from her, of course – Coventry Tom? Aaaagh! – but he might see gratitude, compliance, attraction, prospects. Perhaps there was a moral choice here, too: shouldn't she stay far from him, consider no deals, seek no billet for Will?

Gazing past Helen through the windscreen, Petra said: 'Oh, I can see both of them parading, the good lads, Helen, and you would never think they'd ever seen each other before. I mean, this is acting. This is *so* subtle. I'm really fascinated. Isn't it ... yes, *fascinating*, Helen.'

'No, don't point at them,' Helen said. She could see both men, too. Yes, it was a good show. Preliminaries they were grand at.

Helen thought that if she did stay far from Coventry she had better stop moaning to herself about these driving sessions and Will's criminality, and about Chris's likely tumble into criminality after him – into what the sociology experts called 'status zero', a violent wasteland for undereducated unemployable kids. Oh, God, couldn't Chris be saved somehow from that, saved even this late in the day? Could he? Somehow was right. How? Somehow might be Coventry. And if, instead, she stayed far from him and his offers she had better start thinking now about Chris's immediate safety. Each screened slide Coventry had shown her of Chris and the policewoman's car spoke a threat. For Coventry, this was where any deal began. And the murder of Tim Denton, which Coventry Tom so earnestly denied, was of course Coventry Tom's weapon to terrify her about Chris. It worked.

Helen turned to speak to Petra in the back of the car. 'If Will wants us to have a walk, we'll do it the same way – separately, I think. No recognition signs of any kind.'

'Well, he wants your verdict, not mine,' Petra said. 'Me, I'm just along to fill the car. Helen, you look sad.'

'A bit tense.'

Petra nodded. Then she said slowly: 'Oh, I put it on, bright and enthusiastic, because I get the feeling they need that – I mean all of them, not just Jake. Poor Jakey definitely does. He's such a prize. He laughs and jokes, but he needs something to make him believe in himself.' Her snub, neat, mobile face settled into a wince. All at once there seemed much more to her than girlish bubbliness, though some of that still showed.

'Yes, they need a boost,' Helen said. 'They've got spirit and talent, some talent, but they do need back-up now and then.'

'Perhaps you put it on, too, do you? Do you? Like a wifely duty? Great! But then I worry about it – I worry that if I encourage Jake – encourage him just because he needs it, you know, not because I've really thought it out – I wonder if on account of me he's going to let himself in for something that could turn out pretty terrible. Honestly, Helen, I don't know how you see it, but this doesn't look much of a job to me. So, well, I mean. . . . *cumbersome*. There's a shithead element to it, you ask me. Sorry if you believe in them all-out, the way you seem

76

and Will being numero uno and all that, but...I would never say any of this to Jake or the other two – but, I mean, manhandling this stuff, wardrobes, sideboards, maybe, cabinets, then getting rid of it for a nice price. It's so tricky. And using insider info. First thing the police will do is grill every bugger working there. Is that going to lead? Make sure Will gets rid of those sketches and whatall as soon as it's over. But these people – insiders – they're often soft as custard, Helen. Leaking's all they're good at. They can't handle interrogation. These are people who name names.'

The sudden show of shrewdness and anxiety shook Helen. Of course, at the Bordeaux she spotted that Petra was damn sharp behind the noise, but this was a hellishly clear-eyed and ruthless slab of insight.

Petra said: 'Jake tells me all the time – four or five jobs like this and they'll have enough to quit and start something legit. Great! But...well, I expect they all say it.'

'Something gets in the way, that's all,' Helen said.

'And you've got a kid. This is a worry, is it? Why you look sad?'

'I don't look sad all the time, do I?'

'Of course not.' She grinned again, gave a sort of whistle of pleasure. 'There's some real flavour to this life, or I wouldn't be in it, nor you, I guess. These are good-looking boys, even Oscar. There's something bright and tough and free in their faces. Sometimes you, Helen, you're just full of...that *gleam*. At the Bordeaux the other night, so full of richest, riotous, ritziest gleam. I couldn't keep up. I'm younger but I envied you. And yet a kid is serious. What I mean is, you can't move on.'

'You might?' Helen asked.

'Jake and I – well, I think we both know this might not be for ever. I don't think we're that sort of people. Here he is now, the hero.' She shoved open the rear door and Jake climbed in, panting, grinning. 'Good, darling?' Petra asked.

'Great. Great. A pushover, like we always thought. I can't wait.' Petra kissed him again. He eased her back on the seat gently and pulled his mouth away. 'Pet, I'm on such a ripe high, you know what I wish, I wish we could have it off now, here. Now!' His hand went up her skirt like a cat up a tree.

She freed herself. 'Broad daylight, bystanders watching, Helen watching! But, yes, yes, yes, I do feel like that myself – so excited, Jakey! Adrenalin.' Her voice did passion quivers. 'However – however, restraint! Please, restraint! An hour we'll be home. Keep it for then, yes? We mustn't get the car remembered, you know, and I think it would be if the soles of my feet are suddenly wide apart, toes curling, on the window.'

'Ah, I forgot that,' Jake replied, 'the secrecy bit.' He drew back and sat respectably away from Petra. 'A ton of lovely-looking stuff coming out of that van in there.'

Will rejoined them soon afterwards. 'Good, darling?' Helen asked. He looked as he sometimes could look, dazed by self-pity and pain.

'Did you see who one of those guards is, Jake?' he said. 'They must have brought him in new. My fucking luck. No dossier for him.'

'Who?' Jake asked.

'This is Carl Date. Drive us back now, Helen, will you?' His voice was a squeak.

Petra said: 'Oh, but Will, look, Helen and I were going to have a little inspection on foot, too. Scene of crime – flavoursome. We won't be long, will we, Helen? Please, Will.'

'Take us back, Helen,' Will replied.

Petra said: 'What is this, Will – some unexpected bloke in a security uniform and everything's – ?'

'For fuck's sake shut up, Pet,' Jake replied. Helen took them out into the traffic. On the way past the depository she tried another survey, but was it needed?

'You sure it's Carl?' Jake said.

Will was in the passenger seat and turned to stare at him. Again for a second, Helen thought Will would flare and go for Jake. Then he said: 'No question. How the hell did you miss him?'

'What is he?' Petra asked.

'This is Carl Date, for Christ's sake,' Will answered.

'But you can handle him, can't you?' Petra said.

'This is a bloody mad man,' Will said.

'But you boys can handle him, I know it, know it, know it,' Petra replied, as before clapping her hands repeatedly just under her small chin.

'It's really bad is it, love?' Helen said.

10

Eventually, Kerry decided she must have a delicate go at her Controller for some up-front money to offer Liz. There would be nothing from her otherwise. Liz had smelled gain and meant to hold out for it. These were children who had picked up skills very fast. They believed they knew how the world ran and that it ran on cash and not much else. Contradicting them effectively was difficult, though Kerry did try now and then with Chris and might try with Liz one day: not now. When she thought of Liz she mainly recalled a pair of untrusting, unconfiding dark blue eyes behind those pink-framed schoolgirl spectacles. If Liz ever did beat the terrible odds and get to be an architect she might or might not turn out talented, but she'd know how to screw clients for fees. Kerry loved her toughness, determination, insolence. She thought Chris probably liked Liz, though he would make no show. And Tim Denton must also have liked her. Did Liz really know anything about Coventry Tom? Even if she was bluffing, Kerry still admired her sauce.

Of course, Doug Quinn, her Controller, turned Kerry down. In his gentle but definite way, Doug made it clear that he and the Registrar of informants above him already wondered whether they were getting enough from Kerry's 'dear little laddy' called Duke. Dear meant expensive. They jibbed at also paying out to a friend of his who might or might not have something. 'Sorry, but I've spoken to Superintendent Bell and he won't wear it,' Doug said. 'He did contemplate for a while suggesting you could work both kids with a co-handler, so everything's subject to checking.'

'The children will talk only to me,' Kerry replied.

'He thought you'd say that. *I* thought you'd say that. All handlers do. You want to keep your source exclusive. It's understandable. You'll have heard of the Stockholm Syndrome.'

'The what, for God's sake?'

'Of course you've heard of it – where handler and informant have been through a lot of stress together and start bonding. The detective begins to feel that the proper rules governing the running of a grass are stupid and a dead-weight. Do I sense that in you, Kerry?'

Well, maybe he did. She became desperate. 'All right, possibly I could operate with Vic Othen as co-handler,' she said.

'It would have to be an associate who doesn't know you.'

'Oh, look, I – '

'Anyway, it's not relevant. Finally Mr Bell as Registrar said no.'

Kerry pleaded, argued, promised, and Quinn stayed attentive, very considerate, wonderfully benign-looking beneath his glossy cream baldness – and inflexible. There was another factor. As Vic had warned, people at the top were suddenly nervous and getting more nervous about the secret use of child informants. Doug began worriedly counting on his fingers: 'Kerry, we've got the Home Affairs Select Committee, the National Association of Youth Justice and the National Association for the Care and Resettlement of Offenders all asking hard questions. Plus the Press. You tell me this girl's going to talk to you about Ingle-Blake – *if* she has anything to talk about at all.'

'I do think she has, sir,' Kerry trilled. 'Know it.'

He nodded, acted out surrender by holding up both hands behind his desk, and said: 'If so, it's a hazardous area for youngsters. It exposes them – and so it exposes us: to big blame if things go sour.' He grew gentler still, and embarrassed. 'On top of that, it's not properly a solo area for you, Kerry, is it? There are top figures here still preoccupied with Ingle-Blake. I don't know how they'd take it – you digging undirected.'

'But it *is* directed, sir,' she replied.

'Not by them. Look, why don't you get your prosperous little Duke moving on something a bit more modest and easier, while there's time?' Now Doug used a finger to point up through the ceiling to the Registrar's office: 'Harry Bell's got to make a case for keeping our kid tipsters, and making a case is now no push-over. We need to show some gains from them, Duke included. Duke especially. The Chiefs' Association will bring out guide-lines on the use of kid informants without parental knowledge. Harry's under pressure from our Chief to put things on hold until we get the ground rules. The Chief adores ground rules. There could be a freeze on young grasses – or a freeze on the money they get, anyway. Same?'

Afterwards, she had a cup of tea in the canteen and must have been looking down in the mouth. Claire Bater and Andy Norman came and sat with her. 'Doug been talking harsh at you, Kerry?' Claire asked.

'Talking wisely at me, I suppose,' Kerry replied.

When she came out to her car in the headquarters yard at midday Kerry saw Chris crouched by the offside rear wheel. She climbed into the front and opened the door near him. He crawled in, this time lying out on the floor. Kerry had her long raincoat on the passenger seat and she pushed it through to him. 'Hide yourself until we're past the barrier, Chris,' she said.

'I've given her the money. She'll talk. She's all wrapped up and bought.'

'What money?'

'Tree money,' he said. 'For Liz.'

She started the Cavalier's engine, let it idle for a moment.

'Not all of it,' he said. 'Enough. A fee. It seemed like a . . . like a way to help you.'

He stayed on the floor and pulled the coat over himself. Kerry got out of the car and made a bit of a performance of closing the rear door, as if it were faulty and had somehow opened on its own. Looking down at him she thought suddenly of corpses she had seen covered like this at the roadside after an accident or shoot-out, and she gave a little hoarse gasp and grabbed at the door pillar for a second to steady herself. He heard the sound and stuck his head out from under the coat, grinning with excitement. In a moment she grinned herself. It was an instant comfort to see him move and look so lively. 'What's wrong, Kerry?' he asked. 'This coat smells of Red scent. Nice. Of *you*.'

'Everything's fine.' Back behind the wheel, she said: 'But I'm not sure it's sensible for you to come here. Police gossip like anyone else, you know. More. Or someone might see you coming into the car-park. Word could drift back to your dad, to anyone.'

'How else to get to you? I can't keep ringing up. What's he going to think, this voice asking for you all the time, and obviously not a woman friend?'

There was an almost comical sexual undertone to what he said, as if he was a pushy rival to Mark, but she didn't laugh.

'I wouldn't like it if I had a girlfriend and she was getting private calls like that,' he said.

'They're not private, are they? They're business calls. Private business calls. Mark understands my work.' And he did, pretty well and off and on. He certainly would not get jealous about a boy voice on the phone. 'But listen, Chris, you scamp, we fix a timetable and straight away you break it twice. You're a – Oh, never mind. We'll get away with it. Just stay down.' She used her card on the barrier and drove out.

He did not get up, speaking to her from under the coat and through the gap between the two front seats: 'Well, it was real simple, wasn't it, Kerry? I should of thought of it straight away. All this cash lying there, doing nothing. So, I decided give some to Liz and say it came from you. Which is right, yes? It *did*. Like I was just the messenger with it. You should of seen her, Kerry. You really should of.' He was chortling. 'This is a kid who never had that much cash in her hand, I could tell. Her glasses all misty and she's wetting her lips with her tongue all the time – you know the way people do when they're nearly too excited to talk. Like a snake on *Wildlife*. I don't know if she'll keep it for being an architect or spend it on girls' stuff, you know the sort of stuff they buy. Red scent.'

'How much did you give her?'

'Only a fucking century. This is only her first time. I wouldn't put her on to top rate just like that, would I, Kerry? But I said you said maybe another if the stuff she comes up with is any good. She said, "Of course it's bloody good." You know what she's like, some big mouth. But I said, "You say it's good but Kerry's the one that got to say if it's *real* good. Only she knows that. There's people above her watching her. There's people above her who want to mess her about because she's getting

82

on so fast although nearly young."' He thought about that. 'What I mean is, Kerry, *really* young as a cop, but older than us, me and Liz, obviously.'

'You're very helpful and nice, Chris. Thanks.'

'Seemed the best way, that's all. I mean, in case your bosses were tight with the money. They might be, Kerry.'

'Yes, they might.' Sometimes she wondered whether Chris would make so much effort if his handler was a man, no tits, no smell of Red. How did you deal with a thirteen-year-old admirer? 'When can I see Liz?' Kerry asked. 'Will you be there?'

'You want me there?'

'Of course. She's *your* contact, isn't she?'

'That's right,' he said solemnly. 'Well, it can't be tonight. They got an aunty from America at her house or something like that so she got to be home for cups of tea and that, nice family stuff, telling the aunty about being an architect and her friend knifed to death by the pal of royalty. Architect. Quite a good idea. She can make sure they don't build no more shit tips like where we live. Or if they do she'll get some of the loot for it. I expect they *will* build more like that. Of course, she'll never get there. Ever hear of a kid from here who got to be an architect or traffic warden, anything like that – sort of higher jobs? See her Friday. This money, I'm kind of lending it back to you, that's all, Kerry. If she got something really suitable you'll be able to draw a couple of hundred for her, won't you, from the grass fund – they'd really open up then, your bosses, wouldn't they? – obviously – nail Coventry – would they? – they want to nail him? – I hope so – and then you can give me my hundred back and give her the other one? She will of earned it. Or give her fifty and me fifty for lending you the hundred. Make sense?' His muffled voice went into a teaching tone. 'Kerry, you heard of a middle-man at all? This was something I heard of on a video. That's what I am, a middle-man, and a middle-man gets paid.'

'Where Friday?'

'The usual? Half-past two?'

Briefly her memory showed him again covered by the coat. 'Chris, I told you, I don't like using the same place all the time.'

'You and your worries, Kerry. All right. Where?'

'Say outside Rex Centre.'

'If you like.' In the mirror she saw him come out from under the coat, rise on to his knees and squint through the windscreen. 'Look, don't take me too near my street.'

'You and your worries, Chris.'

'Mum's edgy. I can see the signs. I think dad's – '

'No,' Kerry said. 'You don't talk to me about that. I've told you.'

As to signs, she thought of warning him to tell nobody about Liz and the money and Coventry Tom. She knew this would have enraged him, though – an accusation that he might grow stupid and boyish and gabby. She said nothing but pulled up in a side street not far from his house, a spot she and Vic had used as a change for watching the Mallard place the other night. As he left he said: 'We'll get him, Kerry, we're a team, you and me.'

'Right, Chris.' She did not tell him, either, that any day now she would be seeing Coventry Tom and Timothy Denton's mother at a meeting designed to probe, in civilised style and setting, all the rumour and all the differences between Sonia Denton and Ingle-Blake. Kerry considered this might have enraged Chris, too, and would have at least disastrously confused him.

She went to the shops. It was three years today since she and Mark moved in together, and they always exchanged presents to celebrate. She wanted something to suggest long-lastingess. She had felt very unsure lately that this was how things would be. The doubt depressed her, made her want to spend a lot to dispel it. They were good together, weren't they, real partners? A ring would not do because they had bought rings for each other at the very beginning. She lashed out on a genuine black fountain pen: gold nib for use with real ink. Gold nibs went on for ever, didn't they? She inscribed the gift tag with it, as a trial: *Mark, all my love, Kerry.* Her handwriting looked elegant. The pen as she used it looked elegant. It was perfect for Mark. Briefly, she contemplated going to his office now and getting him to write something with the pen, something loving and a promise of permanency – something she could keep if they separated. Probably, though, he would be out to lunch somewhere. Tonight would do. She had a quick café lunch herself and went back to work.

In the afternoon, she was called up to Harry Bell's room. She thought, Oh God, here's the end to child informants: Doug Quinn was spot on.

Harry said: 'We've had a bit of luck, Kerry. I think we can arrange credibility for your young grass, Duke. He needs some of that.'

She said: 'Duke's an informant who – '

'Who's quite difficult to justify. He doesn't come up with what we want.'

'He will, sir.'

'I gather Will Mallard and his little crew are considering a raid,' Harry replied.

For a second she thought Vic Othen must have told him and was amazed at how betrayed she felt. He had promised not to report what he suspected. The eternal hunt for *gloire* had made him talk to Bell after all?

'We've got three bits of information that can be set alongside one another,' Harry said. He was slim, grey-haired, big-voiced, almost as benign-looking as Doug Quinn but three times as devious. Harry was also five times as powerful, although nominally they were only a rank apart, Quinn chief inspector, Harry superintendent. Harry must have made a study of how power works, and he made it work for him. As head of CID and Registrar, he held that list Chris Mallard spoke of, the one which paired real names and code names. 'I heard just now from a friend of mine in the trade that Oscar Knight has been asking about furniture vans. You know Oscar? Nice fellow. Works with Will. Vans are risk, Kerry – big and noticeable and slow and not easy to hire without starting talk, and not easy to steal and keep concealed. So, we assume a job with take large enough makes the hazards acceptable. I asked our antiques people to check if there were any especially attractive collections that might attract Will and Oscar, and probably Jake Lowe. Apparently there's some lovely stuff in the Sidney Waters depository, but only for a few days.'

'Does Will do antiques?'

'He'll do anything if it looks a goer. He might have someone inside briefing him.'

'But selling stuff like that afterwards?' Kerry said.

'It can be done. Antiques do get taken, you know. Will's not a great one for looking all that far ahead, anyway. His wife is a different body, but Will is Mr Leadership. Status. It has to be protected. She'd let him run things, probably. That's how the love of women works, don't you think, Kerry? I've a little force waiting there discreetly and someone keeping an eye on Will's house, so we can get alert each time he goes out.'

She felt so pleased to hear Vic was not the source that for a while her mind failed to follow all Harry said.

'This will be the kind of neat, bloodless ambush we want – the kind judges and juries appreciate, and, crucially, the sort that might convince the Home Secretary and others that the child grass system is a plus. Especially it might convince them that it can be good for us to have dealings with a child informant even when the parents are unaware of it. How would we have got Will if he'd known his son grassed?'

Now she did pick up what Harry was telling her. 'I'm pretty sure Chris Mallard talks only to me, sir, and he's never mentioned anything about his father's activities.'

'Not to be harsh,' Harry said, 'but I sometimes wonder what he *does* talk to you about. This is some long-term project to nail Coventry Tom? And then the little girl Liz Something comes into that as well, am I right?'

'It's a possibility.'

'Not your realm, Kerry, as I hope Doug told you. And not the kind of case I could use to argue for child informants. Too dark. Too political. Whereas...' He grew matey, sort of man-to-man. Yes, sort of. 'Kerry, come on. You're not telling me, seriously, that the boy never even hinted to you his father and crew have an operation in hand?'

'Never. I know he wouldn't.' She said it plain. Denials should always be that. Interrogators saw deception in wordage.

Harry kept the same tolerant, professional-to-professional tone: 'You might lie to me about that, anyway. Naturally. You want this lad to help you land a biggie. You'd hate to have him blamed for an ambush on his dad. It would make him conspicuous. It might make him dead. People are fond of Will, the blundering prat, and someone could decide he would not want such a son left alive. Where would that leave you, Kerry?'

86

'No, I'm not lying, sir. I can't believe any child – any informant at all – would finger a relative.'

Behind the big cheapy desk Harry had a giggle about that. 'Of course they do, Kerry. All ages. A money matter. Know the phrase "he'd sell his grandmother"? It's about grasses.'

'Duke wouldn't do it.' She disliked calling him by his real name, even with Harry.

'If you like. But the point is we can *say* he did this time,' Harry replied.

She was appalled. 'How?'

'The tip on Oscar Knight came to me, personally, today from an old chum. He expects no credit. Would want no credit. We have a different sort of arrangement, he and I. After the information about Oscar and the van, the rest is deduction, isn't it? No competing grasses. We can credit Chris with giving us the lot – place, probable timing and excellence of the take. Sorry: giving *you* the lot. This is very much your personal grass, Kerry. We manage a plus for you and a plus for Duke when I draw up the balance sheet for those I have to convince. This is valuable.'

'He just wouldn't,' she said.

'It doesn't matter, does it?' Harry was into mild jubilation. 'Here we have one of those situations where what's perceived is what counts. And what's perceived will be what I tell them. Who's to contradict?'

'Me?' she replied.

He stared at her for a while. The matiness had disappeared from his narrow face – that pretence at equality.

'I don't follow your reasoning, sir,' she said. 'You tell me people are afraid child informants might be exposed to retaliation. But you intend publicising that this boy betrayed his father.'

'Publicise? Not *publicise*, for God's sake. I'm not going to give it to our Press department. This will be for the Chief only.'

'And for some of these outside bodies anxious about child grassing. As you said, sir, they have to be won over with a balance sheet. To be credible that needs detail.'

'Some detail.'

'Names, sir. That kind of information can spread.'

'I'll make sure the boy is looked after.'

'Sir, I – '

'I'll make sure the boy is looked after. Kerry, you're fast track. People expect things from you. Important you deliver or the idea gets around that you've burned out.'

In the evening, she gave Mark the pen and asked him to go to the table at once and write her a loving letter with it. She watched him. He composed without hesitation, as though he had been waiting for ever to set down his feelings and had needed only a gold nib and ink. *Darling Kerry, After three years and a bit all I know is that I want to be with you more than I did when we began, and I wanted to be with you then more than I had ever wanted anything. We have our style differences and job differences and temperament differences but nothing shakes us or can. I would not let it, and I don't believe you would. We have a love which is that – a love, a love, a love, and everything else has to take second or tenth place to this and if it doesn't it can take a running jump.*

She went and stood behind him, reading it over his shoulder. 'I like my jumps quite slow,' Kerry said.

'To start.'

'Oh, yes. No complaints.' She folded the sheet of notepaper and put it in her bag.

They went out to a meal at the Bordeaux, a spot Mark loved. Last time she was near it she and Vic had tailed Will Mallard here. That was all right. You had to expect overlaps. Mark had bought her an Edwardian pendant brooch on a fine gold chain and with a central single diamond. She wore it tonight. It was lovely, set off by her plain, high-necked lavender satin dress which Mark said made her look 'almost demure'.

'Three years,' he said, over his sheep's brains. 'I don't know why we don't marry.'

'No, I don't.'

'Honestly?'

He had pressed her before, spoken about a family, and she had dodged. Marriage had not seemed necessary, and a family not on the cards. And then lately out of nowhere had come this yearning for permanence. Legalised permanence? Perhaps it was the effect of seeing households disrupted, imperilled:

Sonia Denton's neat place, the Mallards' endangered peace. Perhaps Liz's household now. Did Kerry want to set up something solid and safe to show it could still be done? *Could* it still be done?

The strange tremor that came when she thought Vic Othen had let her down worried Kerry. The recollection of it had come back for a second tonight when Mark suggested the Bordeaux. Vic was, say, twenty years older, divorced but maybe partnered now – maybe partnered for years, decades, and content. Why didn't she have the facts on this? Surely it could only have been a professional thing, a police thing, that sense of injury. She hated the notion of inconstancy. Was she reaching out to Mark now as a barrier against that? Was it enough to justify marriage? This was *marriage*, not just living together. The barrier notion would do as one reason for going ahead. There were plenty more.

'Yes, honestly,' she replied.

'You've got a timetable in mind?'

'We've decided in principle,' she said. 'We can settle the rest of it later?'

'Of course,' he said.

11

Helen Mallard went alone this time to look at the Sidney Waters furniture depository and without telling Will. Oh, obviously without telling Will. To make sure there'd be no questions about the absence of the car she travelled by bus. It carried her right past the depository and she examined the building and yard from an upstairs window, but saw nothing to alarm her. All the same she felt very unhappy. At the next stop she dismounted and went back on foot. She wanted to stay unobserved, yet did not really know how to manage it. If she approached by side streets she would still have to emerge at some point, and might even be more noticeable when coming out unaccompanied at a junction. Instead, she kept close to a small group of people walking on the pavement of the main road, trying to appear part of it.

She did not know exactly what she was looking for. The woman detective on Coventry Tom's slides? Would Helen recognise her? The pictures had been murky. Yes, she would recognise her, because the detective would be hanging around waiting and acting as if she was not waiting. She would possibly be in a car, probably close to the depository. Did they use girls on ambushes? Maybe there would be other people lurking near her, heavy people, heavy male colleagues. They might be especially bulky around the chest, because of flak jackets and concealed armament. Like Helen, they could have uncertainties about whether at some stage Will and his team would turn to guns.

Helen was here now, peeping, spying, searching because a sharp appalling dread had jabbed her lately. What if when Chris joined the woman officer for one of those trips in her car he told her of the planned raid by Will? Helen knew he was a grass and grasses grassed. Perhaps Chris talked of other things than Coventry and the death of Tim Denton, more immediate things, things easier to deal with. When this thought first came to Helen it had savaged her. It still did. Could Chris know about the raid? He had been at home for some of the time, hadn't he, the day the first meeting took place? Oscar and Jake were loud and careless when excited and their voices boomed around the small house. Chris had even stuck his head into the room where the job conference took place.

Then there was Oscar, out searching for a suitable van. She did not rate Oscar for subtlety, and because of him the police might have heard another signal about a possible break-in. They'd put the two indications together. They could be waiting now, ready to collar Will basically on the word of Will's child. Yes, this idea had savaged her: not so much the idea that Will would be caught and possibly hurt or worse, but that he would realise who had betrayed him. Although she was only into criminal life by fluke and at a distance she had absorbed some of the contempt these folk felt about grassing, and especially grassing on family. God, she could not allow so much darkness into her home.

90

But perhaps in a sense it had already entered: if Chris had spoken to his girl cop of the raid, wasn't that itself the start of betrayal? Possibly, but *only* the start: Helen had to stop it becoming known and obvious and disastrous. Her husband must not be made to hate her son, and perhaps to act on that hatred. Such a shadow would chill all the rest of her life – make her life a waste. Perhaps to conceal treachery was only a very small victory, seen against the treachery itself. But the big gain was that her family would go on looking like a family, a good, intact family, whatever else happened to it. This much would content her if that was the best available. She did not deal in absolutes. Who did?

The woman detective was not on view near the Sidney Waters building, nor anyone else who was flagrantly police. This might only mean they were skilled at concealment: the prey must not see the trap. And naturally they *were* skilled at concealment. They were specialists. She kept going. It was morning. Perhaps they sensed that the raid would take place at night and only set the ambush then. If she saw any hint of a reception party she would go home and work on Will to abandon the robbery. He already seemed uncertain, jittery – a pattern with him, and the other two. They would enthuse about a project and then when the day came close the actuality of it unnerved them. That glimpse the other day of a new security guard appeared to have shattered Will. If Helen now told Will she, also, had come to feel uneasy about the Waters raid, it would influence him, perhaps kill the plan. Naturally, she would not say why, or not the true reason. She would tell him – tell them – she had bad doubts: the selling-on problems, the bulkiness of the cargo, possible exposure by the inside voice. These might be enough. They might be enough even if Jake's girl Petra kept telling them that she *knew, knew, knew* they were unstoppable, the daft, clever nomadic bitch – and kept making Jake feel he had to be heroic to hold on to her.

In a minute she would need to turn and walk past the building again. So often from the car she had watched Will and one or both of the others do this kind of survey, often for a job that never took place. She used to smile at their hammy attempts to act casual. Now, she found she was trying to act casual herself, someone out for a bit of a stroll, window-shopping.

And it was as reflections in a leather fashions shop window that Helen thought she saw for a couple of seconds a man in an attic across the street staring down the road towards the depository. This was a workish, tense stare. She remained where she was. He disappeared, then returned. Now he had another man with him. Both seemed dressed for outdoors in what might be the same kind of blue anorak, perhaps a police kind. The two men withdrew. They were in their thirties, she guessed, thick-necked and heavy-shouldered. She did not think they had looked towards her. Both were preoccupied with Sidney Waters.

By now she had done her thorough study of the leather jackets and skirts and moved on, taking one very quick glance up at the attic. It might be a store room for the shop below. There were no curtains. She did not think the place was lived in, except, possibly, by a police contingent who had taken it over for a time. In the side street nearby a large green van stood parked with a woman in dungarees at the wheel smoking a cigarette. She appeared very relaxed, and uninterested in what was going on outside. Perhaps she was listening to a radio, or to conversation from behind her. Almost certainly this was not the woman detective who knew Chris. She might even be a genuine delivery driver or interior decorator. Of course she might. Helen went to the bus stop.

Later that day, at home, Will came into the kitchen where she was cooking tea and said: 'Know what I think, Helen? What I think is I think I'm going off this Sidney Waters operation.' The jokey wordiness of it was meant to thin out the shame: make the admission sound less like cowardice. He sat down at the table. Chris seemed to be out somewhere.

'Oh?' Helen replied.

'Jake's keen, Oscar so-so. With Jake half the enthusiasm's from Petra.'

'You worry about the new security guard?'

'He's one factor, I don't deny it, Helen. But there are many.' He waved an arm to show range. 'I have to try to see past the thrills of a brand new project. Those thrills are natural and even valuable – they give drive. But they can also bring some confusion, some lack of care.' Discretion got a grip on his larynx. 'I have to be alert against this, not just on my own account, but Jake's and Oscar's, especially when Jake might be influenced by his girl.'

'What is it about the security guard? Carl Date? Is that what you called him? You say he's mad?'

Will seemed touched by a mixture of rage and terror when she spoke the name. For a moment she sensed a danger that rage might rip away his control. He said: 'Leave him, leave Date, will you?' Will's breathing faltered and the words came feebly. He had a round, neat, often cheerful face, but it tightened hard now and grew pinkish-grey and threatening. When he looked like that she always found him part frightening, part laughable. It was hard to be wholly scared of someone pinkish-grey. You could, though, love someone pinkish-grey, partly *because* they were pinkish-grey – love had to contain some pity.

Helen wondered whether far back this man had defeated Will in some way, physically beaten him, possibly, humiliated him. At any rate, as a subject he was off limits. She said: 'What concerns me about the Sidney Waters job is – '

'You're right. Totally. We tried to ignore your objections because – well, because they'd fuck up morale, and morale's central. But you're a kind of partner, Helen, and we damn well ought to listen. Yes, the selling of stuff like that and the possible tracing, these are real snags.' His anger appeared to have gone.

'Plus, Will, I – '

'The voice from inside. I know. Yes, they'd wring him out, no question. Their first move. And Oscar looking for a van. Dicey. Oscar's great, always has been great, but – well, he's bound to be a worry.'

Helen, preparing mackerel, stated: 'Often the anti points to a job don't reveal themselves until quite late on, Will. At that stage it takes real resolution to say the downside is too much.' God, the bullshit.

'It does, it does,' he replied. 'But that's what I'm at the head of this outfit for, isn't it, love? Caution. Not *only* caution, obviously. I bring the new ideas. Concepts. But there is, too, this other function.'

'Jake and Oscar value that in you as much as they value the creative side,' Helen said.

'Yes, I believe they do. There is the initial disappointment, but then they do appreciate the point. They're good lads.'

'Grand,' Helen said.

'And I have this duty to look after the pair – despite themselves sometimes.'

Helen dished out the fish and vegetables and put a meal in the oven for Chris. She said: 'Sure. These responsibilities, Will – hard. Now and then I wonder...' She fiddled with some bones in her mouth and used the moment to work out how she would say the next bit. 'Look, I know what having your own personal team means to you and – '

'Everything, Helen,' he said. 'Second only to you and Chris.'

'Yes, but I do wonder whether it...Whether things would not be easier if you could join someone else.'

'Me, *join* someone?'

'Don't get wild! I don't mean just go on their payroll. That's definitely not you. No, I'm thinking of a kind of merger, as happens all the time in business. Move into some other outfit, perhaps a bigger one. It might mean the burdens of leadership would be...not relinquished, you could never do that, I know, but spread, shared, so they are not all on you, Will.'

'Oh, they're burdens all right.' She recognised the pain and self-pity, the battle weariness of a commander, the dear, sweet near-nobody.

'And the money might come in a bit more regularly,' she replied. 'I'm not complaining, Will. Never. We do all right, fine. And yet sometimes I think you worry about providing for us in the way you would want.'

'Every man worries about that now and then.'

'You especially, Will.'

'Perhaps. What bigger outfit?'

'There must be all sorts who'd jump to take you aboard,' she said. 'Experience. Special skills.'

He nodded. 'What bigger outfits?'

'Not my area,' she replied. 'But you must know the up-and-coming people, the healthy-looking firms.'

'Yes, they might want *me*,' he said. 'I've got to consider Jake and Oscar as well, though, haven't I?'

She laughed. 'Ah, still obsessed by leadership obligations, even when we're talking about shedding part of that load!'

'Built in,' he said.

Chris appeared not long afterwards and joined them for their meal. He was full of chat about nothing much. Did he sound like a boy who would sell his father, look like a boy who would sell his father? Hundreds would be a lot to a thirteen-year-old and Coventry had said hundreds. Occasionally today Chris mentioned school, as if he had been there. She liked it when they ate together. She liked feeling communal, and she liked it that Will sat at what could be considered the head of the table. Eating mackerel he seemed solid.

In the early evening Helen went out to a telephone box and rang Coventry Tom. 'I think Will might listen to an approach,' she said. 'Take it gently.'

'I'd given you up.'

'I had to do some thinking.'

'Your laddy is still seeing her, you know, and now he's introducing another kid, a girl.'

'More slides? No, I don't know, don't know anything about it.'

'But you haven't spoken to the boy, have you?'

'I'm going to,' she said.

'When I say I'd given you up I mean I heard you drove hubbie and the other two over to look at a target. As if you still want to help keep his little company independent, regardless.'

'You've had me tailed?'

'And then over there again.'

'He's not going to do it,' she replied.

His laughter barked. 'Of course he's not going to do it. You know him – an ideas man. Meaning he doesn't get beyond. He'd never risk coming up against... Well, they've got a guard there now your husband won't want to run into.'

'Will's not afraid of any – '

'He'd dodge this lad.'

'Who is he?'

'I doubt whether Will would tell you. Goes deep.'

'Who is he? Will would not be frightened off by – '

'And then others seem to have found out what's supposed to happen and are waiting.'

'Yes, I know.'

'You're the clever one in that team. He's no wizard, your man, is he?'

'He's got real abilities though maybe not the sort he – '

'The point is, I'm not sure many firms would want to take him on. He stops short too often. He could be a liability.'

'Honestly, he's fine. He'll – '

'But I've promised you I'd do it and I know how to stand by my word.'

'Thanks. He's worried about what happens to . . . '

'To the other two?'

'Yes.'

'What am I, the Job Centre?'

'He might insist.'

'He doesn't insist, can't insist, about anything. You know him better. But, all right, there's probably some fetching and carrying they could handle – for a while, anyway. Very short term contracts, while they look around, so your hub doesn't have to feel he's dropped them.'

'Thanks.'

'And you'll call off the teenage hunters?'

Again she had a feeling of grubby complicity with him. It was stronger now. Walking back from the phone booth Helen found she was trembling. She and Coventry were definitely tied into secrets together. Partners. Oh, Jesus. Urgently she consoled herself with the thought that they were secrets meant to profit her husband and her son. Over their meal she had pushed Will towards doing what he already longed to do – call off the Sidney Waters raid. If he did back out of the job through fear – back out *again* from a job – if he did drop this one, it was liable to destroy a bit more of his self-belief, a bit more of his spirit. She would watch him shrivel. But if Coventry Tom was in touch to make an offer wouldn't that give Will a lovely boost, especially if Coventry worded it right, made Will sound a potential partner? Coventry had a fine firm going and would not invite duds in. That's how Will would think, and Helen would help him think it. She wanted him happy, confident, whole, hers, safe. She wanted him to be a positive father, perhaps able to take her and Chris into a better area, and Chris into a better school and a bit of a future – in the way that Helen's own father had managed now and then to get the family into nice surroundings and herself into worthwhile schools. These were gains that justified a deal with Coventry, surely. And this is all it would be, a transaction with clear boundaries – quid pro quo, not quim pro quo.

12

Coventry Tom appeared at her front door in Daniel Street a couple of hours later. Helen was amazed, horrified, at the speed of his response, and at the method. The house still reeked of mackerel. She had expected Coventry to send one of his people to sound out Will very gradually, very carefully, very ambiguously, most likely bumping into him as if by fluke in the street or a pub, not at home. And yet when the doorbell rang something in her must have whispered 'Coventry,' or screamed, 'My God, Coventry!'

Will, Chris and Helen were watching *EastEnders*, caught up as on many evenings by a brisk story of incest, theft and brutality. She was the one who immediately stood, convinced she must get to the door ahead of Will or Chris, above all Chris. Where that certainty came from mystified her. It was not as if the way he rang the bell proclaimed someone lordly – not the long, insistent blast of a man who knew the royals and emperored a range of magnificent, steady businesses, some of them dirty. He only touched the button, barely more than a hint. Perhaps, though, he reckoned there was such a good bond between him and Helen now that a hint would do, a master's brief whistle to his dog. When she thought about this afterwards, it horrified her. It horrified her more because her speed in answering showed him right. Had this sod colonised her subconscious?

Coventry came alone in a small battered-looking car – a grey Ford or Vauxhall – and one of her thoughts as she opened the door was that he should have done better than this, for heaven's sake, if he was going to park right outside their house. A wealthy visitor ought to look like a wealthy visitor. The tailoring helped. He was in what her father would have called 'a country weekend' suit: a green-brown tweed with high waistcoat and narrow trousers for tucking into riding boots, although he wore brogues. It looked custom-made, a London job. His trilby was tan and high-crowned like a horse race commentator's, and he had on a check shirt and plain green silk tie. Friendliness and honour were in his face about fifty-fifty, his grey eyes warm, the smile cheery yet sympathetic. 'Mrs Mallard,' he said. 'Is this desperately inconvenient? I wondered if your husband were at home and might have a minute. Or should I come back at another time?'

She muttered at him with frantic spit around her front teeth: 'Look, this isn't the – '

'He's here? I may come in briefly?'

He pulled the hat off with full politeness and she moved aside for him, then had to push past so she could go ahead into the living-room. Will and Chris looked around from the television screen. 'Will,' she said, 'it's – '

'Will,' Coventry Tom boomed, 'grand to see you, and on your home patch. And the lad himself.' He had his hand out towards Will but gave Chris a good nod, a boys-will-be-boys nod.

Will stood and shook hands. He wore a purple sweatshirt and looked youthful, energetic, hellishly downmarket. 'What is it, Mr Ingle-Blake?' he said. 'I wasn't expecting anything like – '

'Oh, as ever, I'm in need, Will. I'm looking for a bit of help.'

'Help?'

'I was talking about it to colleagues, trying to sort out where such help might come from and someone said, "Tom, have you thought of Will Mallard?" ' He twirled the trilby a bit in his right hand. 'No, no, that's not it exactly. Not it at all, as it happens. The fact is your name had been in my mind for a fair old while, Will – naturally it had – but I'd told myself regretfully that Will Mallard was too damn busy with his own projects to be available for other commitments and, yes, I admit I'd felt it wisest to drop you from active consideration. To avoid disappointment, really, I suppose. And then a colleague – a wise, perceptive

98

colleague – this colleague and friend mentions you during one of our conferences and, of course, all my hopes are suddenly rekindled. I thought to myself, why not? Will might at least have a moment to listen to my proposition. That doesn't mean he's going to accept. But I'd have the chance to put it to him. Simply, I jumped in the car nearest the house and drove here direct, before my confidence weakened. I know you'll tell me if I was wrong, Will – wrong and presumptuous.'

Will stood up, gasping a bit, his skin very pale against the purple, like a sick bishop. 'Wrong? Well, no, not exactly, not at all, Mr Ingle-Blake, not necessarily. I'm not someone who'd shut his mind to any new idea, I trust. At this point in time don't we all need to be open? This is the thing about the coming millennium – opportunity.'

'A domestic context did not seem a bad idea, since this proposal is bound to have family implications,' Coventry remarked.

'Helen and Chris are crucial to my thinking,' Will said.

Chris appeared bewildered, claustrophobic. Helen could see he wanted to get out of the room. For now, though, he sat there staring, mainly at Coventry but sometimes at his father. Would he tell his detective lady about this? 'I'll make some tea,' Helen said. She knew the room probably looked cheap, but she loved it, had furnished it and arranged it with all the care and flair she owned, and if she caught this sod Coventry acting snooty she'd let him have the whole fucking pot of Earl Grey over his wide crooked head. She was not one to take snubs. Hadn't she been bourgeois off and on? One chair in here she felt particularly fond of, proud of. It was Victorian or Edwardian and she had bought it from a junk shop as a wreck for seventy-five pence. Will had grumbled a bit about the cost of doing it up in blue velvet, but she had kept on at him and now the chair was as handsome as anything in Coventry Tom's place. She had been sitting there herself when the bell rang and it was unoccupied since. She did not want him in it. This was a decent piece. All his green-brown would clash. She indicated the loose-covered sofa for Coventry before going out into the kitchen.

Chris followed in a hurry. 'Him,' he said. 'He shouldn't be here, should he? Not in our house. Why does dad talk to him like that, so smarmy? What's he want?'

'Search me. He said help.'

'What help? He helps himself.'

'We'll hear, I expect,' she replied.

'Dad's not going to . . . well, not going to . . . like be *with* him, is he?' His voice squeaked, pleaded for a No.

'Your dad will decide for himself.'

'He kills. Coventry Tom kills.'

'Your dad's heard all the stories, I'm sure,' she said.

'Stories?'

'That's all they – '

'I don't want to be in the house while he's here.'

Helen said: 'They'll be talking business, I expect. You'd be bored.'

'Do *you* like him then?' He gulped. 'Oh, you don't like him, do you, mum?' He looked disbelieving and scared, his thin face pinched and thinner, his eyes a mile off tears but unhappy. It was a long time since she had seen Chris cry.

'I don't really know him,' she said.

'You don't *want* to, do you? Mum, I see him looking at you.'

'Oh?'

'Looking at you like, looking at you like . . . ' She watched him search for the word. He came up with the best he could do, the best he could risk with her. ' . . . like a friend. Dad might get cross.'

'It'll be a business matter, not really to do with me, Chris. I just handle the catering.' She made the tea and put the pot on a tray illustrated with colour drawings of Long John Silver and Jim Hawkins. She thought about bringing out the proper china and crockery but saw Chris was watching so added three mugs and the EPNS sugar bowl with the usual milk jug and spoons. Chris left through the kitchen door and the garden. When Helen went back in with the tray, Will was saying in that great solemn way he had sometimes: 'Well, yes, a certain quite tricky little scheme has been occupying me lately and still does. I should say occupying *us*, because Helen is very much part of the business structure here. And then there is staff also involved, of course.'

'Exactly what I feared,' Coventry replied. 'I arrive too late.'

'But I have to say that, as schemes go, this one has some doubtful aspects,' Will answered at once. 'Only recently come into view. Helen and I both think this. It's not a scheme that will necessarily go forward, at least not at this stage.'

She handed out the mugs. 'There could be snags,' Helen said.

'Timing is so important,' Coventry replied.

'A point Helen and I were discussing earlier.'

Looking massive in the small room, Coventry leaned towards him: 'What I'm seeking is someone who understands such things, Will – timing, balance of circumstances, tact – someone who has a mastery of all these during the setting up of business agreements. Now, obviously, I hope I understand them myself. I don't think it's immodest to say I've had some successes in that kind of work.'

'Thomas Ingle-Blake is a name famed for such achievement,' Will replied. 'Isn't it, Helen?'

'We do hear things,' she replied.

'Well, thank you,' Coventry Tom said. 'Over the years one is bound to build certain aptitudes. However, the company – companies – have reached a complexity where I can't really handle everything of that sort in person. Will, I need to depute. That's the nub of it. Julia, too, thinks it is time for me to relinquish some immediate responsibilities and share more time with her. She has been patient, but I don't wish to strain that patience.' He sat back seeming relieved by this admission. Will nodded. Coventry said: 'And there is another matter that comes into consideration.'

Helen went and sat down in the blue velvet chair. She felt confident there.

Coventry sipped his tea for a while. 'I don't quite know how to phrase this without making it sound damn snobbish, Will. However... You may be aware that as the companies have grown I've developed in as it were tandem an increasing interest in charitable matters. Through these one has made certain quite distinguished connections. I am referring to people who can and do perform remarkable services for this country, to the lasting benefit of many.'

'We've heard something of this, too,' Will replied. 'Definitely.'

'I value these connections and prize my own chance to help with those services and be part of their as it were selfless campaigns. These people act according to the dictates of *noblesse oblige*, Will.'

'This is certainly worthwhile,' Will said.

'One doesn't want to alienate such folk,' Coventry said. 'One has to move with some delicacy. There is among them still – even now in the late twentieth century – a feeling rather against what they call "trade", you know. By that they mean the whole range of what most of us would see simply as commerce – perfectly respectable and, of course, absolutely essential business activity. In a way, I have to say their attitude is...well, at least quaint and possibly foolish. However, it *is* their attitude, and I have to take account of it – a morsel of old aristocratic Englishness. For them "trade" is dubious.' He gave a different kind of smile, a forgiving, tolerant smile. 'To be brief then, Will, I need someone who can act for me, take over certain aspects of my work which until now I have looked after myself. I wish with some urgency to move back a little from hands-on participation, so that I do not give any of these folk uneasiness or embarrassment.'

She saw Will go guarded. He would have enough brain and caution to know that this proposition might not be as simple as Coventry made out. Coventry was Coventry. Will smoothed his jaw then got the mug up in front of his face for a while. 'As I say, Mr Ingle-Blake, I'm already committed to a project of my own, and there's the matter of colleagues to be considered.'

Coventry ignored this now and said: 'The kind of role I have in mind for you, Will, would certainly be demanding as far as negotiation skills are concerned, I cannot hide that. And why should I? One is confident you could cope with this, and so are those who advise me. But, to in a sense compensate for this admitted stress, Will, is what you might consider an attractive change from your present situation. That is, there would be virtually no personal exposure to risk. Such activity could be exciting and rewarding when we were younger, no denying, but you might feel it is time to move above that. In any case, you would, of course, always have reasonable back-up with you and more on call.' Coventry sat forward once more and his voice grew confiding. 'Will, I know you've had some very trying experiences, like the distressing episode with that lunatic thug...what was the name...Date? Carl Date? Yes, Carl Date.' Coventry pondered. 'I wonder what the hell happened to him, Will – Carl Date. That was it, wasn't it? Still around?' He dismissed Date with an abrupt wave of his empty tea mug. 'No matter. He's not going to be part of this new picture. What I'm talking about is across-the-desk work, subtle, civilised, entirely unphysical. It would naturally carry not just salary but benefits to cover the family.' He glanced around admiringly. 'This is a beautiful and comfortable house, but it might be that you have thought of something a little bigger, as your own and your family's life develops. I hear kids like to have a special room for their computer gear and Internet stuff these days. Ah, progress! But fine. And possibly schooling might be more suitable in another area.'

Helen loathed him for those brilliantly amassed mentions of Date. She saw Will fold down into himself and the sweatshirt, saw him shrink as Date's name kept coming, as though out of Coventry's shaky memory but really out of his jolly, browbeating fucking brain. Will was unable to speak. She would have liked to speak for him, so often her duty. Saying what, though? She wanted Will saved by a move into easier work, didn't she? And it was the thought of running across Carl Date again that seemed most likely to make Will accept this offer. The essential game was to terrify Will into a niche where he need never be terrified any more – where his intermittent belief in himself would become more than intermittent, would become stable and dignified. She could believe non-stop in him, then, too. She longed for that. She needed it. Chris could not be expected to understand. Will put her near the centre of his life, and this was gorgeously different from the way Duncan had treated her. But it was vital that the life she was put at the centre of was worth being at the centre of.

'There would be roles for one or two of your staff, naturally,' Coventry said. 'They know your methods, your thinking, Will. They will respond instinctively whereas some of us will need time to learn how to keep up with you. Clearly, their work will not be as responsible as yours. I would regard them as aides in your office, but valuable nonetheless.'

13

It came back to Kerry: the terrible dread of violence elsewhere if Coventry Tom were installed in Stephen Comble's house one evening with an all-round unbreakable alibi. God, was that why he had enthused about the meeting? He'd get a giggle from the idea.

Kerry felt the life of more than one child lay in her care now: Liz Farnes as well as Chris. She should have insisted on a change from Holt's Corner when she picked them up. Perhaps she would have felt slightly easier then. Slightly: the general anxiety about child informants reached her, unsettled her. Of course it did, after those rough interviews at headquarters. Maybe it *was* wrong to use children in this sort of work. Would she like it if she found a child of hers was a professional grass? Some question. What did *she* know about children – except as grasses, that is? And liabilities. Vic Othen had said every detective anguished non-stop over an informant's safety. He meant adult informants. With kids the stress grew spikier. Vic would really blast her if he heard she repeatedly used the Holt's Corner rendezvous, in full view. Well, he wouldn't hear, not from her at any rate. Like Liz, she worried about the Mondeo.

Kerry had done some research on Liz and drove with Vic now past the Farnes' house, a spruce semi on a newish private estate, one or two social steps up from the Mallard home, and one or two steps was a lot. Two recent cars stood in the drive, one last year's reg, and a pair of russet porcelain horses reared on their hind legs in a downstairs window, like the call of the wild. Perhaps the parents would get her into architecture after all, as long as she stayed in one piece. 'Yes, I'll do a bit of a watch on this place and Chris's while you're with Coventry and the great and good,' he said.

Vic had not known about Liz until Kerry told him. There was nobody else for her to tell. In any case, she had *wanted* to tell him, and wanted him to come on this little unofficial patrol now.

It comforted her some. It gave a closeness, and she found she liked that. She was surprised at how much she liked it, but she had been surprised before at her reactions to Vic the Potential. Oh, this was still nothing more than job comradeship, surely. No? 'So then, we're not certain he knows Chris talks to you and we're even less certain he knows about Liz. That it?' he asked in a sharp, do-you-deny voice.

The words hurt. Had he suddenly turned harsh? Was he waving his endless experience at her and his age-old cop scepticism, his previous enthusiasm for her 'burn' and cheek and push abandoned? She said: 'Yes, Vic, but – '

'You're totally right. We assume he does.' He nodded and his silver moustache seemed to flicker red and consoling in the sunset, like a lifeboat's port light. 'Naturally we assume he does. That's what a network means and Coventry's got the smartest crooked network ever.'

She felt happy again, confident in his regard for her, but said: 'I don't even know she has anything.'

'*He* might know she has,' Vic replied. 'Or might think she has. Or might think someone bright like you wouldn't bother with her if she hadn't. As far as the girl's safety goes they're the same.'

'You can't draw armament for this, can you, Vic? It's not a proper duty – not a disclosed duty.'

'No, not a proper duty.' He started to snarl. 'I mean, Kerry, how could it be a proper fucking duty, protecting two youngsters who might help us do the impossible and put Coventry Tom away?'

'He's shielded?'

'He's Thomas Ingle-Blake. You've heard of presumption of innocence? He's cornered the market.'

'So, how will – '

'But perhaps I can make this task coincide with something else that *is* a proper duty and requires me to pack a safeguard weapon. Then I might just be travelling to this very proper duty past the Farnes' house or the Mallard house and see by fluke something that needs immediate armed intervention, such as an attempt at child slaughter.'

'Well, I hoped you'd say something like that,' Kerry replied.

105

'Yes, I thought you did.' He touched her arm very briefly as she drove. It was enough. He needed his right hand for smoking most of the time. She turned and grinned at him for a second. He grinned back around the stub of cigarette. He was pulling at it in his mighty, last gasp style, the back of his hand outwards and thumb and forefinger gripping the fragment like crab's pincers. It was the jail way of smoking, aimed at concealment. Why hadn't he chucked the habit, like nearly everyone else? Except when he smoked she could think of him as not impossibly old. His body did not look old. A lot of men went grey and even silver early. But smoking as a *vocation* – people did not do that any more. Or not the people she met. This was the addled behaviour of another generation: Bogart dragging away and flashing his ciggy case in *Casablanca*, December 1941.

She said: 'I've discovered what good policing is.'

'Oh, Lord.' He cowered in the passenger seat, his grey suit crinkling around him like a cocoon.

'Certainly,' she said. 'It's to recognise the supreme wisdom of the limits we work under – firearms controls, for instance. Yes, to note their wisdom, and find a way round them.'

'You *are* fast track, Kerry.'

She described Liz to him. 'They might try for these children at their houses or in the Square or Rush Street.'

'Ah,' he answered, as at a revelation.

'She says she saw Tim Denton later than anyone we've spoken to.'

'Strong if it's true. The girl could be crucial.'

She said: 'Perhaps he knows it. Vic, there are two of Coventry's people worth looking out for, Raymond Nide and Jack Sonntag.'

'Ah,' he replied, as at a revelation.

She had been about to describe them also. But, of course, if even Chris knew what they looked like Vic was sure to. 'Yes, well,' she said.

They were passing the Mallard house now. An old grey Escort stood outside. Vic held the last bit of cigarette between his lips and brought from his breast pocket the squashed cardboard centre tube from a lavatory paper roll. He studied this. She glanced down and saw it was covered with inked figures and letters. 'One of Coventry's cars,' he said. 'Now and then he goes man o' the people. Sort of penance not disguise.'

'Calling on them? My God, Vic.'

'It's too open for trouble.'

'But why, then?'

Vic put his *aide-mémoire* away and took the cigarette end from his mouth. 'Pressure?'

'Coventry himself?'

'Probably.' They drove out of Daniel Street. Vic chain-lit another Marlboro. 'Perhaps he's doing a deal – a nice job for Will if the boy is stopped from nosing. Will's got difficulties and might welcome an approach from on high. Coventry would be quick to sense that. Or he might have had a prompt.'

'From?'

Vic's mind seemed to stray. 'You know, Kerry, I was wondering the other day what escutcheon motto Tom might pick if he was ennobled. I came up with, "On the smart guy shit don't stick." '

'We'll see.'

He crowed. 'That's what I mean, Kerry – you've got optimism. Did you hear Will was thinking about an antiques job? Of course you did. Everybody's heard. Oscar blundering about. Harry tell you? Doug Quinn? Obviously, Will's going to chicken out of that. He chickens out of most things. More so now. There's a lad at the furniture depository who scares his soul from way back – a knife and pliers session on Will when he was even more tender. An innocent then. Some gang wanted a workplace key or a code out of him. They got it, I expect. Possibly Coventry sees a chance to recruit Will when he's shaky, and perhaps please Mrs Mallard, too. A way of getting at Chris.'

She pulled up near headquarters for Vic to walk back. Kerry said: 'You *will* get some armament, won't you? There might be more than one of them.' Were her worries for him bigger than for the children?

He touched her arm again, just as briefly as before, then left the car, giving a small thoughtful wave. After a couple of steps he turned back and came around to the driver's window. 'Have you thought how it will look when Will calls off the antiques raid because he's scared and/or because Coventry offers him a

107

job which Mrs Mallard pushes him to accept? She's an organiser.'

'How it will look to – ?'

'To Harry Bell and maybe Doug. Harry's got an ambush in place there. He'll be pissed off when Will and his team don't show.'

'Too bad. Not my fault.'

He gazed down at Kerry for a while as if politely waiting for her to do a brain kick-start. He said: 'Will they know it's not your fault, Kerry? Might Harry imagine you told your friend Christopher, who told his father?'

'That's mad. Why would I?'

'You have to keep good relations with the boy, yes? Is this possible if you stay quiet and let his father drop into a police trap? That's how Harry might see it. Harry told you about the ambush, did he?'

'Yes, but – Impossible. Christ, Vic, if I warned Chris and Chris tipped his father what does it tell Will about his son? It screams Chris is in touch with a cop. Only one source for ambush information.'

'*You* understand that and so do I, Kerry, but will Harry Bell see it? Harry lives in dread of leaks and betrayals. It affects them all at that level. Probably wise. Remember Adolf. Remember Julius Caesar. *Let me have men about me that are fat.*' Vic straightened up. 'Be ready to look after yourself,' he said, then snorted: 'Hark at me Dutch uncling! Of course you can do it – look after yourself. You're sharper than all of us, and uniquely dedicated.'

She drove back to Liz's street, feeling unsharp and ununique but dedicated. Those porcelain horses flashing to the street stuck in Kerry's head and troubled her. She could not altogether sort out why. Or – put it another way – she had no bloody idea why, not at first, anyway. They would be mass produced knick-knacks of not much value and the wish to feature them was naff. But at least these folk did want to make a display. Kerry liked that. Liz's parents had pretensions. They might have hopes for their daughter. They would be appalled to find Liz was involved in what she *was* involved in – if she was – and that she took money for it. Kerry found she wanted to go up their clean front garden path, knock the door alongside those fine animals and demand that Liz tell her now, today, what she knew: what she said she knew. After all, according to Chris, she'd had the fee. If her information did add up, disclosure could make her safe, and Chris. An immediate move against Coventry might be possible, and the sick meeting at Stephen's superfluous. Then, Liz would go on living behind the proud ornaments and eventually reach that time where she'd start redesigning the world, the way the young ought to, had to. Who else? Kerry felt another doubt. Was her main worry about Liz's safety, or about the fresh stuff Liz had on Tim – said she had – and which might be lost with her in any disaster?

She drove past the house slowly, went around the block and drove past again. Pointless. Idiotic. But it would have to do. Or it would have to do as far as surveillance and protection of the living went. Instead, she turned her car and went out towards the stretch of field and hedge where Timothy Denton's body had been found. This was another impulse that baffled her, another dim, sentimental, irresistible exercise. Perhaps she simply did not want to go home yet. Mark would be there and she felt unready to meet him. Some of her reactions to Vic Othen confused her. She told herself again that her pleasure in his company had to be a work thing, just as this trip out to the death site was a work thing, though not very pressing now: there wouldn't be any clues here after so long and so much fingertip searching. Never mind. It was where she wanted to be, for the moment.

14

Someone else wanted to be there for the moment or longer, too. Kerry saw a woman walking the field, near where the shroud tent had stood. She parked and watched her from the car for a while. Her back was to Kerry. The woman seemed to be hunched forward, her head lowered. Perhaps she was weeping. It looked like a kind of homage. The idea pleased Kerry. At first, she thought it must be Sonia Denton, making one of those visits described by Liz. She looked as tall as Sonia and the shape of the head might be right. Kerry was not sure she wanted to intrude and not sure Mrs Denton would put up with intrusion. To her Kerry might typify all police, police who did nothing about the death of her son. Or did nothing but fix a meeting for her with Coventry Tom in a comfy house at which all the pain and suspicion and certainty could be chatted away.

Kerry wondered whether she should wait or go home after all. But then, in a while, she began to feel it might not be Sonia Denton. There was something about the clothes. Weren't they too middle-aged fashionable, too expensive, too wrong for a field? Sonia liked leather bomber jackets and trousers. This woman had on what appeared from the distance to be a beauti-fully tailored blue or turquoise three-quarter length silk jacket and a navy skirt. Kerry left the car and began to walk towards her. As Kerry drew closer she knew as a certainty that this was not Sonia Denton. Fine – an extra tribute to the dead lad. The woman turned. Perhaps she had heard Kerry's footsteps on the grass. It was nobody Kerry recognised, though another of those intuitive surges told her that perhaps she should. Suddenly the silk jacket looked all right for the field. This was a genuine caller. Yes, she had been crying. Her face was long, slightly masculine, maybe used to pain.

'Ah,' she said in a shaky voice, 'you are drawn here, too? But you can't be Timothy's mother – too young. As a matter of fact, I think I have seen his mother here. One would not want to meet her, not in the circumstances. You – you knew the boy?'

Kerry said: 'I'm sorry but I wondered what – '

'But, of course, you will be the police. I expect you watch this spot, even now, so long after.'

'Did *you* know Timothy?' Kerry replied.

'I come here very rarely,' she said. 'Well, you'll be aware of that if you patrol the spot. I come here to...oh, I suppose to keep in touch, as far as I can. Foolish? I mean, what is there here? But my visits are by no means obsessive. Certainly no guilt. Certainly not that. Why should there be?' Her voice soared, struck at Kerry. 'Just to restock one's memory.' For much of the conversation she had her head lowered as before, but lifted it now and stared at Kerry for a few seconds. 'Yes, police,' she

110

said. 'Your eyes have that huge acreage of disbelief. You'll probably think it quaint that Tommy Ingle-Blake's wife should come out here at all. I mean, in the circumstances.'

Kerry said: 'No, indeed. I can see you might be affected.'

'Yes, I'm *affected*.' She seemed to weigh this term for a moment. 'I expect you're the girl officer who's setting up this get-together, so everything can be put right. And *can* everything be put right so easily, do you think? Tommy has mentioned you – someone to do with the case, young and quite pretty, pushy. You fit.'

'There's to be a meeting, yes.' Perhaps Kerry had seen Press pictures of Julia Ingle-Blake before, photographed with Coventry at some function. That would explain the feeling, half-feeling, of recognition. The forceful nose and olive skin were memorable: something Spanish in her blood?

'I don't expect I'm invited to this meeting,' Mrs Ingle-Blake said.

'Certainly you are,' Kerry said. 'Why not?'

Mrs Ingle-Blake glanced down at the ground. 'Are we near, or even actually *on*, the spot where he was found? You'd probably know exactly. I trust I don't seem...troubled.' She gave something between a groan and a laugh. 'How stupid, of course I seem troubled. What am I doing crying alone in a field? Yes, troubled, but I hope I don't seem...' The thought tailed away.

Kerry waited. Then she said: 'I think the death of this boy upset many folk in the community, people not obviously linked to him in any way. There has been an all-round response.'

'Oh, folk in the community,' she muttered. She said it as though reading a label on a soup can, a soup she did not want. 'Your official voice? I'm not one of those, not part of folk in the community. I'm Tom Ingle-Blake's wife.' What did it mean, what did it mean? That she was a cut above the community? That she was a cut below? That she knew something private about the death?

Kerry said: 'Please, do come to the meeting.'

'Are you entitled to offer invitations?'

'I've just made myself entitled.'

'A community meeting,' she replied.

'That sort of thing.'

'They teach community on your courses, do they?' Mrs Ingle-Blake began to talk like the lady from the big house. Abruptly the tone had become breezy, now-hear-this, take-it-or-leave-it: 'Timothy Denton did some messenger work for Tom, as you'll know. Nothing too involving, obviously. At that age. I would meet him sometimes when he came to the house. A fine, fine boy.'

Kerry said: 'Yes, we did know about the messengering and so on. It would be natural that you'd bump into him.'

'Natural. Quite. Bump into him.'

'In fact, I've no idea why you raised the possibility of guilt just now, Mrs Ingle-Blake,' Kerry replied.

'Oh, guilt. It's modish. People go about wondering if they were blame for this or that and they consult shrinks to find out. No, I don't suppose you do understand why I mentioned it.' She turned away. 'My car's down at the other end of the field. Goodbye.' Her walk now was brisk, her head up.

15

Helen Mallard knew she must talk to Christopher, and couldn't do it. Couldn't do it yet. Heart-to-hearting about treachery, oh, God. But there would come an opening when she could, surely. There had to come an opening when she could or Coventry would turn vindictive, withdraw all offers, douse all clemency. He had that dirty, traditional unstoppable power.

Although the offers mattered, they did not matter much because Will would always find something. Clemency to her grassing son mattered. That was everything. Only she could look after him. The police? He was *their* boy, too, wasn't he? The thought dazed her, but, yes, he was. So, would they protect him? Could they? Doubtful, both. Did they protect Tim Denton? They could not even catch whoever killed Tim Denton, and they did try, didn't they? Did they? Her certainties and uncertainties fought one another, like a lifesaver and a threshing swimmer. Which was which?

But how did you ask your child if he had helped place a cop trap for his father? Ask? In words and pictures she would be telling him she knew. The words would be hers, the pictures, Coventry's slides: she could not show him those but they were hot in her head and she would describe them to him if he denied grassing. Of course he would deny. So of course she would have to say she knew about Holt's Corner and the old Cavalier, had seen the evidence, had seen the woman detective. No need to tell him whose the slides were. Chris would know they must exist and that they spoke true.

And then how did she explain to her son that he must stop trying in his childish way to prove who killed Tim Denton because, if Chris backed off immediately, his dad would fall into a foolproof job – with the man who slaughtered Tim Denton or had him slaughtered? His dad could do with a job and it needed to be foolproof. *She* might like him to have a foolproof job, too. So should Chris, if he would see it. He wouldn't. What was he going to make of her when she spoke to him like that, outlined this juicy bargain? Could she ever recover from it in his eyes? Could Will? Would Chris want to live in the same house as the two of them any longer? Kids much younger than Chris left intolerable homes. They disappeared, drifted to London and cardboard shanty towns, went arse tart. Her role was to keep this family happy and whole and loving, not poison it. She had been good at that. Now?

Will said, his voice merry and big: 'Do you know what I'm going to do then, Helen? I'm going to get on the phone later to Jake and Oscar and tell them straight the antiques caper is off. I'll ask them over here again so I can explain why in detail – they're entitled to that, definitely – and then afterwards we'll all go to the Bordeaux as before – yes, exactly as before – a brill party, I want that – because this will be no dark miserable occasion. Here we have something to celebrate. Absolutely!'

'I think so,' Helen said.

'We celebrate a damned exciting move forward. Not an abandonment or a defeat, an achievement. An operator of true

113

renown and well known to royalty so admires the work of my small team that he wants to welcome us into his own considerable empire. Posts and prospects for all of us, myself, Jake, Oscar.'

'I expect Coventry is a damn shrewd judge of personnel.'

'Absolutely that, and I know Jake and Oscar will see it as a compliment, too. Oh, there are some uneven sides to Ingle-Blake possibly, yes, uneven, but show me a businessman you can't say something like that about and I'll show you a stick-in-the-mud businessman. If J.F. Kennedy's father hadn't been a bit of a wheeler-dealer tearaway could that lot have bought the White House? This is the creative aspect, not just something for strict rules. Nothing to stop Oscar and Jake bringing the girls with them even to the prelim meeting here. After all, there are no security worries if the job's not going ahead. It's the past, the foolish past. I see that now, thanks very much to you, Helen. Oh, Lord, you can analyse! Those girls – Lesley, even Petra, the fly-by-night – they're entitled to hear about the career development suddenly available to their menfolk. It's their future, too – their standard of living, their long-term peace of mind, suppose Petra is long-term about anything. True, Jake and Oscar will be down a peg or two from me in the Ingle-Blake structure, but they would expect that, I'm sure. There'll be opportunities for them to rise, probably. I shall look for opportunities to rise myself. I notice that at this stage Mr Ingle-Blake didn't mention or even hint at full partnership – well, naturally – these are very early days. But I felt there was that kind of promise lurking not far out of sight, didn't you – a recognition of a sort of like spirit?'

'Give it a year or two. He mustn't offend others in his firm by bringing you on too fast, Will.'

'Right. And the crucial thing is that even from the position he's offering now I'll be able to look after the interests of Jake and Oscar very well. Not partnership yet, but this is a spot with clout. There's no question of forgetting my obligations to comrades.'

'Nobody would expect you to, Will. You're not made like that.'

Oh, God, I must, must talk to Chris.

114

16

This time when Chris telephoned Kerry was in the flat by herself, a day off. 'We're going into Coventry's place,' he said.

'You're what?' Kerry yelled.

'It's Liz's idea, but not bad.'

'Chris, what do you mean, going in?'

'You know, *going in*.'

'Breaking in?'

'That kind of thing,' he said. 'Don't worry. They're away for the day. The races. We checked.'

She was terrified for him, for them. 'You can't do this, Chris. It's –'

'Oh, a bit illegal.'

'Dangerous,' Kerry said. 'Hideously dangerous.'

'What's that – hideously? Wow! That's a new one for me. Look, I shouldn't tell you, but we've done houses before. Liz more than me.'

God, didn't she hate children, their bounce, their daft joki-ness? Well, no, she didn't, she fretted about them. Fretted? Feeble word. She was appalled. 'This is not just a house, Chris, for heaven's sake. This is Coventry's house.'

'I told you, they're away. Liz thought maybe find the knife that done Tim. Like important in a trial? Police are always looking for the weapon, fingertip searching with dungarees on. I'll take a leather sheath with me, in case. Have a look around. Not taking anything else. Just a look around. The thing is, Kerry, your lot can't do it. You'd need a warrant. Police got to sort of behave. Liz thought – help you. She's a pretty good kid. I mean, she'll do this for no money. I mean, she *wants* money, and she's not talking no more without money. But she'll do this because she gets a buzz from it, burgling. Adventure?'

'It's silly, Chris. Don't do it. No, no, no. People like that – they don't leave knives about.'

'People like what?'

'People like Coventry.'

'People who kill kids, you mean? So, how we going to catch them? Look, pick us up at the corner. And don't worry. No alarms at the house. We checked that as well. He couldn't because if he had an alarm and it went off the police could go in, and that's just what he don't want. See you in a couple of hours? In case we got something urgent, Kerry. We will have. Definite. We got him, Kerry.'

'Where are you?' she said. 'Stay where you are now and I'll come.' But at his end the phone was down. It could be traced, but what point? They would be on their way. She felt responsible, as if she was sending them. She saw why people thought it bad to run underage grasses. They got shoved into risk. At once she drove out towards Coventry's place. If she was quick enough she might catch them on the road.

But she did not. She took the car right up to the house and parked in the forecourt alongside the old grey Escort and a red current registration Toyota estate. It was a peril. If Coventry and his wife came back they would be alerted at once – that is, supposing Chris and Liz had it right and the Ingle-Blakes really were away, in another car. She would have preferred to leave her Cavalier out of sight somewhere and walk, but no time. If she had got ahead of Chris and Liz they might be put off trying to enter as soon as they saw her vehicle here. Kerry left the car and began to look for signs of a break-in. No dogs as well as no alarms, apparently.

She walked slowly right around the two joined cottages but saw no smashed window or forced door. So, perhaps she *was* here before them. Perhaps they had come and given up. Perhaps they had not even come, deterred by what she had said to Chris on the phone. She thought of jumping into the car and getting clear. There was something that said to her, though, that even if Chris considered giving up, Liz would not. She was flint. They were either inside somehow, or they would arrive soon.

A small conservatory had been built on to the front of the house. You went through that to reach the front door. The conservatory door was ajar. She went inside among the potted plants and garden tools and at once saw that the key was in the lock of the house door. Coventry would leave his place available

116

like that? It baffled and alarmed her. She turned the knob and the door opened. The key operated a mortice lock, which had been released. She saw now that the button on the self-locking Yale above had been pushed up to keep the tongue back. She went inside and closed the door behind her. She was in a hallway with bright rugs on a boarded floor. A vase of fresh-looking flowers stood on a Pembroke table. For half a minute she remained still and listened. The house seemed silent. There was that pleasant smell here, Coventry's breath smell – liquorice, myrrh? It was a darkish house. They had kept the old, small windows, or had been made to keep them by the planning people – authentic Victorian shadowiness. She called out: 'Chris. Liz.' It was not much more than a whisper. Mad, really. If you called someone you ought to do it so they could hear. The fact that Kerry was in the house at all meant she believed Coventry and Julia were absent. They were not going to hear anything. She called again, but just as quietly. Again the house stayed silent.

Where would they look for a knife? The kitchen? But how did they expect to recognise a murder knife among all the rest? Was that kind of logic beyond them? She could believe it might be beyond Chris. Impulse could run him. Not Liz, though. Kerry had seen the kitchen through a window on her outside tour, at the rear of the house and to her right now. She began to move slowly that way, keeping close to the wall, as though that might offer shelter. In the flagged kitchen she found nobody. Everything looked neat, undisturbed. Briefly, she looked out over a wide field sloping away from the house where sheep grazed. She paused and listened once more. She might be alone. She hoped she was. What should be the programme – search the house properly now she was in here?

She turned and walked back towards the hall. A door opened slowly a little in front of her and on the right. Chris pushed his head out, took a look and then emerged. Liz was just behind. They seemed to be carrying a couple of video cassettes each. 'Kerry,' he said, 'we heard you. We was busy.' He waved the cassettes. 'I said we wouldn't take anything, but this is different like. Could be snuff movies. You heard of that? Maybe we'll see how Tim died, maybe other kids. In a locked cupboard. Liz got it open. Only a plastic card. No marks. We locked it again.' He said this clipped, offhand, to show how simple everything had been.

'I don't think snuff movies,' Liz said.

'Why?' Chris asked.

'I just don't,' Liz replied.

'Let's get out,' Kerry replied.

'Sure,' Chris said.

'You looked for a knife?' Kerry asked.

'How can you find a knife in a house?' Chris said. 'It could be any of them, couldn't it?'

'I thought you were looking for a knife,' Kerry said.

'Changed our mind,' Liz replied. She gestured with a thumb over her shoulder. 'Tasty furniture in there. This is a man with taste.'

'Go to your place, Kerry?' Chris said. 'Play the tapes. The boyfriend there?'

'At work.'

'Great,' Chris said. He was a mixture of excitement and coolness.

At the front door he put the Yale back on to self-locking, closed up and engaged the mortice. He took out the key and put it under one of the flower pots in the conservatory. 'We saw where they kept it when we did a little visit to find if they had alarms or dogs. You can watch the house from them bushes over there. There you are – that's a tip for you and other police, Kerry.'

She drove them to the flat. In the car Chris said: 'If they're snuff movies you could get him, couldn't you? I mean, even if it's not Tim, and even if we don't see Coventry himself snuffing anyone. He should not have videos like this. So, you could go in and really dig into him, the way police do.'

'How does Kerry tell her bosses where she got the videos from?' Liz asked.

'Let's see what's on them before you start worrying,' Kerry said.

At the flat they watched Kerry's Cavalier on the screen and Chris waiting at Holt's Corner and Chris climbing into the car and disappearing from view on the back seat. Then they saw

Chris and Liz waiting at the Corner, climbing into the car and disappearing from view on the back seat. Chris screamed with fright when he first glimpsed himself and threw up on the sofa. Kerry stopped the tape, brought a bucket of water and a cloth and cleaned away the mess. She would have ended the film show there, but when he had recovered Chris wanted the rest. 'Did you tell him we met there?' he asked. 'Was Liz right about all that – the Mondeo?' He sounded appallingly sad, and she felt that impulse to put her arm around him again, despite the insult. This was a scared, confused child. Kerry was scared and confused herself. But she had *two* children to look after now, and must keep things equal.

Liz said: 'He's going to come looking when he finds those videos gone.'

'He might,' Kerry replied. 'But he doesn't know where to look.'

'He can guess.'

'He might not think kids would be capable of it.'

'That's true,' Liz replied. 'We're pretty exceptional, really.'

'I want to go home,' Chris said.

'What shall I do with the tapes?' Kerry asked.

'What you like,' Chris said. 'And with this.' He pulled a ten-inch kitchen knife in a sheath from his belt and put the knife on the sofa.

'You *did* take one?' Kerry said.

'Well, we were in there. Might as well. It could be the right one, couldn't it? Couldn't it?'

'You ought to keep that, in case he starts stalking you,' Liz said.

17

In the evening, Helen listened while Will telephoned Jake and Oscar. He spoke jubilantly, as though broadcasting a coup. In coded terms he mentioned cancellation of the raid, because time made that a matter of urgency. But he did not say in detail what was on the plus side, just mentioned there was one. 'We've done what every business tries to do,' he told Jake. 'Made beautiful gains purely through reputation and merit, no fragment of our organisation put at risk.'

At the other end of the phone Jake seemed to argue. Perhaps Petra was in the room and he had to make a show. 'No, no,' Will said angrily, 'I'm not calling it off simply because of that one element. Would I? Look, I don't want to discuss him on the telephone.'

Oscar and Lesley arrived at Daniel Street first. 'It seems a pity, Will,' he said. 'There's been a lot of work – the reconnaissance, the furniture van. I handled that with . . . well, I say it myself, but real care.' He looked and sounded more than ever like an old-style clerk craving praise for blot-free books.

'No question,' Will replied. 'The van's not why I'm stopping it, Osc.'

Lesley said: 'What do *you* think, Helen?' Her plump, plain face was bright with friendliness and dependence.

'On balance against,' Helen replied.

'That's good enough for me,' Lesley said. 'Helen sees right the way around a situation.'

Will said: 'She's inventive, but not foolhardy. I rely very much on Helen.'

Petra and Jake turned up soon afterwards. Helen made tea. There was not enough alcohol in the house to go round. 'What good news then, Will?' Jake asked. For once he looked sullen, not close to a laugh. Petra must be getting to him.

'Posts with Ingle-Blake,' Will replied. 'He's desperate for us to join him.'

'Is this the slug they call Coventry Tom?' Petra asked. She was in a cotton shirt and dark wool trousers with a cerise sweater over the shirt which could be cashmere. Some money had been spent. The impact was statelier than last time. She was sitting in the big mock leather armchair next to the sofa and looked a bit high life for the room. She would stand out even in the Bordeaux.

'A few call him Coventry, yes,' Will replied. 'To do with his home town, probably, and the cathedral.'

'I thought I heard some knife work London way,' Petra said. 'And he killed a kid in these parts, didn't he? A famous case.'

'Petra's one who does fret about that sort of thing, Will, and I can understand it,' Jake said. 'Was it necessary?'

Will stood in the centre of the room wearing his good navy suit and talked to them all like a preacher, very mild, very reasonable. His tone pleaded for tolerance. 'The dead boy, Petra – this is evil gossip. People like Ingle-Blake – rumour always settles on them. Envy.'

'Yes, probably,' Oscar said.

Petra said: 'Well, working for someone of his sort! I mean, isn't it, well, sort of slimy? I heard even an incident in a charity ball.'

'What sort of posts, Will?' Oscar asked.

'To be finally determined,' Will said. 'He's so eager to sign us up it wasn't clear what exactly we'd do in the organisation. He just wanted us aboard.'

Her face alight with affection, her skin shining, Petra said in a burst: 'Do you know, I've always seen Jake – well, all of you, really – but I've always seen Jake as sort of free – like someone who does the job he wants when he wants and without any boss. There's a leader, yes, of course, of course, namely your good self, Will. But not a boss. This was always the zing in Jake for me, and in all of you, really. Remember that terrific movie, it comes on TV, *The Misfits*, with that lovely Clark Gable, and he plays a plucky cowboy who just drifts around and hates the idea of "wages". That's something like I always thought of you three, not people who take "wages", but who pluckily do their own projects as and when. Gives a soul dimensions.'

Helen said: 'Will feels it might be wise to use a period on Mr Ingle-Blake's staff to consolidate and possibly consider the future, while in guaranteed work and with no pressure from money shortages.'

'Ah.' Petra grinned and pointed her finger at Helen, an accusation, but lighthearted: 'Did you persuade him to drop the antiques sortie?'

'That right, Will?' Jake said slowly. 'This Helen's decision? I mean, Helen is great and – '

121

'Of course it's not fucking right,' Will bellowed. 'I don't take orders.'

'But influenced by her?' Oscar asked.

'Why not?' Lesley said. 'She can think.' Although she had no looks her skin, like Petra's, was as smooth as a child's.

'Undoubtedly,' Oscar said, 'but all the same – '

Will seemed hurt and puzzled. 'You want to go ahead with the antiques regardless of my recommendation against it, Osc?'

Occasionally Helen had heard them argue with Will about a decision, nothing too fierce. Now, things seemed changed. Yes, Petra must be the difference. She and Jake seemed in a competition to welcome risk, even though when Petra talked to Helen alone the other day she had sounded so doubtful about the little firm. It had become a sex thing, an image thing. And then Oscar, so proud of his van duties and wanting the vehicle used. His dark eyes were nervy behind the glasses. It would trouble him to oppose Will. Oscar wasn't one to have a life apart.

'Now, I'll tell you what – why not a vote?' Petra cried, clapping her hands in front of her chest, thrilled by this sudden vision.

Will said: 'Not our style.'

'But, Will,' she replied, 'surely, surely, surely in something as – '

'Keep your fucking button nose out of it, will you, you know fuck all, Petra,' Will replied, bending to shove his face close to hers.

'Hey, Will, I don't want you talking to Petra like that,' Jake said. It was a bit of snarl, a bit of a sad reproach. Jake was sitting on the carpet alongside Petra's chair, his back against the wall, long skinny legs out half-way across the room. He didn't stand up but looked as though he was thinking about it. Once or twice there had been fights here. Will usually came out of them all right. He moved back from Petra and gave a little wave of his hand, a sort of apology.

Lesley said: 'This is getting rather noisy, don't you think? Look, if there's a vote who's in it? Girls as well as boys?'

'Didn't I say, not our style?' Will replied. Jitters showed in his face. Helen saw he felt this meeting going from him. Lesley had swung?

122

Giggling, Petra called out as if she had not heard: 'Right then, ladies and gentlemen, who says do the S.W. place?' Jake put his hand up. Petra raised hers.

Jake reached up and across and pulled her arm down. 'Just the heavies, love,' he said. 'The ones who stick their balls on the line.'

Oscar lifted his hand, then lowered it to scratch his centre parting, pretending that was why he had raised it. But then he pushed it up again and left it there. Behind the glasses there was something half-way to resolution in his eyes.

'It's on, on, on,' Petra yelled. She stood. 'Now the Bordeaux again? Yet another festive evening. Great. Last one before the night itself, tomorrow.'

Chris pushed the door open and looked in: 'Everything all right, mum?' he said. 'Only I heard funny shouting.'

'It's all right, it's all right,' Will said. 'Shut the door.' Chris glanced towards Helen and then went. In a way, she wished the boy would at least acknowledge that his dad was in the room. But she was glad Chris needed her, especially her, only her.

'So, tomorrow, Will,' Oscar said. He sounded petrified. It might be the job. Also he would know the dangers in talking down Will at home. Helen could not give it much thought. Didn't she have a choice to sort out here, but no choice? If she let them go ahead they would be caught: at least caught and perhaps worse. And Chris would have caused it, most likely. On the other side, if she warned of the ambush – stopped the raid – they would ask how she discovered the trap. That meant telling them she knew her son grassed, so she had rechecked the store.

'You can't do Sidney Waters,' she said. 'Suicide.'

Petra pouted. 'Oh, Helen, it's settled, sealed.' She moved towards the living-room door. 'Come on. To the fleshpots!'

'Right,' Jake said, clambering up. 'All agreed.'

'The police are waiting at Sidney Waters,' Helen said.

There was a silence and nobody moved. Then Petra grunted: 'Oh, come on, Helen, don't try to pull a – '

'I've seen them at the depository,' Helen said.

'You've been back?' Will asked. 'Why?'

'I was worried.'

'You're certain – police?' Oscar asked. 'Uniforms?'

123

'No, but police,' she said.

'How the fuck do you know that?' Jake said.

'Wouldn't you?' she replied. 'Lurkers.'

'Someone tipped you off they were there?' Petra asked.

'Yes. Coventry Tom,' she said. Of course, she saw risks in that lie, but not as many as in the truth. Best she could do.

There was some quietness. Then Will said, sincerely puzzled: 'How do you mean, Helen, love? When did you see Coventry Tom again – Mr Ingle-Blake?'

'Lately,' she replied. 'He told me.'

'How did Tom know there was an ambush?' Oscar asked.

Helen said: 'He's got voices everywhere, including inside the nick.'

'But, look, Helen, I don't get this – how come you were seeing Coventry?' Will asked. There was more rage than mystification in his voice now.

'Is there something going on I don't understand?' Petra said.

'Of course there fucking is,' Will answered. 'Didn't I tell you that at the beginning?' He did not look at Petra, kept staring at Helen.

'But you don't understand either, Will,' Lesley said.

Petra stood up. Her face was wise and angry, her tone madly reasonable, not girlish-goofy any longer: 'I'd like to see this personally. I'd like Helen to show me this ambush...yes, personally. I mean at once. I mean while there would still be time to go back to the raid plan. We don't write it off. I'll drive. The rest of you wait here. We can do without a gang. Too obvious.'

This nobody girl would love to take over. Helen began to detest her. This nobody girl did not know how things ran here. She did not realise it was Helen's brain that governed this team, a partner's brain. 'The ambush is in place,' Helen said. 'OK, go and see it, Petra. By yourself. You don't need me. You know what a plain clothes cop looks like, either sex.'

Petra was boxed into anger now, had to complete her challenge. 'Helen, remind me where the place is on our street map in the car, will you? Can I ask you that much?'

Jake said admiringly: 'Petra's a damn determined character – once she got something really in her head. Be careful, love. You want me to come?'

'Stay and talk collapse with this lot,' Petra replied.

Helen and Petra went out to the car. Petra did not get in at once. Helen said: 'So as not to be obvious they may have shifted the ambush vehicles from where they were when I was there but you'll see a van and – '

'I'm not going. I'll just drive around here for a while,' Petra replied. 'Helen, for God's sake, I had to talk to you on the quiet. He'll kill you. Did you see his face?'

'Will?'

'When you said you'd been with Coventry Tom. I mean, Jesus!'

'Not "been with". Spoken to. Get into the car. We'll drive. I'll say I changed my mind and went with you.'

When they were moving, Petra said: 'No, not "been with" – I didn't mean that. I don't think I meant that. Not as a certainty. That's your business, anyway. But it's Will. What does he think? I was watching him. This was hate and fear. These boys – Will, Jake, maybe not so much Oscar – but Will, Jake, that's what they live by, mostly fear but some hate, too. They hate anyone who makes them feel small – because they *are* so small, and know it. You go to Coventry Tom on the quiet for talks or whatever – that makes Will feel like nothing, like shit. This is the man who knows the royals and now he's pulling you, Helen, even if it's only for talks. This takes you out of Will's realm.'

'Yes, only for talks. It's a complicated set-up.'

Petra spoke at a rush. 'Now, listen, if Will goes at you about this, and he's sure to, as soon as we've left tonight or sooner – why I wanted to get you out of there, love – if he goes at you don't for Christ's sake say to him, "It's a complicated set-up." That makes it sound like this is something he can't understand – only you and Coventry can understand – sort of above and beyond Will?'

Yes, it was a bit like that. Helen saw she had been right about Petra from the start. She would act woolly and wild now and then, her role as charmer, but she never stopped thinking, never stopped watching.

'Will's going to wonder how you know stuff from Coventry even if you're not fucking him – and Will's not going to believe you're not fucking him, anyway. There's something nice about

125

Will – modest. He'd *expect* his woman to be fucked by someone else. Will's got self-knowledge. It must be unbearable. What's he like?'

'Will or Coventry?'

'Coventry. Like Mel Gibson? Like Arafat? Like Ross Perrot? Old? Young? Fat? Thin? Bald? Toothless? AC/DC? The sexy scent of success and power. I heard his wife's unsatisfied to a major degree. Gone a bit deranged? My Jake in there – he probably thinks you've been bedding Coventry and pillow-talked something about the project. Then Coventry says, "Thank God you told me, darling. The police are on to that. Warn them." This is the way Jake's wary little mind works. He can be evil, Helen. Will could think it, too, wouldn't he? This is dangerous, yes?'

'Yes. It was necessary.'

'What – do something perilous to damp down something more perilous?'

'Like that.'

'To do with your boy?'

'Complicated,' Helen replied.

Petra drove and did not speak for a while. 'I'll be moving on. Jake's fine, really fine, in many ways, but . . . It's getting to be a deep mess here. If you've been murmuring things to Coventry, obviously it will be so Will lands something decent and well up in the outfit. That's your natural priority, I don't complain. You love him – Will, I mean – so you look after him. Where will Jake and Oscar be, though? Jake can be real fun, but in some shit job can he be fun? This is going to be measly work and front-line dangerous. And then you have to ask, is Coventry safe? All right, the police don't touch him, not so far, but I heard a news-paper reporter's around asking big awkward questions, the way they do. Not some local hack. From London. They'll dig and dig if they think there's a scandal, and death of a boy grass is a scandal. Some of these papers want to put the world right, which could mean blasting Coventry Tom.' She turned back towards Daniel Street. 'So, look out for yourself tonight, Helen. Get some good words ready. Oh, love, what can we do for you? What? You can't come and sleep at our place. No reason. No *obvious* reason.'

'I'll probably be OK.'

'Go sexy? Tell him his dick is the biggest and hardest and longest-lasting ever. That usually works with the poor sweeties – makes them forget for a while what bits of debris they really are.' At the house, Petra announced: 'Yes, Helen's right. They've got a bloody disguised army there. Helen was nice enough to come with me after all, identify the enemy. Oh, look, I've given her and the rest of you a lot of bother and I'm really sorry. This is a job that can't happen.' She grew high-pitched. 'Can't, can't, can't.' Instead of clapping she gave three thumbs down in front of her chest.

18

'Is he taking you away from me, Helen?' Will cried out. He was crouched forward in the three-castor rexine armchair where Petra had sat, his face in his hands. 'Perhaps I deserve that. I've failed you, Helen, whereas Thomas Ingle-Blake can – '

'Coventry's a slug,' she replied – Petra's word. 'A killer slug.' The others had gone. There had not been enough drink for a party but she found a couple of cans of Stella and they sat opposite each other in the living-room tidying the ends of the day. The Bordeaux visit was shelved.

Although she did not want Will too close to her, Helen thought things might turn out all right. Now and then self-pity would daze him, make all action impossible, including thank God violence: hard to recall at those times how rage could take him over, turn him hellishly inventive. Will had variety. There was a flimsiness to him and there were those flashes of daft lower league power. She did not mind the mixture. It gave her a chance. She watched him continuously now but felt more or less comfortable. Things had worked out pretty much as she wanted. He was safe. He had a job. His friends had swallowed it, more or less. Lesley had swallowed it. Things were working towards a good change. Helen had applied some brisk management, as ever.

'I see myself as finished,' he said. He took his hands from his face, as if to leave himself unprotected, a doomed victim of whatever came next.

'Mad,' she replied. 'We're at a brilliant beginning.'

'I could despise myself, Helen.' He held up a hand with the Stella can in it to stop any contradiction. 'I could. If I let my mind go a certain way I could find despair. I can believe my colleagues despise me. Jake. Perhaps even Osc. Women despise me. Petra.'

Helen laughed: 'Hardly. Do you know what she referred to you as in the car? She called you "the Supremo" – no micky-taking, she meant it. "Balance, audacity when appropriate, decisiveness."' The terms hung proud in the air a while. 'These are what she sees in you, Will. She listed them like that – balance, audacity when appropriate, decisiveness. This was a thoughtful appraisal. That "when appropriate" is *so* crucial. She pretends to act gung-ho, but she knows care is needed, she appreciates judgement. And, listen – this is damn cheek, but listen – looking at me, she said she could tell from my total contentment that you had the biggest and hardest and longest-lasting dick this side of the Atlantic. Envy there? And of course I said, Who the hell's better in the States, then, and book me an air ticket? Joking.'

He had the Stella tin to his mouth now but hardly drank anything. She did not like that. Generally, he improved with booze, could get in touch with his backbone. She had been hoping to see his face gradually pick up its usual cheerfulness, start showing belief in himself again. 'Did I tell you about Carl Date?' he asked.

'Date?'

'The guard at the depository.'

'Oh, him. Does it matter, Will? That's the past.'

'He won't disappear.'

'We don't have to cater for him. We're not in that sort of game any longer. That's the beauty of things now.'

His eyes seemed to have moistened. *God, don't let him weep.* She had seen him cry once or twice before. Her father had taught her contempt for men who broke like that. Will said: 'When you were talking to Ingle-Blake I wondered whether he told you what Date had done to me. Did he tell you that, like tête-à-fucking-tête? It's the kind of thing Ingle-Blake would do. He's sniffing around you, or beyond that by now, so he'd want to shrink me down to fuck all, wouldn't he – show you how I could be terrorised, and then do me a kindness – like to the disabled – make a kindly opening for me on the staff?'

'It's not that kind of post – you know it. We didn't even talk about Date.'

He giggled, but his face stayed solid: 'Do you think I'm really going to take some poncy job with – ? You and him together fixing up Will Mallard! You think Will Mallard is going to play at that? I'd have thought you'd know Will Mallard better. There's something inside that would never allow him to accept some pissy spot with a man who's been taking precedence with Will Mallard's wife.' He pressed the tin of Stella to his chest. 'Yes, deep inside, but always there and ready to show. How could I know that was the situation when he called? This was the unspoken between you two. I hate that, Helen.'

She stood up. 'You don't like drinking from a can, Will. Primitive. Never have.' She went into the kitchen and took a pint glass from its shelf. Then she picked up a short-handled Kitchen Devil knife in a plastic scabbard and slipped it into the pocket of her jeans. Perhaps Chris had heard her move out from the living-room and he came quietly downstairs to the kitchen now. When she turned to go back to Will her son was there behind her.

'What's wrong, mum?' he said.

'It's a business matter. Nothing much. Complicated.' They both whispered.

He struck the kitchen unit with his fist, gently. 'When those two come here, Jake, Oscar – always afterwards there's some kind of – I can feel it.'

'Nothing's going to happen,' she said.

'Is dad – '

'I've got to talk to you, Chris.'

'If you like. What about?'

'Who you meet.'

He seemed to falter. 'Meet? Have you seen – ' He stopped himself.

'Seen what?' He'd viewed the slides? But how?

129

Chris recovered. 'You mean meeting kids at school, the teachers?'

'Talk later,' she said. 'Dad and I are discussing something.'

'If you want, I could come and sit in there. Things couldn't get too bad then – I mean, not as bad as just the two of you, if he's...if he gets...you know what he can be like.'

'No. You'd be bored.' She returned to the living-room and gave Will the glass. She heard Chris go as noiselessly as he could back upstairs. She poured some of the Stella into the pint pot for Will and then returned to where she had sat before, that decent distance.

He spoke as though answering a question, very matter-of-fact inside the dark suit. 'When I was clerking, Date and his chums wanted me to get some keys for them and stuff about alarms at the firm I was with. They'd pay me. They *did* pay me. But then, oh, I don't know, I decided it was wrong. Or I chickened. I'm not sure now. A bit of both.'

'Doesn't count, Will. It's years ago.' God, some mistake to have made up her tale that Coventry told her of the ambush.

Will drank and nodded. 'No, you're right, Helen. Doesn't count. You're a strength, do you know that?'

'We're a strength to each other,' she said. Yes, things might be all right.

'Absolutely. So he got me into some workshop he was renting and tied me with cable, hung me from a rafter with a gag in, and then went to work with pliers, the big kind of pliers you can get. You know that kind of pliers? This is all over the body. All over. I gave them what they wanted. They paid me in advance then cut me in as they promised for another chunk but more, because Date said I'd coughed so fast and not caused a lot of inconvenience or blood in his workshop, or chewed up the gag too badly. That story went around – what he said. Coventry tell you this when you're frisking about, the two of you? The bonus I got? It's like you said, he knows everything on this patch.'

'We had proper simple business discussions, Will, that's all,' she replied. 'Nothing complicated. About the jobs.'

He nodded again, drank a bit more, put the glass down. 'Who went to who first? You to him? You thought, That useless sod,

Will, is going to foul up again, this time at the antiques, so I'll get over to the fine friend of majesty and me and ask him to grant a favour on behalf of the fucking liability I keep at home, and his liability pals.'

She said: 'He sent for me, Will. He wanted an intermediary to make a deal with you. He didn't think you'd listen to him direct, being so well placed already. Then he comes to our house too early – so damned eager to recruit you, before I've had time to say anything.'

'What are you carrying?' he said, nodding at her pocket. Not once had she touched it or looked towards it. She thought she was ready for him if he moved but when he did, out of his chair and across the room at her, it was so fast that she couldn't react. Perhaps she had glanced away momentarily, thinking she heard Chris downstairs again and near the living-room door. She heard glass break and feared Will had smashed the pint pot to make a weapon. Her hands went up to her face to keep off the carving. She forgot the knife. At once his fingers took her throat. He must have kicked over the glass and smashed it with his shoe when he lunged. She brought her hands down and tried to tug at his wrists.

He jammed his mouth to her ear and bellowed. 'He's having you, but of course he doesn't want to have you full-time, not make you his steady woman, he's got one of those, and who are you? Who are you? How can you rate, except as meat? So, keep poor flimsy Will, look after Will. That's his scheme. Then, when you're ditched there's someone for you to slide back to, and maybe in a nicer house and a nicer area, so you give no trouble to darken his gorgeous name.'

She could not break his hold on her. His weight was forcing her down into the chair. His fingers on her neck did not slacken. Ten death jobs – she was conscious of each finger and the thumbs as a separate, berserk killing item. That meant her mind was clear, she had not even started to cloud yet. And if her head was clear she should use it. Abruptly, she released his wrists and instead reached up and locked her hands around the back of his neck, jerking his face down towards her. She cracked him twice on the bridge of his nose with her forehead and was immediately drenched in his blood and maybe some of her own, blinding her, filling her gasping mouth. His fingers did loosen now but the blood clogged her throat, half choked her. He took one of his hands away, perhaps to comfort himself, check on his shattered nose.

Or perhaps to fight off Chris. She heard her son yell, though couldn't see him through the blood. The din must have brought him – Will's glass breaking, his body crashing on to her in the chair, the filthy shouting. Chris screamed: 'Mum, use the knife. Use the knife. Oh, God, I had a real one, a bigger one.' Helen rolled a bit to the side under Will and managed to get her hand into her pocket and pull it out, still in the plastic cover. She drew the blade. She fancied jabbing up into his mouth and tongue through the soft bit under the jaw, to let him know he couldn't call her meat.

She heard what sounded like a heavy, tidy blow and instantly Will toppled off her to the left. There was a mixture of noises – a groan, a double-stage impact with the floor, like someone slumping down seated for a second and then tipping over help-lessly. She wiped her eyes with her free hand. She spat, not caring where it went, but longing for it to be on Will. She saw Chris bending over him near her chair. In his right hand Chris still held the stout black masonry chisel Will kept by their bed in case of burglars.

God, she thought, some family tableau. *Mother and Child With Weapons, Father Fucked Up.* Poor Will, beaten by a schoolboy and a woman. She put the knife back in its holder, cleaned herself more or less, then saw to the room, then Will. Her head was split all along the front line of her hair. She found some cotton wool and gave herself a dab or two. Will had begun to come round. His eyes were closed but he muttered: 'Who hit me? That creep kid? I'll – '

'Take it easy now,' Helen said.

'It was him. He with you against me? You and Tom against me. The boy against me. I'll get him, you know. He knows I'll get him for this, the creepy kid.' He drifted down into sleep again. Helen and Chris helped him upstairs and she undressed him. In the night he seemed to stir and half wake once more. She turned towards him. 'Silly. Nothing but business, Coventry and me, Will,' she said. 'How could there be? Would I go to someone like that? Petra's right. Haven't I got used to the biggest, hardest, longest-lasting dick in the region?'

'Well, I suppose you have, love,' Will murmured. He began to snore the snores of a man comfortable with himself and a bit concussed but able to take it.

19

Kerry said: 'No, I can't talk to you about things like that. And you know it. There's a Force Press officer. All newspaper reporters get their information through him, including you. You shouldn't be here.'

He acted out apology in the hallway of the flats, a sort of small, coolie-type cringe from the waist, a guiltyish smile. This lad was a star, a freak but a star. He looked about Kerry's age, twenty-eight or nine, and had a Welsh accent, refined Welsh: say Newport, Gwent, plus Jesus, Oxford, that Welsh-flavoured college. He replied sheepishly: 'Well, yes, I – '

'I don't like being doorstepped by the Press.'

'No, I understand, believe me, and normally, of course, I'd – But there did seem to be a personal element here. That's really why I took a chance and called.'

'Personal? What's personal?' she asked.

Again the small, deferential arching of his body inside that heirloom suit: 'I'm puzzled. If you could just clear up one or two basic points for me, Sergeant Lake. Have I got that right? It *is* Detective Sergeant Kerry Lake?' She did not respond – give this one no openings. Why would he be here trying to get into the flat if he was short of her name and rank? He had journalist eyes: thoughtful, thoughtless eyes that knew too much and believed next to nothing, especially not what he wrote.

He said: 'Look, one of the local reporters passes on stuff to us in London now and then – our stringer. He rings when there might be a nationwide angle in something, often something too tricky for his own paper here to handle. Apparently he told our news desk you were dancing with Ingle-Blake when that fierce business happened at the Heart ball. This is a detective sergeant dancing with Tommy Ingle-Blake and getting involved in a scene about child murder. Have I got it right, please? Deemed to be significant by my masters up there. Perhaps not.

'Of course, the stringer knows we're watching Ingle-Blake, and have been for a long time. But no progress. Well, so are most London papers watching him, heavy and tabloid – we're intrigued by the royal bit as against...well, I don't know whether you're a friend of his and I certainly don't want to offend...but this famed royal connection as against the kind of...oh, call it *swashbuckling* business he does – call it *commodity* business that he does, too – and the ripe stories about his past. On the face of it a newsworthy mix – royalty, loucheness.' He giggled. 'All right, some of my best friends are louche – but, of course, they don't hobnob with royals, only with people like me. So, anyway, my boss's ear starts to flap, Kerry – sorry, Sergeant Lake. I mean, I can imagine it – mention Ingle-Blake and he's mesmerised, thinking, Are we on the edge of another Fergie-scale imbroglio here? *Hold the front, back and centre pages and make sure we're first.*

'Then some more, isn't there – the stringer tells us your boy-friend is big in the firm that catered for the ball and his chief's a pal or almost of Ingle-Blake. Does this take us yet further on? A double link with Tom? Any news editor would think Ingle-Blake has bought up this town. London suspects that's par for the course in most provincial spots, some big-time not too scrupulous money-bags taking over. So, sharp orders come: *Get on an Intercity, Charlie, boy, and have a little investigative browse there. To our cleansing task again!* That's what I meant, you see – the personal element. Your Press officer can't really help me on this.'

'I can't help you either,' Kerry said. She began to shut the door. His tone scared her, so damned playful. Children's lives might be only an assignment to him, another sortie.

When she had first answered his knock and opened up just now Kerry immediately thought he looked such a freak – the suit, the hair – that he could not really be such a freak and that he must know things and might say things which would appal

134

her. The only things able to appal her would centre on Chris and Liz, and she had sensed they interested him above all. Sensed it how? She could not have said. But a vague, general, petrifying fear had taken hold of her lately that all sorts might know about Chris, even know about Liz. All sorts could include Coventry Tom and possibly this odd-looking caller. Those Holt's Corner meetings – so obvious, so regular. But if Coventry knew, he had done nothing about it, so far. The status quo suited him. She could understand that. But she had wondered, what if this lad confronting her now and announcing himself as a reporter began to disturb the scene, began to up the pace? News hounds were trained to disturb scenes and up the pace. They lived by it. Chris and Liz might die by it. She had told herself, get rid of this oddity, get rid of him, but hadn't.

In fact, he had not mentioned Chris and Liz, not at the start, but said he wanted to ask about Ingle-Blake. His office had sent him here from London because of a couple of 'strange items' they'd picked up on Ingle-Blake recently. That was when she had tried to give him the official bum's rush and referred him to the Press office.

Now, as she at last tried to shut him out, he did not push a foot over the threshold in standard style – too crude – but his voice rose fractionally, though still unstressed, the Welsh bit stronger, more lilting and creepy. She fretted about this kind of talk bombing around the landing and up the stairwell to other flats. He put out a hand and leaned against the door frame, still not actually preventing her from slamming, very relaxed, con-spiratorial, just the two of them. She loathed this notion. 'Obviously, any guidance you could give me and my paper on this would be totally off the record,' he said. 'Background – like Deepthroat. Look, I feel I must be specific. All right? I can't fool someone like you, high-flier type, trained sceptic. So then, what really fascinates us, of course, is the death of this boy, Denton. Big story and every paper gave it the treatment.' He shifted his stance a bit but kept the arm out, propping himself. It was so chummy still. 'Or at least we know all about it except who did it and why. I'll say things even more clearly – we wonder whether it ties into the stuff about child informants that's causing grave worry on all fronts at present. Given the child murder, this is a mighty topic, a topic of legitimate national interest, I think you'd agree. We're a campaigning paper, you know.'

'I'm sure, but the proper way to – '

'You see, Sergeant Lake, I wouldn't want to go clod-hopping into what could be quite delicate areas as far as you're concerned by making an official call on your Press department – mentioning the closeness – yours and your partner's – with someone at least a bit dubious, like Tom. A bit? Oh, come on!' He frowned, tensed momentarily, signalled regret. 'Does that sound like tabloid Press strongarm? But no, it isn't at all. This is sincere concern for your situation. I hope you'll believe that.' He bellowed an outright laugh, punched the wall feebly, and became at ease again. 'No, of course you won't believe it! Do *I* believe it? To you I look like one of what Denis Thatcher used to call the reptiles, when he was still newsworthy, poor old bugger. Remember him at all?'

Keep *this* reptile out, keep him out. His face was not especially reptilian, more canine: a square, slightly flabby construction, like a boxer dog's. He had other stuff to spill, worse stuff, and she did not want to hear it. Yes, she did, did, did want to hear: it could be vital to hear it, counter it, if it could be countered. 'Delicate areas?' she replied. 'How would it be delicate?' Sure, it was delicate. This character in his old and infinitely old-style suit could bring youthful funerals. His lapels were duvets. He dressed like *The Forsyte Saga* and some of the dandruff on his collar should be Edwardian.

'Believe me, Sergeant Lake,' he said, 'I'm sure there was nothing *really* off-key about dancing with Ingle-Blake. Sure, the mother yelled cruel abuse at you, supposing an alliance, business or sexual or a mixture. But she was worked up and always liable to go haywire. Perhaps, in fact, you were dancing with him as a kind of detective ploy, buttering. You went through the accelerated promotion course at Bramshill, didn't you?'

He wasn't like Vic: brought out no prompt notes. It was as if her career was naturally familiar to everybody, like Madonna's.

He said: 'I'm in favour of women getting on fast in the police, very. I bet they teach all sorts of fancy techniques to the gifted at that coll. How could Mrs Denton know what was going on? Too subtle for her, especially in that state. This is a woman seeing

136

only enemies. You're with her enemy, so you're her enemy, too. Crazy. And, then again, clearly I don't say it's sinister that your boyfriend's firm caters for a function in which Ingle- Blake is so prominent.'

'Kind.'

Two hands raised, another cheeky surrender. He was fair-haired and ruthlessly crew-cut. It seemed mad with the outfit: a hulk's escapee who'd pinched some bank manager's clothes. But his cheeks were too plump for bread and water. Carefully he puckered up his face. 'In some ways this is a disgusting bloody job I do, you know, even worse than being in the police – the dredging, the tricky footwork, the intrusion. Once, I thought of stockbroking, and not just because I had this suit. But that seemed such a huge ambition for someone with my background – ever been to Cwmbran? – and so the drift into laptop and modem. Sad.'

'Please don't weep here. Did you consider going on the stage?'

He said: 'Anyway – as to you and your boyfriend's silver-service firm: we have to consider not necessarily how things actually are but how they might be perceived. That's the buzz word these days. *Perceived*.'

He talked like Superintendent Harry Bell.

'I'm sure you can see how these links might appear if they were carelessly presented, sergeant. Suppose Ingle-Blake's grubbier side were emphasised rather than the good works, and suppose you and your boyfriend were shown as hand-in-gloving with him, you dancing, the boyfriend catering. We do need to guard against that.'

'Do we?' she asked.

'The public would not understand. These days they're looking all the time for dirty links between police and villains. You could find yourself on the end of politicians' questions, Home Office inquiries.' He glanced down lovingly at the navy serge. 'Oh, OK, you'll say I could get rid of my suit if I've chucked the idea of broking, but I like the impression it gives in this trade – sort of puzzles, disarms. This is not doorstepping gear. People get uncertain, even you with your hard and chirpy brain. You're thinking of asking me in. Oh, true, you're also thinking of telling me to piss off. But at least I've a hope. Where would I be with denim?' He gave the waistcoat a fondle and said: 'Yes, I think you'd want to avoid any mention of your own name in the paper alongside Ingle-Blake's. After all, Kerry, you've got a family to think of – mother, father, young brother at a good school and the older ones both undergraduates with smart careers ahead if things go nicely. They wouldn't enjoy reading stuff like that about you. Families hate taint. Even tainted families hate taint, but a spruce family like yours – daddy an MBE – they really dread the remotest contact with the rotten. Your older brothers – as I said, I know how careers can be pushed off the planned golden road if there's the wrong sort of pressure.'

Again no notes. She said: 'What is this? You've been nosing into my – '

'In the office they believe Timothy Denton died for putting the word around about Ingle-Blake – how they interpret the outburst by his mother at the ball. They might be right or totally adrift. I feel it could be something else. If you and your boyfriend are in touch with him – I mean only socially in touch, no imputations whatsoever, naturally – but if you're in touch with him you might be able to give me some idea whether the office estimate of the situation is reasonable. It's not something I can ask Ingle-Blake, is it, even supposing he'd see me? Certainly I'll try to interview Tom, but only when I've got something to put to him.

'Of course, I do realise that if he's a chum you might feel you must tell him I've quizzed you, but, OK, that's one of those risks. The local reporter knows things up to a point. He saw what he saw at the ball, and was the only journalist there after royalty left. Good conscientious lad. But he can't tell us everything. As a police officer having at least some sort of connection with Ingle-Blake you would be much better placed to offer help. You might convince me the whole thing about him and juvenile grasses is nonsense. If so I could be on my way back to London tomorrow.'

Say goodbye? Say, as he suggested, Piss off? Or should she ask him in and try to get some boundaries to this, smooth it over, stop him flailing about – yes, clod-hopping. But even if she did talk, would it stop him flailing and clod-hopping about? The London office wanted to expose underage informants and their handlers. He had to provide. The office wanted names. She was confused. Despite his denials, did he think she might be bound somehow to Coventry, perhaps part of a 'pact' – police blind-eyeing to protect the man who knows the royals? So why did he imagine she would help him? Perhaps as he said he had to gamble at some point.

At some point most folk had to gamble. 'You'd better come in,' she said. 'It's going to be brief. My partner will be home from work soon, and he won't want to listen to shop talk.'

He dropped his hand from the door frame but did not move forward at once, as though giving her time to backtrack. 'It's not really like you think, you know,' he said, with another frown and then a smile which had such prolonged sweetness it could have been more or less real. Like the crew-cut, it seemed monstrous perched on top of horse bus clothes. He said: 'We're a tabloid, yes, but a tabloid with a real sense of serious mission. Like the *Mirror* of the 1950s.' He introduced himself formally then. 'Charles Highton. My areas for the paper are crime, social issues, a bit of politics now and then. And you, I know, are who you are and your boyfriend is Mark Taber, a director with Stephen and Peter Comble. Excuse me, Mark doesn't mind you working so closely with your dapper colleague Victor Othen?'

She ran through a short prayer that Chris would not telephone while he was here. Highton followed her into the flat. He said: 'I accept totally that there will sometimes be a case for using child grasses. Anything I write will be balanced, believe me. We realise all kinds of gambits are necessary to catch the biggies.'

'I don't know much about any of that,' she replied. 'You could be wasting your time here.'

'Please, about any of what?'

'Informants. Young or old. Only much more experienced detectives run grasses. It's a high skill.' True, too. Claire Bater had been amazed and envious to find Kerry might be operating a grass.

'But you'd hear the buzz about informants, I'm sure.'

'What buzz?'

'About informants.'

'But there is no buzz. Talk's forbidden. It's too dangerous.'

139

'I meant perhaps the buzz said Timothy Denton was done for grassing, or the fear he might grass,' he said.

'If we had a motive we might get nearer to an arrest.'

He sat down and made appreciative grunts about the comfort of the bucket armchair, then looked with pleasure around the room. She watched him memorising for what they called 'colour' when he wrote something. She sat opposite, offered no drink or tea. Keep it short. He said: 'The stringer thinks there's quite a gang of kids selling information, without parental knowledge.'

Here it comes.

He said: 'This is the gossip around the youth haunts, apparently. Rush Street, the Square, the Welcome.'

'Not my area.'

'I had a glance at it. Looks the right sort of crowd. I've asked him to keep at it there.'

'Who?'

'The stringer. He's local and wears their kind of clothes – the denim. He's only twenty-two. We do need kids who can tell us how they operate as grasses – in their own words. Names – possibly coded names – are the guts of this kind of story. Otherwise it reads like a woolly, concocted Press yarn and loses any chance of changing policy. No good to a responsible paper.'

'Your responsible paper could kill a child, children.'

He nodded very gravely. 'You're saying that Tim Denton was definitely done for grassing, then?'

'I'm saying you'll turn kids into targets. Kid A, Kid B! For heaven's sake, don't you think some clever villain could work out who they are?'

'Which clever villain?'

'Plenty of them.'

'And there are other kid informants around the Welcome and so on, are there? My Intercity trip was worthwhile?'

'I told you, not my level.' She had come to feel that dealing with the Press was not her level, either.

'Yes, you did tell me, you did.'

'You should have done broking.'

'The stringer whispers two names,' Highton said.

'Of children?' Who was this perilous, gifted twenty-two-year-old local mouth in denim? Had he seen Coventry's slides? Get this scribbler promoted fast out of the town. Did he understand what harm he could do? Well, of course he did. Their trade was to harm someone.

'I'd never write them down – the names,' Highton said.

'Does your colleague write them down?' And when she tried to visualise the stringer's notebook she suddenly saw not Chris's name but her brother's, Simon Lake. Could she only worry fully about Chris if she thought of him as Simon? No. No. She did worry about Chris.

'The stringer write stuff down? I suppose that's possible,' he said. 'He'd have a lot of material to keep in his head. Do you know, I'm damn reluctant even to pass on the names to you.' He guffawed. 'Yes, even to you, a detective officer. Well!'

'So right,' she said.

'I don't mean because you might have a link with Ingle-Blake. No, I don't think I really believe that. But it's simply that it would be hopelessly slack, since these kid grasses are not *your* kid grasses, are they – you not having kid grasses at all or any other kind of grasses – you've told me that, haven't you? – I understand you right? – and so this would be a breach involving the two kid grasses and their detective, whoever he or she may be? That a fair summary of things?' He had put on a very plodding, logical tone. Kerry saw he was near to laughing, the well-informed creep.

She went grave. 'Security is crucial and has to be one hundred per cent where informants are concerned. I know nothing about them from personal experience, but this is the basic and obvious teaching on running tipsters of any age.'

'The boy is a Christopher Mallard,' Highton replied. 'And then there's a girl called Liz Farnes. She's the one who's done the talking – mostly about the pay she expects. How we got the identities. I'm not going to speak to them either, at this stage. Not until I get some kind of confirmation.'

She tried to stay blank-faced as he spoke the names but could not count on it. 'How's that going to happen?' she asked. 'Confirmation.'

'Quite.' He pulled a handful of coins from his trouser pocket and jangled them in front of her. 'It might be a matter of offering even more money than the grassing stipend. Do you know them at all, Kerry?'

'I don't run grasses,' she replied.

'No, you said. But the boy's father is a small-time crook. I wondered if you'd run across the family. Mallard,' Highton said with great definition. 'Will Mallard. Jinxed. Lunatic temper. Daniel Street. The wife-mother, Helen.'

'Not my area,' she said.

'Where *is* your area?'

Terrified and angry, she gave a huge yawn and stretched her arms high for a while, as though uninvolved and therefore uninterested. When it was over she said: 'Do you know, I believe you're here to propose some deal, aren't you, Highton?'

'These kids are *your* grasses, aren't they?' he replied. 'That's what I'm advised. You've done pretty well to line them up – as you say, so early in your career.'

'Advised? You're obsessed about grasses. Can I ask you something – have you or a colleague hired a Mondeo?'

'But the grasses *are* yours, yes?'

She got another grand yawn from somewhere. 'And if they were, which they're not, but if they were, I suppose you'd like them and me to describe how it all works,' she said. 'Barmy. Do you understand anything at all about police operations, police security?'

'I detest that word "deal". A brokerage term, not appropriate to serious journalism. What I would like, Kerry, is for you and me and, yes, the two children to sit down together and draft an account of this beautifully tidy grassing system you've built. These will be articles on which you personally can exercise a fair degree of shaping. Or more than that – major shaping. If you say something should be kept out, out it will be kept. If you say something should be stressed, stressed it will be.' He flexed inside the redolent suit. 'These articles could do you good – show that although young you've progressed with grasses.'

God, yes, yes, she should have told him to push off at the very start, as she had been trained to tell any potentially damaging bit of the Press. 'The articles could kill two kids,' she intoned.

'Oh, I think Coventry Tom knows about Chris and Liz already. Yet he hasn't moved against them.'

'What?' She was horrified to hear him speak her fear. 'How do you know he knows? You said you hadn't talked to him.'

'No, not yet,' Highton said. He expounded in that unsettling mix of accents – Welsh, cockney, junior common room. 'He knows because he's Coventry Tom. Someone that big – it's their function to know, isn't it?'

She longed to squash the idea but said: 'Even if he does know, can't you see that if your paper publishes an article, articles, saying two kids have incriminating information about Coventry he will have to get them out of the way? Press reports like that might force the police to act against him at once, in a panic. There would be public pressure. Suddenly these children become potential witnesses in a murder case. He'd silence them. Please, Highton, think.' She heard herself begin to yell.

'Might not be a bad idea to get the police to act against him, at last,' he said. 'One purpose of the Press should be to force action.'

'We'll act when we're ready.'

'Really? *You* might be willing to act. But your bosses?' he asked.

'Look, drop it,' she said.

'Besides not naming them I might manage to avoid naming *you*, Kerry, he replied. We'd have our Child A, Child B and Detective C – not even your gender. I would not disclose, believe me, even under threat of jail.'

'It's maniacal.'

Highton folded the folds of his face into sadness. 'Kerry, if I can't convince my office that you'll co-operate – that this is the most effective way to handle the story – we're pushed to a free-for-all situation. In that case, I fear I'll have to get the tale by whatever means I can and publish it as I see best – and as the office sees best. Although I'd try to hang on to the assignment as mine only, because it's so worthwhile, I don't think I could rely on that. There might be reinforcements. Difficult to contain matters when there's a pack. There might even be a decision to use names in the paper, and to hell with self-censorship. What that would mean, of course, is that if you ever brought a case against Ingle-Blake and you tried to use evidence taken from these kids – '

'They'd be dead.'

'If you tried to use evidence provided by them the judge would probably chuck it out because of the stink that articles like these – I mean possibly tactless, unduly explicit articles – the stink these would create around your operations with child grasses.'

'That's going to happen if you do any kind of articles about child grasses, named or not.'

'Names would make it so much worse. You're in the witness box and some QC asks whether you are the same Detective Sergeant Kerry Lake as in the recent newspaper revelations about child informants. That's the kind of questions QCs love – the ones they know the answers to. What would a jury make of it – suppose the judge ever allowed it to go that far?'

God, he could be so right and she wanted Highton out of the flat. God, she wanted him to stay, so she still had a chance of talking restraint at him. She wished she had never let him in. Oh, she was glad she did and had discovered what he knew. 'Here's Mark,' she said. She had heard his key. In a moment he joined them. 'This is Charles Highton, a London journalist,' she said. 'He's interested in Tom Ingle-Blake.'

'Oh?' Mark said. He looked amazed that she should have admitted Highton and was talking to him.

The reporter stood. 'But we don't get very far,' he said. 'Look, I won't intrude any longer. It's been very kind of you, Sergeant Lake.' He produced a card and wrote on the back of it. 'My hotel number. Should you recall anything further I'm there,' he said.

'And she hasn't even given you tea?' Mark said, looking about for cups.

'Ah, Sergeant Lake mentioned you were mighty in catering,' Highton replied.

'I'd have thought fashion not crime reporting was your specialty,' Mark said.

20

Kerry decided Stephen Comble said his piece as well as it could be said. 'I am delighted you could all come,' he told them. 'I trust nobody else will be offended if I say I'm especially delighted that our two principal guests are here, despite many factors which might have intervened.'

Stephen had a lot of presence, especially in his own home, but, more than that, she felt a real sensitivity in his voice and words tonight, a genuine, anxious reaching out for hope. Stephen was old enough and rich enough to believe in hope. The big drawing-room's white-based décor and the wide windows must make it a light and hopeful room in the day. 'By "principal guests" I mean, of course, Sonia Denton and Tom Ingle-Blake,' he said. 'It's also my pleasure that Tom has been able to persuade his wife to accompany him. My own wife would have been here, too, I assure you, were it not for a visit arranged long ago to one of our daughters and our grandchildren.'

Stephen's hair was grey, but jaunty grey not deadbeat, and he had it cut *en brosse*, which gave him a thrustful, upbeat look. He was standing alongside the tall mahogany Regency cabinet in his drawing-room, a class item, hugely too high for council house ceilings. Stephen was tall, too, and kept himself leanish. He and his cabinet set each other off.

'What we seek here tonight is some degree of clarification and, through this, some degree of reconciliation, also. I phrase it guardedly, because I don't think our expectations should be unreal. We are not an official body – have no power, no status, no means of legislating for change. And yet change is what we seek. We crave an abiding peace in our city. We desire safety for its people of all ages, we desire an end to threat, violence, dark rumour, poisonous hate.'

He glanced nervously towards a curtained window. 'As to rumour, I have to tell you it might be increased at any time: there is a London newspaper reporter in the city. He has approached me – has tried to: in my view it would be wrong to encourage him with information. I trust he does not know of this meeting and that he confronted none of you on your way here. No? Good. Just the same, please be alert when you leave.'

Positivism took over Stephen again. 'But regardless of this journalist, regardless, indeed, of all the difficulties, I believe that with goodwill – and your attendance here tonight proclaims that goodwill – with this goodwill I believe we could move matters a little way towards the kind of cleansing and harmony I know we all wish for. One thinks of the Putney Debates during the King–Cromwell Civil War – talk sessions without formal powers, and yet *so* influential.'

Sonia Denton asked: 'We've got a procedure?' She was in a double-breasted navy pin-stripe tailored suit tonight, not the bomber jacket, and looked like the manager of a Motor Show pavilion. Kerry found it a bit sad, as if Sonia thought she must act up to Stephen and Mark and the fitments. Kerry wore jeans and a collarless black shirt, but then Kerry had nothing to prove here, except that Coventry Tom killed Sonia Denton's son.

After the Putney stuff, Stephen had sat down in an armchair at the far end of the room next to his son, Peter, and Peter's wife, Alex, as though keen to get swallowed up in family and not dominate. He said: 'A procedure, Mrs Denton? Ah, yes, well – '

'An agenda,' Sonia said. 'You know, something I can wrap my legs around?'

Stephen said: 'Well, this being almost a casual kind of – '

Sonia Denton said: 'I see what you mean. You'd think to yourself, this woman sneaks into a silver ticket ball and starts screaming at a prime guest despite the recent presence of royalty. And if she'd been able to she would have sneaked in earlier, while royalty was actually there – she'd have *really* fracassed. So you'll calculate thusly – *What we don't expect from her is acceptance of rules and/or decorum. Play the grieving bitch by ear.*'

Sonia had been offered a chair, of course, but so far stayed standing near the grand piano. Now and then as she spoke she took a couple of small paces, away from her spot and towards some sort of blue and yellow abstract painting on the wall – a genuine job, not a print – then back, like a twitchy lecturer. Her

146

face showed she was having a fight with herself. Perhaps she regretted coming. Perhaps she feared it would all be jiggery-pokery and politeness. The skin was pulled very tight on her nose and chin and she clamped her teeth together occasionally, sucking the air in through them with a little anxious noise, like filtering. Kerry longed to go and comfort her, put an arm around her – as she often longed to put an arm around Chris Mallard – but knew this would be even more of a mistake with Sonia. To her Kerry was the enemy, like the rest here.

Mark said: 'Naturally, Stephen has in his head an ideal picture of how things might go this evening, Mrs Denton – how he, and we, would *wish* things to go – but, yes, in a sense you are right, he declines to impose a, well, iron framework. This has nothing to do with the incident at the Heart ball. It is simply that he recognises – we *all* recognise – the existence of extremely emotional material in this meeting, and would feel uneasy about stipulating a, well, yes, unduly precise framework.'

'Exactly,' Stephen said.

'"Material",' Sonia Denton replied, '"emotional material." Right. Yes, there'll be a chunk of that, I should think.' She paused for a second and seemed to lose some of her steel and contempt, but only for a second. 'When I say agenda I... What I hear when you speak, Mr Comble – it's a public voice, you know. You're into health of the city, regard for its history, traditions, the happiness of the general folk – all that. It's great. It's horse shit. What I've got is a personal thing, you see. I've got a dead boy. I've got a spot in a field where he was found – this particular spot. It concerns me more than the general civic fabric.' Her voice stayed steady. She'd worn the suit but wasn't jinxed after all. Her rage and sadness made sure of that. It heartened Kerry to get a slice of her scorn.

Julia Ingle-Blake said: 'I know this spot in a field, too.'

'Of course you fucking do,' Sonia Denton replied.

Coventry Tom said: 'Julia has been *so* affected by the young lad's death.'

'Of course she fucking has,' Sonia Denton replied.

Coventry was seated modestly on a straight-backed ebonised and parcel-gilt side chair, perhaps also Regency, his knees together. He seemed serene enough. Maybe he had not gone looking for the video tapes yet. Maybe he and Julia had not noticed that the house had been entered and a major kitchen knife was missing. Coventry had on a grey-black three-buttoned woollen jacket and navy-black slacks with an open-necked white shirt, like obsolete gear from a pre-colour movie firm. He said: 'I don't know whether I should address Mrs Denton's point about procedure, agenda, Stephen. I am an interested party, I suppose. But perhaps I might permissibly say this: there are, of course, public issues involved here tonight, and there is an agonisingly personal one, too – the loss of a son. But it does seem to me, Mrs Denton, Stephen, that no contradiction is involved. This meeting has been called, Mrs Denton, because Stephen and Peter and Mark – others too, perhaps – they see these two aspects as only one – as wholly involved with each other, each as cause, each as effect.'

With a chuckle Stephen said: 'As to agenda, Mrs Denton, you have in a sense initiated one – by raising forcibly – justifiably forcibly – the very matter of agenda, procedure! We are into them, I think!'

'I can put up with it if the death facts are given now,' Sonia Denton replied. 'The cop woman's here. The cop woman who dry-rub dances with Coventry and so on possibly. I don't know what the boyfriend makes of this, and I don't ask. She was in on Tim's case from the start. She knows it all. She knows more than she will tell us, probably, but she'll tell us *something*. I've been over it with them, of course I have. It can't hurt me hearing it again.'

Mark said: 'This is in no way a court. Stephen would not want that.' Kerry did not mind too much the way Mark mediated, spokespersoning. If you were a company director one direction you directed your mind to was interpreting the direction of the chief's mind and directing your own mind in the same direction.

'What I'm grateful for, Mr Comble, is no attempt was made to body search me at your front door,' Sonia Denton replied. 'The girl cop could have done that. Are you trained in frisking, sergeant?'

'The basics,' Kerry said.

Sonia Denton said: 'Enough, thank you. I wouldn't want you squinting up my arse in such an extensive property. But I could

148

be carrying a knife to finish the sod, a nice step on from shouting at him in a dance. Or *try* to finish him. It's no push-over to kill with a knife. And not just a matter of strength. Butcher's skills. Ask Tommy. But you have faith in me, Mr Comble, and it does you credit. I don't expect you searched Coventry, either, though, so I imagine you thought if this former mother pulls something Coventry will pull something better, he being Coventry and named after a time when he pulled something better than the other guy. Tom's a cosy friend to have.'

'We wish you to be at ease here, Mrs Denton,' Mark replied.

She sat down suddenly at one end of a big settee covered in bold, assured purple, gold and green floral patterns. ' "At ease", yes, that's the ticket. Or should *I* tell it, not the sergeant – the prelims, then the death?' she asked.

'Yes, you, Sonia,' Kerry said.

'If it were *my* son I believe I could do it, would do it,' Julia Ingle-Blake said. 'This would be a statement of our closeness.' She wore a blue bias-cut crêpe dress with spaghetti straps: looked like somebody almost at ease. 'Yes, I'd recount the approaches to his death because my knowledge of these approaches was to me a matter of pride, comfort, intimacy. I'd wish to share this knowledge and retain it.'

Coventry said: 'And we all *do* share the sorrow and the wish to know who has done this thing, so that the shadow can be lifted from our lives.'

Sonia Denton stood up, went back to her place near the Bechstein, gazed about almost fondly. She said: 'I try to imagine this gathering if I was not here.'

Mark at once cried out: 'No, no. We would not have gone ahead without you. I know I speak for Stephen on this. It would have been absurd, gross.'

'Impossible,' Coventry said.

'Of no value,' Stephen said.

'I'm not talking about suppose I'd turned down the invite,' she replied. 'I mean, what if I'd topped myself right after Tim's death? This was on the cards once or twice. I had tablets, you know. I didn't mind the taste. If I'd done it, the stink would still be around the town, and maybe more – first the boy, then his single-parent mother. Stephen, in his fine way, might have

149

wanted to do the cleansing and renewal just the same. It would be important to establish for his own satisfaction as a leading figure and for the satisfaction of those close to him that a major citizen like Coventry had not killed the boy and caused the boy's mother to see herself off in despair. Perhaps instead of me Tom would have been standing here, explaining how he could not have done Timothy because of his, that's Tom's, welfare nature, and because he was somewhere else, in any case, continuously in sight of eight witnesses who can swear to it without payment.'

Peter Comble said: 'Mrs Denton, is this a profitable way to – '

'I see it as a triumph that I'm here this evening,' she replied. 'I think you have been brave and considerate, Stephen. And your firm and family. I expect you feared I might feel impossible anguish at occupying the same room as the man who killed my son. Nonetheless you decided to go ahead, and I am grateful. It would be terrible and endlessly defeating to think we had a dead boy but no idea who was responsible. To know it was Coventry and to have him here on show through your splendid efforts, Stephen, brings the sadness within limits – what Mark might call a framework. We do not have to think that somewhere outside is the unnamed and unknowable vileness that killed Tim. He is here, neat and nasty, in this tasteful room. We can get a focus on him. Don't you think there is something nightmarish about uncharted horror, everyone? But Coventry gives it comfortable shape and exact boundaries. He parlourises evil.'

'There *are* good sides to Thomas,' Julia Ingle-Blake said. 'Neatness, yes, that would be one of them. Great bathroom neatness. Never pools.'

Stephen stood and went to Mrs Denton. He gently took her arm. 'I certainly don't wish to curtail what you say in any respect,' he told her, 'but possibly you are assuming matters to be true which, really, we are here to discuss, weigh, perhaps establish, perhaps not. The whole purpose of our gathering, you see. I feel that Kerry, for instance – our as it were professional – thinks you are moving a little fast.'

'She made some interesting points,' Kerry replied.

Mark said: 'Yes, but, Kerry, love, the unproven nature of – '

'Best let things run,' Coventry Tom said. 'One can learn from animus.' Stephen made a little so-be-it gesture and returned to his chair.

Julia Ingle-Blake said mildly: 'I certainly could not stay here and listen to allegations that Thomas is shit all through and from top to toe. Not one hundred per cent. Nobody could convince me of that, not even Mrs Denton with her gifts. This, after all, is the man one lives with, sleeps with more often than not. He would have been the father of my children.' Julia's tone stiffened and her face seemed to grow longer, pleaful. She turned towards him. 'No agenda, so you – now – *you* Thomas, why don't you grab precedence, dear, to tell us you are tolerable? Speak at once. Oust her. Push her from the piano. Claim innocence, do. Display your saving graces and alias. If you wish to sit in meekness, darling, sit in meekness later, when you have actually proved to us that meekness is your bag. I for one believe you can probably do that. Oh, definitely probably.'

Coventry smiled and glanced around, perhaps trying to gauge what others thought. Sonia went on with her address: 'I want to talk to you about Timothy from two different perspectives. There's the immediate – the day he was killed, where he had been, the exact times, the places, the whole null investigatory rigmarole. And then the larger scene: home life, school, his friends – especially his two best and worst friends Chris and Liz Farnes – perhaps it's unwise to draw attention to them, I worry about them – but I'm sure Coventry knows of them – yes, Tim's friends, and, finally, the connection with Coventry and his wife – this is all necessary. I'm going to begin with – '

A telephone rang on another bit of mahogany, a small, fine side table with a twin-flap top and brass-handled drawer. Stephen looked annoyed and flustered. He did not leave his chair. 'Excuse me, friends,' he said. 'This should not be, should not be at all. An entirely private, undirectoried number. Mark, take it, please. Say we cannot be disturbed. I thought I'd made that clear to everyone who knows the number.'

Kerry grew very scared.

Mark went and picked up the receiver. 'Yes,' he said, and listened. 'Who are you?' he asked. 'Well, how did you know of

151

this line? he said. 'Very well,' he replied. He put the receiver down and said: 'Oddly enough, it's for Kerry, Stephen.'

She would have bet it was but felt worse to hear him say so.

'The damn Press?' Stephen asked.

'Someone who refuses his name, Kerry,' Mark said.

'Excuse me, but did you give out the number, Kerry?' Stephen asked.

'I don't know it,' she said.

'And I'm sure *you* would not disclose it, Mark,' Stephen said. 'A mystery.'

When Kerry picked up the phone, Vic Othen said: 'The boy's gone.'

'I don't understand,' she said.

'Disappeared.'

Mark had remained standing nearby, as if feeling responsible for her and for this interruption. She had embarrassed him again. Perhaps he wondered if Stephen suspected him of spilling the secret number. The others in the room watched her.

'Someone has officially reported this?' she asked Vic.

'The mother saw me hanging about the street – you know, guarding, in case. She asked me if I'd seen Chris. Described him.'

'But he'd often be away from the house. Why the...'

'The panic? When she described him she said he'd be carrying a holdall. Perhaps she knows he's taken clothes with him.'

'I see.'

'There might have been trouble at home.'

'I'd better come.'

'I think so. I'd have called sooner but it took me a couple of minutes to dig out this fucking confidential number. Look, Kerry, I – '

'Not your fault. You're watching two.'

'Yes. I suppose he waited until he saw the street was clear, when I was over at the girl's. Kerry, when his mother was telling me what he looked like she used a phrase I thought strange. Worse. She said: "You wouldn't mistake him. He looks haunted."'

'I see.'

'I asked what it meant. She said: "Death in his eyes. Death in the stoop of his body." She ran up the street still looking, crying maybe, but came back almost at once. She stuck her head in at the car window and said: "But, of course, you know him already, don't you?" '

'I see.'

'She said: "If he comes back keep him here, will you? Don't let him go into the house alone. His father's there.'

'She knew who you were?'

'I'm waiting in a car in Daniel Street so what else would I be but police? And I've been about the town a long time. People know me. She went up the street again and around the corner. I had to start work trying to reach you – Comble's number. I'd have stayed with her otherwise. She hasn't come back. Have they had refreshments yet where you are? You wouldn't want to miss those – from a professional.'

'Where are you?'

'The boy's street.'

She realised he must suspect this special telephone did recordings. He had spoken no names. 'OK,' she said and replaced the receiver. 'Sorry, Stephen.'

'Not the Press? A colleague?' he asked.

'I'll have to go, I'm afraid,' she replied.

Stephen said: 'I really must look into how – I'm sure it's urgent – well, clearly, if you have to leave – but – unsettling. Mark, take this up with the telephone people tomorrow, please. I shall want the number changed, obviously.'

Sonia said: 'Oh, my God, not those two kids I mentioned, is it? Well, is it? Did you say "watching two"?'

Julia Ingle-Blake said: 'What will be the use of showing your nicer sides, Tommy, if the tight-arsed committed cop's not here?'

21

'I don't ask what it is, darling,' Mark said. He had followed Kerry out from Stephen's drawing-room to the porch. 'Rest assured everyone understands you are subject to these urgencies.' He looked unforgiving and painfully loyal.

'Perhaps I'll be able to get back,' Kerry said. She hated wrong-footing him publicly: Mark deserved the goodwill of his boss and the hangers-on. A career did matter.

'Possibly to do with the fretful lad who phoned you at the flat?' Mark said.

'Your meeting can continue, can't it?' she replied.

'Oh, Kerry – not so much *my* meeting, surely. Not really *mine* at all. You are central, a kind of fulcrum.'

'That what I was? Mrs Denton and Coventry are the principals. Their interaction. That will go ahead – regardless of what Julia Ingle-Blake said just now. You must tell me what happens.'

He seemed about to hold her arm and stop her leaving, or at least delay her. Then he pulled back. She was glad. A noisy struggle in Stephen's porch would be sick.

He said: 'Stephen did feel you were very important to these proceedings. He's mentioned it specifically. I consider this far-seeing of him and, yes, generous in a way.'

She wanted to be far-seeing, too, and surveyed the street in case Stephen had been right and the London reporter and his suit were around.

'In a way Stephen was making an opportunity for you, Kerry. I thought it to his credit that he invited someone like Mrs Denton into his home – I mean, with all the possible, well, unpredictability she would bring. Did bring. Not that one blames her for being emotional, of course, in the circumstances.'

'It was large-minded of Stephen,' Kerry said. As far as she could tell the street was clear. 'But, then, he is by nature large-minded. He'd have room for unpredictability.' *Oh, God, you snide bitch.* 'Mark, I must go, love.' She turned and gave him a good, friendly kiss, absolutely unhurried.

Of course, she drove straight to Chris's bank, not to Daniel Street. If the boy was running he would need money and have to make a withdrawal. His hollow tree stood in a thin strip of woodland the planners had left between a housing estate and a new so-called Industrial Park. She would never have taken Vic Othen here. It was a secret for her and Chris. Some intimacies stayed intimacies. She felt it almost a betrayal to go there herself,

154

alone. Well, of course it was a betrayal. She wished treachery came more easily to her. But, anyhow, it did come.

She recalled the bearings he gave in case she had needed to find the tree when he was dead – or she hoped she recalled them. It was twilight. She brought a torch from the car and followed a sketchy path to where it crossed another. Here, she turned right, found a holly bush and then the beech two trees further on. It was eerie to think of him taking those unearned fees from her week after week and coming out here to top up the store. In the night? 'Make sure you turn right,' he had said, 'not the other way. Lovers and all that go there. You know.' He had sounded queazy, as though she had to be protected from fleshy sights.

She listened. He might arrive while she was here. Crouching down, she pushed her hand through undergrowth that hid the opening and pulled out the treasure. She had guessed what it would look like: a small metal brown and gold locked cash box, wrapped around many times in a large black plastic bin liner for waterproofing. The packet was held by a thick elastic band. Its weight seemed right. There had been a chance that Chris arrived first, had taken the money and gone. With funds he would be able catch a train and make for Cardboard City in London or Manchester or Liverpool. This was the tradition for escaping kids, and he would probably have followed it, even if he had money for decent accommodation. He would think he could live undiscovered if he stayed on the streets there. They all believed that. But these were the kind of spots Coventry would get searched first if he heard Chris had gone and feared he might know something. Shanty lands were insecure. Inhabitants sold rumour, sold knowledge. Everything else they had sold already.

But Chris must have decided to stay hidden somewhere in the town until it was properly dark and reasonably safe to move. Mr Streetsavvy. Naturally. She took the box back to her car and forced it with the tyre lever. At a quick count she thought around seven hundred pounds in twenties and tens, and that would be without Liz's hundred. You could see why Harry Bell might feel pissed off about poor returns. For a couple of moments she considered putting the car out of sight then returning to the beech tree and waiting for Chris. But she ditched the idea. It would be grim to watch his horror when he found the tree rifled. What could she do or say then? Refuse to return the money so he could not get away? Order him home? That would finish things between them – not just the grassing, but any respect and affection he had for her – and she could not face this shame. Kerry would become the enemy, like school, Coventry, the rest of the police force and Chris's dad.

She jammed the money into her handbag, shoved the wreckage of the box and the plastic bag under the driving seat then went back to Daniel Street. Chris would turn up at the tree and have no notion where the money had gone. No certain notion. Anyone could have found it. Hadn't she warned him of this at the start? It was still his money and she would work out a way to return it, but not now. He would have to go back to his mother and father. That was what she wanted, though he must never know she schemed it. Get him off the streets, into safety. He *would* be safe at home, wouldn't he?

Vic was waiting in his Peugeot not far from the Mallards' house. It was fully dark now and Kerry saw the gleam of a cigarette before she spotted the car. She parked a little way from him then walked and climbed into the passenger seat. 'You smell rural,' he said.

'You can't smell anything but smoke.'

'The mother's returned, not the boy.'

'I think he will.'

He laughed a little and shook his head slowly, the silver moustache flashing under the street lamp like semaphore. 'But I love it – the confidence.'

'I think he will,' she said.

He considered this. 'You've picked up his money, have you? He's high-and-dry? So, either he burgles or hitch hikes or goes home. Yes, you're probably right. Home. Takes one clever kid to beat another clever kid. I can remember when I was a clever kid. My God, Kerry, have I fucked up or have I fucked up? I've got excuses, but that's what they are.'

She touched his arm, as he had touched hers the last time they were together. If this was getting to be a relationship it was a

156

muted one. She was unsure yet that she wanted it to move faster. Mark was still Mark, still rated. Well, of course he rated. The ease and warmth with Vic felt so good, that was all. 'Why did she tell you to keep him out of the house when she wasn't home?'

Vic did not answer straight off. 'You want some mind reading?' he asked. 'OK: Will could be perilous I imagine. Why the boy ran? Will might be exceptionally edgy if his antiques operation folded – and it did. Or perhaps Will's got a link to Coventry. Will's volatile, meaning ungovernable now and then as long as the opposition is weak.' He spread his hands, then chain-lit another cigarette. 'I don't know. Perhaps I ought to. I'm speculating.'

Suddenly she longed to embrace him – to comfort him in his spasms of self-blame, and perhaps to do more than that. When she did put her arms around him he turned his face and kissed her lightly on the temple, did nothing to push things on further than that. 'Ah, you're checking to see whether I picked up some armament,' he said. He'd let her disown the bit of impulsiveness, if she liked.

'Did you?' she asked, drawing back.

He opened his coat and showed a loaded shoulder holster. 'But you knew,' he said.

They waited for half an hour, not talking much. Then Kerry said: 'He might have gone to the girl's place. She's smart enough and tough enough to hide him for a while – say they had a garden shed. It's the kind of house that *would* have a garden shed.'

'You mean they'll run together?'

'Could be, both scared. She might really know something. This is a bright kid who was a friend of Tim and saw him late. Coventry or some of his people might have been sniffing around her house while you were here in Daniel Street. Perhaps she and Chris will move now it's night and not so many people about. If she knows something Coventry would assume they both do, as pals. Chris is into big hazard, Vic.'

'I'll accept that.'

'Look, I'll drive over – might spot them. You stay here. If he comes, don't do anything, just let him get inside to –' She had

157

been going to say safety, but couldn't, not to Vic. 'To his parents.'

'You're going to prowl their garden, look in their shed?' he asked. 'That could be damn tricky, if you were caught. Think of your golden career, kid.'

'It might not be necessary,' she said.

It was not necessary. As she drove down Liz Farnes' street Kerry saw Chris ahead of her, carrying the holdall. He reminded her of pictures of evacuees at the beginning of the war with all their possessions in a big case, weighing them down. Chris ran a bit, walked a bit, ran a bit, moving away from her and making towards the Farnes' house. There were lights upstairs. They must be going to bed. She pulled in, switched everything off and watched. It was approaching midnight. Did he really think he could get in touch with Liz so late? They had some arrangement? Perhaps she would join him once her parents slept.

Outside their house Chris put down the holdall on the pavement and stepped into the front garden. He seemed to bend and search there. A note from her fixing a rendezvous? But in a moment she worked out what he was doing. He had picked up two large stones, perhaps from a rockery. Briefly he stood still facing the house, a stone in each hand hanging by his side. Then he hurled them one after the other through the downstairs front window. She heard the glass break and perhaps another sound, the weightier clatter in bits of the proud porcelain horses. Still facing the house, Chris began to yell something, but although she had the driver's window down Kerry could not make out the words from that distance, only the childish anger. He shook his fist up at a bedroom window, yelled again, then turned and hurried back to his holdall, picked it up and ran once more, still in the same direction, away from where Kerry waited. Lights came on downstairs and almost at once the front door was opened and a man emerged gingerly, wearing only trousers. He seemed to be carrying one of the stones. He gazed up and down the street, and in a while moved slowly on bare feet from the front door and crossed to the window to look at the damage. A woman in a house coat appeared in the doorway and spoke to him.

Kerry put on her lights, started the car and drove past the house and after Chris. The man inspecting his window turned and waved at the Cavalier. Perhaps he wanted her to stop and say if she had seen anything. She kept going. In a couple of minutes she picked out Chris ahead, running all the time now, though slowly. He could have taken side streets towards his parents' house but ignored these. Occasionally the holdall knocked his leg and he would stagger. He glanced back twice, perhaps thinking Kerry was the pursuit, and tried for more speed. He looked weary. She *was* the pursuit. Drawing in a little way ahead of him, she pushed the door open. 'What was that about?' she said.

He had stopped and seemed nearly to turn and run the other way. Then he must have recognised the car. He bent down and stared in. 'What *you* doing here?' He had hardly the breath to speak. His voice was half relief, half accusation. He threw the bag on to the seat; fell in, picked it up and nursed it.

'What's the matter with you?' she said. She drove on, watching the mirror. It looked clear.

'You saw?' he asked. 'Of course you did. You see everything, don't you? Do you know what's happened? Well, you'd never fucking guess. That fucking Liz pinched my fucking money. I just been to look for it.' He sobbed with rage.

'What money?'

'The tree money, of course,' he said. 'From you. This is seven hundred and twenty pounds. Gone. So I went to her house and told her in a big shout she was a fucking thief, and told her mother and father and everyone in the street she was a fucking thief, and smashed them fucking stupid poncy horses. If I saw her I'd smash her, too, the cow.'

'*All* the money?' Kerry asked.

'Of course all,' he said. 'She got it for her architect fund, hasn't she? You know what she's like.'

'How did she know where it was? You showed her, told her?' Kerry realised she felt hurt. His safe was supposed to be private to her and him.

'Of course not. Would I show my store to a cow like that? All she thinks about – money. But she could of followed me. That's what I mean – she don't think of nothing but money. The other

159

night I told her I was going to get cash to pay her for you, so she would talk. She could of got behind me and watched. She could do it. You seen them little greedy eyes behind them pink fucking glasses? She could do it without me knowing. She's so clever, that one. She could be an architect, or anything she wanted. She's the sort who would decide she wanted *all* the money, not just this much or that much. I thought she was a fucking friend. But this was a business matter. You can't trust people in business. That's well known.' He sat crouched against the door, no seat belt on, his breathing still harsh.

'So what about it – this lot of information she's got?' Kerry asked.

'That all you think about?'

'I need her to talk to me.'

'Is that all you think about?'

'She might change her mind about talking now.'

'Why? Because she got all the money already, so why talk? Yea, it could be like that.'

'Because you've . . . well, upset her now.'

'Upset the cow? Of course I bloody upset her. Wouldn't you upset the cow if she took all your money?'

'I'm supposed to be meeting the two of you,' she said. 'Remember?'

'She won't come. She'd be scared to come – she'd be scared to see me, now she pinched it all, even if she wanted to come?'

'I'll turn up,' Kerry replied.

'Fucking useless.'

'You?'

'What?'

'Turn up?' she replied.

'What's the use?'

'Turn up, Chris.'

'How can I? I might not be here.'

'The holdall?'

'I got to get away.'

'From?'

'I got to get away.' He turned, suddenly beaming with an idea, his eyes still red from crying. He stuck out his head towards her on that long frail neck. 'Look, Kerry, can you get me more cash?

160

I mean now. Tonight. Like emergency funds. I expect it would have to be your own, personal. Or the boyfriend's. He got plenty, yes? The grub firm. But you could get it later from the police grass cash, yes? Like repay yourselves. This would be what's called "on account" like. Being a crisis.'

'What crisis?'

'Well, running, of course.'

'You ought to go home,' Kerry replied.

'I told you, I can't.' He wasn't beaming now and shook his head. 'My dad. Or could I come and stay with you? Like sleep on a settee, no bother. I got pyjamas and my own toothbrush. I wouldn't get in the way – you and the boyfriend.'

'You ought to go home,' Kerry said. 'Your parents will be anxious.'

'Do you know my dad?'

Kerry said: 'He's not going to do anything serious to you in his own house, for God's sake. He'd get caught.'

'"Anything serious". What's that mean?'

'Oh, you know.'

'He goes mad,' he said. 'He got to prove he's big because he's not. I did something terrible. Hit him with something. And – ' He stopped.

'What?'

'He's like friends with Coventry. I seen it. If Coventry tells him what's on the videos. The grassing.'

She was driving towards his street and he seemed suddenly to realise this now. He sat up and grabbed at the door handle. 'Let me out,' he yelled. 'You can't take me there. You can't, Kerry!' The yell had become a scream and he was almost weeping.

'Open my handbag,' she said. 'It's on the back seat.' She kept going towards Daniel Street.

He turned to look at her, grinning again. 'Yes? You'll lend me some, so I can go? Then down the railway station? I'll sleep there till the first train.' It was a whisper now, scared, unsure, abjectly grateful.

'Open it,' she said.

He turned and picked up the bulging bag. 'God, what's here?' he muttered. He undid the clasp and stared in. After a while, still whispering, he said: 'Mine? Christ, Kerry, *you* took it?'

161

'I...'

He kept gazing down at the cash, did not glance at her. 'I would never of thought that, Kerry. I told you where it was – but, like, in case of I was, well, deceased. I would never of thought you would of taken it. Oh, Kerry.' She thought he would cry again. His voice was shaky, feeble. 'But you're a cop, that's the thing.' He made no attempt to take the notes from her bag. He put his hand on the door handle again. 'Oh, I see – you think it's still yours, do you – because I still haven't got nothing on Coventry? Your boss told you to take it back if possible?'

'Put the money in your holdall,' she replied.

He didn't move.

'When I heard you were running I worked out a scheme,' she said.

'What scheme?'

'Put the money in your holdall.'

He began to do it. 'I can still make a run? That what you mean?'

'When you get home I want you to tell your dad you've been out and done a job. Robbed a shop. You had the bag with you for the takings, that's all. We'll hope he doesn't know about the toothbrush. Say you'd heard one of his own jobs fell through. You thought you'd better help the family funds. You did it solo. Do you understand?'

'A robbery?'

'He'll be proud of you, Chris, chip off the old block, but better. You're like a hunter home with the prey. I doubt if Coventry would tell him about the tapes.'

He was still transferring the wads. 'What shop?'

'Think of one.'

'How did I hear of it?'

'What? The shop?'

'No, how did I hear his own job fell through? I thought they was planning a job, but I didn't know it fell through. Nearly all his jobs fall through, but I didn't know this one. He don't tell me stuff like that.'

'An antiques place. Probably they talked about it in the house. Have his pals been around a lot?'

162

'Yea, now and then.'

'So, you happened to overhear, didn't you? You're not to blame, and especially you're not to blame when you turn up with seven hundred and twenty quid that he doesn't even have to tell his mates about. You were really upset when you heard the plan had collapsed,' Kerry said. 'He'll decide you're on his side after all, Chris.'

'I got to give that bastard my money?' he replied.

'You can earn more. For now, just get safe. You and Liz – you're *not* safe at present, and you especially – on the street and so bloody noticeable.'

'Poor Liz,' he replied. 'Me shouting like that. She'll get grief from her parents. She thought them horses was crap but her parents didn't.'

'They *were* crap.'

Chris said: 'My dad will give the others some. He's a bastard but he got rules. Maybe a hundred each for Jake and Oscar. Or fifty.' She put him down in Joshua Street, next to his own, and watched him walk away. She did not follow. Now and then you had to trust people, though not too often. After ten minutes she drove into Daniel Street. The front door was shut but there were lights upstairs and down in the house. From along the street, Vic's cigarette winked at her. She drove and parked in front of him. He joined her in the Cavalier.

'The boy came back,' he said.

'Great.'

He digested that. 'You knew, did you? How in God's name did you work it? Is he going to be safe?'

'I think so,' she said. 'For now.'

He kissed her as before, on her temple, not much more than a touch of his lips. 'You deserve a drink – and a bloody good meal. Look, I could cook you something at my place. Nobody there these days, nights. I'm gifted in the cookery line.'

She did think about it. 'Well, another time, Vic,' she said.

'Yes?'

'Probably.'

'Very probably?'

'Probably.'

22

When Kerry returned to the flat it was after 1 a.m. Mark had waited up for her, and she was glad to see the lights while putting her car into the yard. Those moments of special contact with Vic Othen continued to trouble her. The promise, half promise, forgettable promise, she had just given him troubled her. God, she had caught herself actually wondering about how his body would look at whatever age he was now – forty-five, fifty, older? – his legs, his chest, his cock, his gut, his arse, his arms. Was decline under way at that age: expansion, shrinkage, softening? Her mind could be very systematic, strong on check-lists. About his breath, though, she would not think. Perhaps it was tact that made him kiss only her temple. Could someone who'd been a policeman – a police*man* – for nearly thirty years still recall tact? And yet, yes, there *was* a tact to him, and not just the dandyism, either. Mind, he did call her 'Kid'.

Why had she started thinking like this, anyway? She was in a good relationship already, wasn't she – or as good as most relationships could be after three years? Mark's body certainly had not begun to signal the start of break-up, and his mind would generally do. Now, immediately, tonight, she wanted the strengths of hers and Mark's love given a bright show. It was needed. The little harmless contacts with Vic excited her a bit and scared her.

In the flat with Mark she would demand first some comfortable talk plus a drink or two: talk about *them*, not a report on the remains of the meeting at Stephen's place. He could tell her in the morning. She had had enough of work. Vic was work and only work, wasn't he?

And then, after the happy talk and drinks with Mark, there would be sweet violent sex, not too prolonged and with no après conversation but followed by blot-out sleep. Waking up, she would have it clear in her mind and the rest of her that it was Mark who filled her life and would fill her future, not Vic.

When she let herself into the flat she found Stephen Comble with him. They were drinking Burgundy and Mark poured her a glass. She flopped down on one of their tube-framed easy chairs which had come from Mark's previous place and were all right or close. Stephen said: 'This is a terrible imposition, Kerry – calling so late. But both Mark and I thought you should know what happened at this evening's gathering after you left. Unpleasant. Even tragic. I must accept it might have been an error to set up that confrontation. I felt I had to be here when the account of things was given, to defend myself, one might say.' Deep in their best armchair he smiled, but perhaps he might mean what he said.

Mark was pacing about with the bottle in his hand though all glasses were full. He must be nervy. 'Everyone well knew it was a risk, Stephen,' he said. 'Yet a risk that was eminently justifiable – a totally original notion which could have taken us forward. I'm sure Kerry thought – still thinks – that.'

'What happened?' she replied.

Stephen said: 'In my own defence, and suggesting no blame, perhaps I could mention that things might have been more balanced, Kerry, if . . . Oh, but this is pointless speculation, something one always seeks to shun.'

He meant, didn't he, that she had ruined his scenario by leaving early, wrecking the balance? 'What *did* happen?' she replied.

'One is worried about what Mrs Denton might do, Kerry,' Stephen said. 'On tonight's evidence, I am not at all sure she can be deemed in control of herself, safe. It's the main reason I thought it urgent to speak with you – as a police officer.'

'Oh, I felt she was teasing when she said she might have a knife,' Kerry replied. She sat up, shocked. 'But, look, she didn't go for him, did she? She *did* have a knife?' Kerry tried to keep jubilation from her voice. She was what Stephen called a police officer, for Christ's sake, unentitled to hope Coventry was injured, dead. The night had been tragic, according to Stephen. Where would an attack on him leave Sonia Denton, though?

Stephen said: 'As far as I know she did not have a knife. And, no, she did not go for him, as you put it. Not physically.' He drank off all his wine at a rush and held out the glass for more. Perhaps he was nervy, too.

'It was tone, mood, implication,' Mark said, as he poured. He sat down opposite Kerry.

'But Mark, love, those were all dark before I left,' she said, 'tone, mood et cetera.'

'Nobody is blaming you for what happened,' Stephen said.

'I had to go,' Kerry replied.

'You say "dark" – that things were dark before you left,' Mark said, 'and yes, they were. Or at least awkward. Mrs Denton was being...say mischievous. That was all right. But afterwards... well, worse.'

'Oh, threatening,' Stephen said.

'Yes,' Mark said. He had dressed in a suit for the meeting and so had Stephen. Although this had not been an official function it was important, a civic occasion. Stephen's briefcase lay alongside the leather armchair.

'Mrs Denton had brought what can only be called a dossier, Kerry,' he said. 'She came to malign and indict Tom – no other purpose.'

'It was embarrassing, Kerry.'

Stephen said: 'It was evil – not a word I often use.'

'Well, yes,' Mark said.

'When I say threatening, Kerry, I mean actual threats,' Stephen said.

'To do what?' she asked. 'Threats to hurt, kill, Coventry Tom?'

Stephen sat grave-faced for a moment. 'I think I'd prefer you did not refer to him as that, if you don't mind, Kerry,' he said. 'It prejudices the discussion. It's what Mrs Denton called him throughout. An attempt to win her case by slur.'

'Threats to hurt, kill Mr Thomas Ingle-Blake?' Kerry asked.

'Of course she timetabled for us the movements of her son on the day he was killed,' Stephen replied. 'She knew every step, every turn of his stolen cycle's wheel – '

'Borrowed, I think,' Kerry said.

'Well, perhaps. Anyway, knew every step and turn up to that certain moment when information fails. In many ways I felt very moved, of course. Yet there was a kind of obsessive accuracy about her descriptions. Well, I say accuracy, but one doesn't know, does one? There was an apparent obsessive *exactitude*. Not 11.30 a.m. but 11.28, like *Crimewatch*, that kind of thing. As I say, rehearsed, and intended deliberately to suggest an impending crime.'

'There *was* an impending crime,' Kerry said.

'Like an accusation, and an accusation aimed unmistakably at Tom Ingle-Blake. He offered no disagreement to any of her timings, detailing with absolute good temper his own where-abouts at each period and citing witnesses. He explained that these accounts of his movements had apparently satisfied the police. He had brought slides made from photographs which he assured us would prove he was elsewhere, though he did not actually show them. No real opportunity: Mrs Denton merely reiterated and reiterated the details she had already given us. Tom saw the state of things – I mean *her* state – and did not respond after his first contribution. He came out of this part of the evening well. Indeed out of the whole evening.'

Kerry said: 'Hardly anyone thinks Coventry – Mr Ingle-Blake – personally killed the boy, Stephen. This would probably be a job for one of his heavies, or more than one.'

Stephen twitched and smiled again. 'If I may say, Kerry, that remark displays the utter absence of anything precise about the death. It was in the hope of ending such damaging rumour that one called the meeting in my home.' He sipped his wine this time. He might feel he was winning here.

Mark said: 'And then a claim from Mrs Denton that there was evidence so far undisclosed to anyone, even to the police, which would...well, which would "settle matters".' He piled on the weight for these words, making them half comic. 'I think that when Stephen referred to the threatening nature of her attitude, he had in mind not just possible physical violence against Tom Ingle-Blake, but this verbal menace, too.'

'What evidence?' Kerry asked.

'This is evidence from a child, apparently,' Stephen said. 'She spoke of a child, a girl. This girl had been to see her lately – had finally felt obliged to talk.'

'What kind of evidence?' Kerry asked. She hoped her face showed nothing. Why was there no dead-pan course at Brams-hill?

'This girl was apparently a friend of her son,' Stephen said. 'Timothy told the girl many things and she might have seen him quite late on the day of his death. Or so Mrs Denton asked us to believe. And, of course, the suggestion was that what this child knew and would say could, yes, "settle matters" as she put it. At first she did not tell us what the child supposedly knew, but we all assumed she meant it would prove a case against Tom. She held back, teasing us again, perhaps, Kerry.'

'Did she name the girl?' she asked.

'Oh, no, certainly not,' Stephen said. 'She claimed that this might endanger the child – put her into the same situation as her son. It's what I mean by "slur".'

'It could be true – the danger to the child,' Kerry said.

'Certainly it *could* be,' Stephen replied instantly. 'It *could* be if the starting point for these suggestions were reliable. But we have only the words of an overwrought woman – perhaps justifiably overwrought, but not a source of unbiased information.'

'Oh, no, she's biased,' Kerry said. 'Against her son's killer.'

'Kerry, perhaps you'd know who this girl might be,' Mark said. 'I mentioned to Stephen that you came into contact professionally with at least one local child.'

Possibly Mark did want to help her and even help Sonia Denton by convincing Stephen that the girl existed.

'No,' she replied.

Stephen shrugged and sipped again. Sign language: it said, Of course Kerry didn't know her because there was no such girl.

'After that things grew . . . well, I'd call it frantic, Kerry,' Mark said.

'Evil,' Stephen remarked.

'She informed us she had been in touch with the Press – with "several London reporters" were her words,' Mark said. 'They had approached her. Apparently an investigation into child informants.'

'This at least is credible,' Stephen said. 'Unsuccessful alone, the journalist has sent for reinforcements, apparently. Kerry, you can see the sort of terrible damage this could do to the city, and certain individuals. These papers know how to blacken people and places without actually stepping into libel.'

168

'She threatened that they would name names, Kerry,' Mark said.

'Her words were that even if the police couldn't or wouldn't get "Coventry Tom" the Press would slice him into little bits. Those actual words – said with a laugh that I think it's fair to call unhealthy. Would you say unhealthy, Mark?'

'Not pleasant, certainly,' Mark replied.

'She's *so* desperate,' Kerry said.

'Believe me, I am not unsympathetic,' Stephen replied at once. 'She has suffered and is suffering. But...well, I'm afraid things became even nastier after this. And at the same time vague, undefined – no dates or times now.'

'Involving not so much Tom as Julia, his wife,' Mark said.

'I'm afraid so.' Stephen paused, shaping his thoughts, picking phrases. 'Kerry, as far as we could make out – and Mark and I have gone over her words carefully together – as far as we can make out, at the culmination of her performance she was screaming accusations of impropriety between Julia and this boy, Timothy Denton: sexual impropriety over a period of months and discovered by Tom Ingle-Blake.'

Kerry felt dazed. 'What?' she said. 'You're telling me Tim was killed by Coventry out of sexual jealousy – a boy of thirteen?'

'I most certainly am *not* telling you that,' Stephen replied. 'We're telling you that's what Mrs Denton said, seemed to say. I realise it's hard to credit.'

'He was killed for grassing,' she said. 'Or because Coventry believed he was grassing, might grass. He's got an empire to keep.'

'I think we'd agreed Tom should be called by his proper name, Kerry,' Stephen replied.

'Sorry, it's difficult,' she said.

Mark hurriedly took up the talk: 'Stephen and I would both admit, I think, that there are ambiguities in what Mrs Denton said. Vaguenesses, as Stephen mentioned at the outset. Nonetheless, we...But in any case you can make your own judgement, fortunately. Stephen thought it would be wise to record the meeting from beginning to end, you see. No need to bore you with the whole thing, Kerry, but do you mind if we play this extract?'

169

Stephen, leaning over to the briefcase and fiddling with its clasp, said: 'I don't want this to be regarded as some sinister procedure on my part, Kerry. Not bugging. I would have told people when the meeting closed that we were all on tape, and would have offered them copies. It was intended only as a reliable record on which we might have built understanding. I don't know whether, as things turned out, I'll be able to make that offer now. Parts of the tape are altogether too hurtful, too malignant.'

'Will you listen, Kerry?' Mark asked. He sounded half ashamed.

'Of course. It could mean something.'

'Thank you,' Stephen said. 'Yes, it could mean something, though what it could mean is unclear.' He brought a recorder from his briefcase, put it on the floor and switched on. The tape began in the middle of a sentence just before what they wanted her to hear. Sonia Denton was speaking:

'...and perhaps you can imagine what a tabloid newspaper would make of all that. Plus there's more. We haven't even reached the centre of this tale yet. But you have a right to hear, those of you who don't already know it. I'm talking about how Mrs Ingle-Blake started taking an interest in Timothy. Yes, Mrs Ingle-Blake. Tim's over at their place supposed to be doing odd jobs and messages for Coventry now and then and, of course, you'll all say it was stupid of me to let him go there at all, given the character of some of Coventry's businesses. All right, I can see I was wrong now. Yes. Careless. Tim needed a part-time job and Coventry was the only one offering. But then things change and Julia begins telling my Tim he makes her think of the son she might have had herself. Tim spoke to me about that, and it seemed all right if it helped her. It even seemed sad. I didn't mind. He didn't mind. But maybe it was a good thing her son didn't grow up if she was going to start treating him the way she behaved with Tim.'

Stephen was right and her voice did go into a scream here.

'This begins with a fondness, an embrace or two, OK, OK, motherly, but then turns into something else, something not right at all, something sickening. And repeated. He didn't tell me about this, of course. But he did tell a friend. That friend is the girl I've mentioned – boasting to her, I expect – and eventually she told me. She considered it her duty then. She's that sort. She said Tim thought it was all a bit of *a laugh. Perhaps he even enjoyed it, I don't know. Flattered? Boys growing up – why not? This rich old bird opening up to him. He kept going there, anyway, didn't he, Julia, didn't he, Coventry? The girl said Tim told her about it months ago. And you, Coventry, saw it and put up with it for a while and then decided it had to be stopped. You thought you were losing your missus to a kid.'*

On the tape a man shouted, *'This is insane...'* It might have been Coventry, it could have been Stephen or Mark. The sound was too far back for identification and there seemed to be a bit of all-round hubbub. Kerry listened hard in case the cry was repeated or in case Julia Ingle-Blake said something. She would have hated to pick the voice as Mark's. In fact, the tape ran more or less silent for a couple of minutes. Then Stephen, undoubtedly Stephen, could be heard stating simply that the meeting was closed.

'What else could one do?' he asked now, putting the recorder away. 'Julia walked out just before the end of Mrs Denton's outburst and Tom followed her. I could not expect them to deal with such – such a...well, such an obscene and absurd charge. Even to deny it would have conferred a status it did not merit. People dispersed. As far as I know, nothing more was said between Mrs Denton and the Ingle-Blakes, not in the house or outside. I believe everyone was in shock, everyone except Mrs Denton, perhaps. Her aim had been injury and disruption, and she had achieved them. Probably I had been naïve not to expect that. This could be a dangerous woman, dangerous to both Tom and Julia. In her current state, it is conceivable that Mrs Denton genuinely believes what she said about Julia.'

'The little girl could be in peril, too,' Kerry said.

Stephen nodded with generosity: 'Let's suppose momentarily that this child is not an invention of Mrs Denton, created to aid in her havoc, in which case, yes, there might be a case for saying she is at hazard, also.'

'Did Julia say nothing?' Kerry asked.

'Absolutely not,' Stephen said.

'How did she react? Her face when these accusations were made?'

Stephen said: 'I was looking towards the speaker, Mrs Denton. But Julia would be horrified, I should think. She left almost as soon as Mrs Denton began to speak of this...this supposed relationship.'

'When she moved out you must have glanced at her,' Kerry said. 'How did she seem?'

'Well, she *was* leaving, wasn't she?' Stephen said. 'I took that to mean she was intolerably offended. She looked...she looked dignified, regardless.' He stood up with the briefcase. 'I'm going to leave you and Mark now. Kerry, you will wish to think over these developments and act as you see fit. One is an amateur in such things and perhaps tonight's meeting has convinced me even more of that. And yet I cannot regret it. We have been alerted.'

When he had gone, Kerry shared the rest of the wine between them. She said: 'How's he getting back? I didn't see his car.'

'I brought him. He'll walk.'

'At this hour and carrying a briefcase? It's across prime muggers' country.'

'Stephen won't accept that such areas exist in this town.'

'Oh, well, they'd only get a loud tape,' she replied. 'Sellable to the tabloids, though.'

'Do you believe it – what Mrs Denton said about Julia?'

'What do *you* think?' Kerry replied.

'You know this girl she spoke of, do you? You can ask her.'

'I might be able to ask her,' Kerry said.

'Why only might?'

'Will she stay alive? In some ways Sonia Denton is wonderful. In some ways she's all dangers in one and loads them on to everybody.'

'Her tale about the relationship is mad, you think?' Mark asked.

'Yes, it might be mad, I suppose. Or it might be what Stephen suggested, deliberately brutal – "evil".'

'But why would she do this?'

'To hurt. Her mission was to hurt, wasn't it? She doesn't believe we can touch Coventry. She's correct? So, she handles things herself. Hurt him, hurt his wife. Two wounds for the price of one.'

'Stephen is right, then?' Mark asked.

172

'Oh, Stephen might get the small stuff right. It's only on the major bit that he loves his awful blindess.'

'Which major bit?'

'Coventry, of course. Stephen still believes in him.' Kerry yawned. 'Five minutes' talk about nice generalities and then I want you to undress and strut about a bit before you go to bed so I can look at your body.'

'And you?' he said.

'Mine's not important. I'm not taking my clothes off, anyway. I'd better have a saunter up by the little girl's house. Coventry might know – I mean *really* know – might know Mrs Denton had it right after all, you see.'

'And Stephen could be wrong, even on that?'

'Of course he could be wrong. He's the sort who doesn't want to believe in mugging on his home ground, and most likely doesn't believe in sex abuse, either. There are folk like that, apparently hard-nosed business people included. They crave rectitude, order. They expect cleanliness and make themselves see it despite the fact that all that's around them is dirt. Stephen expects cleanliness even in the so-called Thomas Ingle-Blake.'

Mark said: 'I'm damned well not stripping for you if you're going out.'

'It will give me something to think about in the long emptiness of the night. Emptiness, I hope.'

23

Will Mallard said: 'Show me a lad who puts his family first and I'll show you a *great* family, a *strong* family, a *happy* family.'

'Right,' Jake Lowe replied.

'The essence,' Oscar said.

'It transforms everything,' Will said. 'Who wants a dogsbody job with a lout like Coventry Tom when there's a lad like my Chris around?'

'Right,' Jake Lowe replied.

'I really love to hear you say it, Will,' Petra cried, clapping her hands in front of her face. 'Flee wages! Oh, flee them, flee, flee.'

'Not to run down what Helen did for us, fixing things with Coventry,' Will said. 'I don't want Helen to feel slighted.'

'Not at all, Will,' she replied. And it was true. To look at him, joyful and vibrant under the unstained head bandage, thrilled her. She felt how Will seemed to feel – as if she and he had escaped something that might have degraded both, degraded them all. She knew the happiness she saw in Will was real, not just a fruit of his concussion. Her own happiness soared with it: she would never have to sleep with Coventry as part of any deal, or even pretend to Coventry that she might consider sleeping with him. Chris had saved her, saved them all, the furtive, lying little angel.

Will touched the head dressing with what seemed like fondness. 'I got this from Chris.' Then he touched the stack of notes on the living-room table with all-out fondness: 'And I got this.'

'Right,' Jake Lowe replied.

'I needed both. Absolutely,' Will said. 'I attacked Helen just because she had spoken to Coventry – spoken to him trying to help us. Stupid.'

'Bandage is so *you*, Will,' Lesley said. 'I've never seen anyone wounds suit better.'

'This boy stopped me from hurting Helen in my stupid rage, you know. I mean *really* hurting.'

'Maybe stopped *me* from hurting *you*,' Helen said. 'I mean killing.'

Will nodded. 'It's as I said, this boy is a family boy. He holds things together.'

'Well, *we're* all together again and this is so great, oh, yes, yes, yes,' Petra said. 'We have more meetings than the fucking UN, you ask me, but great all the same! Chris is a boy with true pluck and the great thing about it is that this pluck will spread to all of us.'

Will said: 'Yes, indeed, Petra, pluck is what he instructs us in, pluck and get-up-and-go.' He glanced at the funds.

174

'When Chris came in very late with this money I cried,' he replied.

'Understandable,' Oscar said.

'This weeping wasn't pain from my skull or hysteria through the blow,' Will said, 'this was – this was a mixture of joy at what my boy could do, and shame that he had to do it. Those tears that soaked my face were asking a question. They were asking who was the breadwinner in this house now. This lad, Chris, had become the breadwinner. I felt pride in him. And I felt disgust with myself that this should be necessary.'

Will looked as if he might cry again. She did not want him crying. She wanted him ballsy, recuperated, full of shit.

Oscar said: 'You're damn hard on yourself, Will. What you're describing is Nature, that's all. Youngsters grow up. They want to be the main part of things. Think of that boy Martin Amis. He didn't stay home reading his dad's books. He sat down and wrote a couple himself, and longer than his father's, I heard.'

Will said: 'Disgust, first, because I was lying on the bed, injured and useless, owing to an injury I definitely deserved. And disgust, second, because a job had slipped away from us – *another*. Had slipped away and caused my son to turn tradesman.'

'You done dead right to call it off,' Jake said. 'I see it now. Our luck was we got good information on that job, and that information said the police was there waiting, and I expect are still there waiting. Not even you can take on a team like that, Will. All right, this information come in a way you did not like, I mean Coventry speaking to your wife in kind of secret – no man's going to like his woman having close conversations with someone like Coventry – but it was good information all the same, Will.' His drooping face got a hold on itself and turned into one of his big grins. Now and then Helen could see why Petra might find him all right for a while. He was too thick to be always a pain.

'Seven hundred and twenty here,' Will replied, touching the notes again. 'Split three ways that's two hundred and forty, and so useful.'

175

Oscar said: 'Oh, but he's *your* boy, Will. I'm going to insist you should take a bigger – '

'Chris would not want that,' Will said. 'I know it. He wouldn't, would he, Helen?'

'Never,' Helen replied.

'I want all of us to get inspiration from my boy,' Will said, 'and this is another reason for keeping things equal. When he pulled that money from his holdall – I mean, he was so sure of a result he took a fucking holdall with him! – this is determination, this is "Be prepared" – I see this money and hear how he got it – a shop – I see this money and I think, This boy is great, this boy I never knew the worth of, and the weeping starts. But I'm also thinking, This boy must be thanked in the way he would understand better than any other way, and that is I have to start – we have to start – start right away with successful work of our own. On our fucking own, not employees. I say immediately for two reasons. First, I want him to see our response and recognise it is that, a response, and something he helped us make. And, second, it's a good time to make a start when half the Robbery Squad is tied up on ambush at Sid Waters' store room, where we're not sodding going.'

'Right,' Jake replied with a hoot. 'I love that way you got of setting things out, Will – first, second. This is organisation. This is leadership.'

'Which shop was it your boy burgled, Will?' Oscar asked.

'You want to do it next, do you?' Will replied.

They all had a giggle, Oscar included. 'Curiosity, that's all,' he said.

'This boy's a professional,' Will said, 'taking a holdall with him and so on. Is he going to tell us location – even his father and mother?'

Oscar said: 'This was money left in the till at night or did he have to do a safe? Can he do safes? Yes, I suppose some of them get sloppy and do leave cash in the till. He's bloody bright to know where.'

'Perhaps he had an inside tip,' Lesley said, 'like in the antiques. He might have a network.'

'He was bright enough for us to think he'd done a runner,' Will said. 'When Helen saw the holdall gone she thought Chris must have quit. It would have been reasonable, after the strife we'd had. She was out looking for him.'

'*Oh, where is my wandering boy tonight?*' Helen sang. 'Now we know. Shopping!'

'You'd think he would hate me for going for his mother, going for his mother about nothing, just dirty suspicion. You'd think he would be scared to face me, after he'd banged my head in. So, yes, he might have decided to disappear. Instead, he's using his mind, *and* he's using his good feelings. He's saying to himself, *No cash flow at home for the moment. It's making dad and mum edgy. Better do something.*'

'Terrific, terrific, terrific,' Petra said. She moved her legs quickly in a kind of short step running action, although she was sitting down.

Will said: 'So, for quick action, and it's got to be quick to maximise, I thought maybe turn back to one of those projects we dropped because some special difficulty came up at the time. We want something where all the research and preparation are done, and where that one snag has gone.'

'Right,' Jake replied.

'For instance, the Intradome,' Will said. 'We were bothered about road works on the escape route. Finished.'

'I always liked that one,' Oscar replied.

'Cigarettes, booze, computers, TVs, videos, cameras,' Will said.

'We can use the van,' Oscar said.

'Absolutely,' Will said.

Helen could have asked as she had asked about the antiques, how they would sell stuff like that, especially recognisable stuff like that, such as numbered computers and top class cameras. But she didn't. She wanted this euphoria. She wanted Will to be on top again. She wanted the freedom from Coventry, wanted it even if this meant risk for Chris. And of course it meant risk for Chris. The whole deal had been about Chris. She had to gamble again. She would have to make sure the boy was looked after. The idea pleased her, as if he were a baby once more, not a nearly grown-up grass pretending to be a robber. One priority was to choke off any more Oscar-type questions about where the money came from.

177

24

Chris said: 'Maybe she won't come. She could be upset, I got to admit that. I mean, them horses. Smashing them horses like that. She could be into the environment and all that for when she's an architect, and smashing them horses would most likely right piss her off, even china horses. There are people who go around slashing horses in fields, don't ask me why. She could be thinking of that. She's deep. And the windows. And shouting in her street she was a thief. The neighbours. Her parents would be on to her about that and the horses. You should of told me *you* had the money and then I would not of blamed her.'

'No time to,' Kerry said. 'I'll drive around the block once or twice more.' They were outside the Rex Centre shopping complex, vast, glassy and twinkling. She felt reasonably secure with Chris here, but did not like waiting anywhere for long in the Cavalier when he was aboard. Chris said he had better hang on, in case she turned up and disappeared again, thinking they had failed or gone. But Kerry was not happy about that, either. She said stay in the car.

'My dad loves me now,' he said when they were moving.

'I'm really glad.'

'You were right. I don't think he ever heard about them videos. Where are they?'

'Gone. And the knife.'

'And the knife? That could of been evidence, couldn't it? But if you say so...Well, my dad *and* my mum love me now but my mum always loved me and now my dad loves me as well and I know he been telling his mates how great I am because of the money. Like I'm one of the family. That's you, Kerry – your idea, so thanks, even though you should of told me you had it.'

'I should think he always loved you, Chris. Some dads don't like making a fuss of their sons, but I'm sure he always loved you. Now, you've come along and helped him. So he can't hide it any more. *You're* one of his mates now.'

'Because of the money – well, not just because of the money, but because of the way he thinks I got it, this really gave him a big buck-up even though his head got a hammering, and now my dad and his mates are going to – '

'Don't tell me about that,' Kerry said.

'No, right. But mum said he's like different – better. Like he used to be. Like younger again. And she's different as well. She's happy. She's like that – she gets happy when he's happy.'

'Marriage,' Kerry said.

'You're not.'

'I might be one day.'

'To the one you're shacked up with?'

'Of course. Who else?'

'Is he the right one?' Chris asked.

'Of course. Who else?'

'Well, he got quite a job, I got to admit it. But don't you ever think about someone in a cop job?'

Did she? Now and then. Or oftener.

'My dad can be a right prick but deep down he got something. I care about if he loves me.'

'Of course you do.' They were into the morning traffic of the one-way system. It would take them about ten minutes to do the circle. Kerry half wished now she had left Chris there, to make sure Liz did not bolt. But she felt glad, too, that he was in the car and telling her about his father. It was so open and warm. Everyone said a boy needed a father, and now he had one. He'd bought one? Maybe that was not fair, not even about Will Mallard. He would have been impressed by the boy, touched. As Chris said, not just the money. This was a bond.

And Kerry had to make sure things stayed like that for Chris. Could she? She saw one huge danger, of course. The reporter, Highton, or one of his cronies would probably call at Daniel Street before long, hunting Chris, and asking Will and Helen whether they knew their son was a police informant and, if not or if so, did they object? That was the journalists' crusading purpose and the grand mission of their paper. They were here to reveal all. Suddenly, Will would know where the money had really come from. God, he'd turn feral. He would be worse because for that short while Chris had pleased him so much.

179

And for that short while he had also fooled Will. Chris would be in peril at home, as well as from Coventry Tom. Kerry decided now as they crept around the system that she would have to take that arrangement with Highton, if it was still on offer: the deal that as long as she and the two children fed him their story he would keep it nameless, traceless. She knew his hotel. She would get to him fast. Apparently more than one reporter had been to see Sonia, though. Did that mean things were out of Highton's hands, as he had threatened? Would his paper spill the lot – their noble free speech duty?

'I might want you and Liz to help write a newspaper article,' she said. 'Help a journalist I know. Don't laugh when you see his clothes.'

At first Chris obviously liked the sound of that. This was importance. 'What article? What about?'

'Just things in general.'

'What things?'

'Things around the town. This is a journalist from London.'

Chris's excitement began to die and his bright brain and sharp memory did their bits. 'About grassing?' he said. 'I seen some of that in the papers already – about underage grasses. That what he wants? I bet that's what the bugger wants.'

'Some of that,' she said. 'We'll be careful. I'll tell him what he can write.'

'*You'll* tell him? They're not like that, people from London newspapers. They write what they like. They don't give a shit. Think of Fergie.'

'It's agreed,' she replied.

'You already talked to some reporter? About me?'

'I told him nothing. But he knew some stuff from elsewhere.'

'What elsewhere?' he said.

'They don't tell things like that.'

'You sure not from you, Kerry? God, Kerry if – '

'Not from me.'

'What kind of things did he know?'

'General things.'

'You're fucking lying, aren't you, you fucking cop?' he screamed. For the reporter and the article there was only hate

180

left now. 'Police and Press. They get together. It's famed. He got my name? He got Liz's name?'

'We have to keep certain things out of the article. That's what I mean when I say there's an arrangement.'

'Here she is,' Chris replied.

Among a crowd outside the Rex, Liz stood looking burly and patient. She had left her glasses off today and without them her face seemed crumpled, older, weaker. She would not be that, though – weaker. Kerry drew up but Liz did not get in at once. Instead, she stared at Chris in the back. 'I don't come if that shit's with you,' she said. 'I'll stay and go to see *101 Dalmatians* in the Centre cinema.'

'I'll explain what went wrong,' Kerry replied.

'I know what went wrong. I was there,' Liz said. She had on a long black velveteen top coat that gave her some age, too.

'I had his money,' Kerry replied. 'He thought *you* did.'

'I had a fee,' she said.

'He thought all the tree money.'

'It was a cock-up, Liz. I'm sorry,' Chris said. 'I was scared you wouldn't even come today. I would not of blamed you.'

'If I've had a fee I'll do what the fee is for,' she said. 'That's obvious.'

'I don't like hanging about here,' Kerry told her.

Liz moved her head back and away, like one of those proud horses before the stoning. 'All right, if it was a mistake, I'll come,' she replied. 'But, listen, I – '

'And like you said, you've had the fucking fee,' Chris said.

Liz climbed in beside Kerry. The car moved away again.

'I thought you could of followed me when I was doing your fee,' Chris said.

Liz worked at this. 'You mean the money I had from your tree was your money, not from Kerry? You told me it had been placed there especially for me. This is not an official fee at all? It comes out of your private store?'

God, Liz sounded bitter, as though she had been caught in some unprofessional act. She might clam. Kerry said: 'Oh, yes, it's official. Your fee was done by a loan from Chris, which, of course, I've since repaid in full. This was a routine business transaction, Liz.'

181

'So why have you got his money now, his tree money?'

'I had a tip someone had found out about the tree.'

'What someone?'

'A matter of getting there first,' Kerry said, 'before it was pinched.'

'Where is it now?'

'A bank deposit box.'

'It should be invested. Interest – to help towards his pet shop.'

'Yes, perhaps.'

Liz said: 'There's other rubbish ornaments in the house you could have had a go at, besides the horses, Chris.'

'Well, I'll come back.'

Kerry drove them to the supermarket car-park where she sometimes took Chris. It was a day for contact with the retail commerce world. They were part of it. She liked all the movement around these places, the gang of people – not just because it seemed easy to stay obscure in the crowd, but she could see and feel basic, harmless life went on, no matter what she was hearing in the car. For a minute or two you could believe here among the high-packed trolleys that life was a simple, alimentary progress from eating and drinking to toilet rolls, not about the slaughter of a child and the agonies and ramblings of his mother. Or not ramblings.

'Do I talk while he's here?' Liz asked.

'I think so,' Kerry said.

'What? Why not? We're a team, Liz,' Chris said. 'I brought you into this team and don't you fucking forget it.'

Liz flicked at her frizzed dark hair. 'I don't think he'll understand about this sort of thing, that's all, Kerry,' she replied. 'This is motherhood.'

'I've heard of that,' Chris said. 'It goes right back.'

'Mrs Ingle-Blake,' Liz replied. 'In a way it's really nice. And sad.'

'She's got no children. Is that what you mean?' Kerry asked.

'Yes, motherhood. It's serious,' Liz said.

'Well, yes,' Kerry replied.

'I don't want any recording of this,' Liz said. She had a good look around the car – dashboard, glove compartment, door

182

pockets. 'Can you lie out straighter on the seat?' she asked Kerry. It was just as eerie when Liz searched her as when Chris did, maybe more. 'No offence,' Liz said.

'I don't know what the shoppers would make of it,' Kerry replied. She sat up again.

Liz said: 'When I saw Tim that afternoon, he's laughing and laughing, but he's scared. He's on his way to Coventry's place, supposed to be to work – odd jobs and that. But, really, it's because Mrs Ingle-Blake wants him to be...well, in the house as often as he can make it. She wants him to be like her son. That's what he said, "like her son". He's laughing. He said she wanted to kind of adopt him, you know, talked to him about that, so she could give him a better life, because his mother is single parent and not much money. Tim said she hates Coventry – the dirty life he leads and having it off in London with all sorts, even royalty, so she's worried about Aids and so on. So she wants to go off and live somewhere else in the town, so Tim could live with her most of the time but still go and see his mother. Also she hates Coventry because he had such a dirty life they would never let her adopt properly before. So, she wants to be away from him and with Tim, for most of the time, anyway. She would be a single parent, too, of course, but she's got money – she would get money from Coventry by saying she would start talking about his firms all round if he didn't cough. This what she was always on about to Tim.'

'And Tim – did he want this?' Kerry asked.

'Of course not. That's why he's laughing. It sounds so crazy to him. He keeps going up there because of the pay and she won't let Coventry sack him, obviously, but he's got a mother and he wants to be with her not with Mrs Coventry. So, why he's also scared. She's getting all frantic because he doesn't want it, and Coventry is dead against it obviously. How would it look if she's living in the town but not with Coventry and with somebody else's kid? This would be what's known as a scandal. Coventry thinks he's going to get a gong one of these days – I mean knighthood, something like that, for works for charity et cetera. Why else is he doing it and giving money away – the lifeboat, all that? That's not going to come if his wife ditches him and is still around in the same town acting like the mother of someone else's boy. They do a real look into people who'll be knights and so on, even if some turds still get through.'

Chris snarled: 'You telling Kerry Mrs Ingle-Blake killed Tim because he wouldn't have it? He wouldn't say yes to being her little boy?'

Liz said: 'See what I mean, Kerry. He's never going to understand such topics, women's topics. Anyway, I don't know if it was her. She's weird, isn't she? All I'm telling you is what he told me that day. A few hours later he's dead.'

Kerry said: 'A sex side?'

Chris bellowed: 'What the fuck you mean, Kerry? He's thirteen. This is a woman who's – she got to be over forty.'

Liz said: 'So? Grow up, kid, will you? *You've* got a dick, haven't you? You get hard-ons, don't you? You're thirteen.'

'Sex?' Kerry asked.

'He didn't say sex. No, just motherhood. It gets some women, I heard. That age.'

'Sex gets them, too,' Kerry said.

'No, he would have said,' Liz replied.

'You're disgusting, Kerry.'

'You've been around to Mrs Denton and told her about this,' Kerry said.

'Yes,' Liz replied. 'I wanted to. Eventually. It seemed right. She told you?'

'You told her there'd been a sexual side?' Kerry asked.

'No. Motherhood. She said sex? She's a bit, well, strained ... and she wants to do damage.'

'A sex side,' Chris said. 'That all you think about, Kerry?'

'Take us back now, will you?' Liz said.

Kerry started the engine. 'Look, are you holding back confirmation of the sex angle for a second fee, later, Liz? Instalments.'

'I'd like to go home now,' Liz replied. 'The Insurance say my mother can buy new ornaments straight away. I want to go to the shops with her so we don't end up with more shit.'

184

25

CHILD INFORMANTS *(Charles Highton's exclusive report continues from page 1)*

where a child grass earns hundreds of pounds per 'tip' from one detective. As is usual in this type of arrangement, the child's parents have not been told of their son's role. Politicians, youth organisations and church officials have expressed alarm at the secret employment of youngsters as informants. They point out that the Police and Criminal Evidence Act (PACE) lays down that when major interviews take place involving police and a child an adult should be present.

But police say that, if the parents were told, a child grass might be forbidden to operate, because of the widespread hostility to informing. Where a parent is himself or herself a lawbreaker the child's life might be in danger if the grassing became known.

Names have been changed or a code letter used in the case which follows, to protect the children and adults involved.

Detective Sergeant A runs a 13-year-old boy informant called Jason. His father is a minor league burglar who usually works with two other men. Slim and with close-cut dark hair, the boy looks like any other schoolboy of his age in his uniform of dark trousers, white shirt and dark tie. But in fact he admits he spends most of his time away from school looking for material to earn him money from Det. Sgt. A.

The detective stresses that no information from Jason about his father is ever passed and would be refused even if it were offered. 'It would be disgusting to use a child to inform on his dad,' Det. Sgt. A said, 'and would, in any case, make the boy's safety very questionable. It would be the very worst thing for a father of that sort to find about his son – that he helps the police.'

Det. Sgt. A uses the boy mainly in an attempt to build up a case against a prominent local businessman who, despite heading several successful and legitimate firms, is also suspected of large-scale drugs dealing and possible illegal arms sales. He might also be involved in *the death of another teenage boy, a friend of Jason, who was found murdered two months ago. Police have so far failed to catch the killer.*

Det. Sgt. A says: 'Jason is keen to help us on this search for the murderer of his friend. He is determined to look for evidence which might be of use to us. He is accepted among his peers and would hear things around the youth areas of the city which might never come direct to us.'

Jason, a slightly built, thin-faced boy with grey eyes, was reluctant to speak to the Press but said: 'I think the man who killed my friend is getting away with it because he is such an important man in the town. People cannot believe he would kill a child. This man is so important he knows royal people. The police cannot get anywhere on this case so far. I want to help them. I do not think there is anything wrong with giving information when my friend has been murdered.'

Jason says that all the money he gets from Det. Sgt. A he is saving to help him with his career when he grows up. He is believed to receive between £200 and £300 for each good piece of information and might have piled up by now £700–£1000. He has a special hiding place for the money away from where he lives.

He has lately recruited another informant for Det. Sgt. A, a girl called Barbara of his own age. She has also been paid. Plumpish and with glasses, Barbara is known to have seen the murdered boy late on the day he was killed and talked to him. She said: 'He told me things which I now realise might help the police in the inquiries, which is why I agreed to meet Det. Sgt. A with Jason. I do not think someone should be able to get away with killing a boy just because he has a big house and is rich and knows royalty.'

Det. Sgt. A said: 'I know there is some uneasiness about the use of child grasses, but it would be tragic if this source of information were shut off. We do everything we can to protect a child who has helped us, though discreetly so as not to pin-point the young informant. Sometimes their information is wrong, but sometimes it is very good. This is true of what we get from all informants, adult or child.

'We are not certain why the friend of Jason was murdered. He was not an informant for me. I would not know, of course, whether he was employed by another detective. That is a very personal, confidential matter. This boy might have been killed for other reasons. We are still investigating.'

Child protection groups and some politicians fear that underage informants are put at acute risk by their activities, especially children who are members of gangs. They also object that if the children are paid they might lie in order to earn more.

Police try to play down the risk element. Det. Sgt. A says: 'A child informant could easily explain the possession of a large amount of money by saying it came from a robbery. This would be believed and would, in fact, bring the child increased status and safety.'

But the Association of Chief Police Officers is so anxious about the situation that it is rushing to draw up special guidelines to cover the handling of child informants.

Additional reporting by Blake Wint and Rosemary Inverness-Chape.

26

When Will had left on the Intradome job, Helen decided she did not want to wait around the house fretting over his chances of doing something right this time and drove out to Coventry Tom's place. She thought she should tell him to his face that all deals were off. It would give her pleasure. And it would give her special pleasure to think – to feel – he had no sex hold on her now.

But most of all she wanted to tell him that he had better not think of any move against Chris. The deals were off, but that did not mean he could turn savage in self-protection. She had with her a cutting of that newspaper report about child grassing, in case he had not seen it. She would point out to him that although he had not been named, the reporters obviously knew who he was and who 'Jason' and 'Barbara' were. If Chris were hurt or worse there would be such Press pressure on the police that they would have to do something, even against the important businessman who knew the royals.

She drove up the lane to Coventry's cottages, parked and knocked on the big, genuine timber door. There were three cars in the yard, so Coventry and Julia ought to be in. Julia answered. She was wearing a neat suede suit over a velvety tan blouse. 'Well, I'll expect you'll want Thomas,' she said. 'He's here.'

She led Helen down the wide hall to another genuine wood door, partly open. Julia gave it a push. It was not the room where Helen had talked to Coventry before but what seemed to be a study-library. Helen saw shelves filling one wall when the door went back. The books were all sorts, some in bright dust covers, some leather-bound, some paperbacks, and they looked as if they were read, not just up for display. Perhaps Coventry had sides to him that Helen would not have expected. It humanised him a little for her, and she felt a fraction of her contempt and anger falter. There were shelves and books like this in some of the houses she had lived in as a child: the houses they had when her father was on the up. She had loved those rooms. Helen thought she might have come to love books, had she been given the chance to stick at them. If this sod started talking books at her now she knew she might soften. It would be like a voice from that other slice of her life, an often happy slice, pre-Duncan and certainly pre-Will.

But in fact Helen saw soon that she would not be getting this kind of problem from Coventry. He sat, head fallen forward on to a small, possibly eighteenth-century desk speckled with blood. His country suit had stains on the shoulders. Coventry's back was towards french windows, open on to the garden. It looked to Helen as if he had been stabbed in the neck from behind, perhaps more than once, and she assumed whoever had done it must have come in quietly from outside while he was working. The rug on which his desk stood had spots of blood on it, too.

'You're cool,' Julia said, standing a little behind her. 'But, then, I suppose it's only Tom.'

'You're cool as well,' Helen replied.

'Well, it *is* only Tom,' she said. 'And I've had time to get used to it. This happened a while ago. I've been able to take a shower and generally remove traces – on myself that is. The room's going to be a different matter. Thomas really loved doing his accounts at that desk. The businesses might be lawless and rough, but the furniture put him in touch with a noble history.'

188

'Have you got rid of the weapon?' Helen asked. 'You could claim it was an intruder.'

'Do I want to claim *anything*?' she said. 'Except that I wanted him gone and he's gone. Of course, he killed Timothy because I longed to set up home with him, mother and child. I think Tom must genuinely have prized me, in his funny way. He couldn't bear the idea I might go.'

'Personally?' Helen asked.

'What?'

'He killed the boy personally?'

'Oh, yes. He'd got the alias and all those folk to swear to it, of course, but total shit. That kind of work – the death of Timothy – couldn't be deputed, you know. It wasn't really a business matter.'

'No, I see that.'

'Plus he put around some filth that I was infringing on Tim. He might have believed it. That's so like Thomas.'

'Infringing?'

'You know.'

'Where's the weapon?' Helen replied. 'I could take it away and lose it for you, if you like.'

'Could you?'

'You ought to call the police then. He's been gone for some time, has he? They'll know that. Tell them you came back and found him. They'll be so glad he's dead they might not push inquiries too hard. Also if you like, I could say I'd seen you out this afternoon at the right time. It would have to be somewhere fairly remote.'

'Quite often I go up to the field where they found Timothy. People know about this.'

'That sounds good,' Helen said.

'Tom had quite a few reasonable aspects, though they're not obvious now, I admit.'

'Could you get me the weapon, please?' Helen replied. 'I ought to leave.'

'The detail?'

'Of his death?' Helen asked. 'No, I don't think so, thank you.'

'Tom took him in the car. He told Timothy it was so he could meet a major pusher who worked with the firm. Timothy would

messenger between him and Tom, that was the yarn. The lad
was excited. This would be a big job for a child, you know. Of
course, Tom never took him there. And he knew I'd realise he
wouldn't take him there. Tom didn't laugh, or anything cruel
like that as they left – he's got consideration – but he knew I
understood. He must have got Timothy out of the car somewhere to do him. No interior mess. I don't know how he kept the
boot clean when he shifted him to the field. A lining, specially
fitted? He's adept, Tom. After all, stabbing makes a lot of blood.
Well, yes.' She nodded towards Coventry.

27

When Kerry came out from seeing Harry Bell, Vic Othen
was waiting for her and they went across the road to a booth
in the Demijohn. He bought brandies. 'Oh, he's ratty, yes, of
course he is,' Kerry said. 'They keep an ambush in place at the
antiques for God knows how long with no result, and then
Will and his people try the Intradome instead, with armament.'
She lowered her head over the plastic cup. 'Oh, God, Vic,
my little lad thinks it's *his* fault his father's dead. If he hadn't
given him the tree cash, Will would still be safe at home, a
wreck but safe. Lord, though, Will Mallard with a .38 trying to
take on the rapid response crew. He was transformed – thought
he had to be worthy of his audacious son.' Vic touched her arm
She straightened. 'So, in a way, Harry's got it right, hasn't he?
He thinks I tipped Chris about the ambush, Chris tells his
dad, his dad switches to the Intradome – which makes Chris
responsible. Chris agrees, but from different information. His
dad dead, Oscar intravenous in hospital, Jake and his girl on
the run.'

'Harry actually came out and accused you of telling the boy?'

'He didn't exactly say it. That would be some bloody charge to
make, Vic. I could have the bugger. Might even be represented
as sex discrimination. So modish.'

'But he *thinks* you told Chris?'

'He also thinks Julia Ingle-Blake did Coventry. But he can't stand that one up, either. No weapon. A decent alibi.'

'Did she?'

Kerry said: 'I expect so. Coventry kills her little boy, she kills Coventry.'

' "Her little boy" – you mean the tale around that she saw him like her dead son?'

'Along those lines. Or something more. I might have been told about the *something more* by Liz Farnes one day. She was running things like a serial – refresher fee for each episode. But she's overstayed the market. We don't want any more information now Coventry's dead. Who's interested in convicting poor Julia? Not even Harry Bell, really. God, Vic, the death of Coventry – we get the right result by the wrong means. Is that anarchy? But, no complaints. I like what I get, even if I did nothing myself to get what I like.'

'That's more or less a pinch from the March Hare, isn't it?' Vic replied. 'As you say, anarchy. I hear Mrs Mallard supplies Julia's alibi. We work in a very tight little circle, don't we?'

'Yes: Harry says my car registration was reported by a member of the public near a night-time window-breaking incident and minor disturbance, and what the hell was I up to?'

'You were and are unaware of such an incident.'

'Exactly.'

'Things will improve, Kerry.'

'Oh, Chris says he doesn't blame me.' She tried to grin.

'How could he?'

'I gave him the money and fed him the story for Will.'

'You might have saved the boy's life. Nobody could guess Will would turn mid-life intrepid because his son slips him a stack of notes.'

'Maybe *I* should have guessed it,' she replied. 'I'm a fast track kid, remember.'

'A big-headed fast track kid. I love it. The future.' Vic put his hand over hers on the table. This was the headquarters pub and not a good place for that. It was not an especially good place even to be seen drinking together in a booth. She pulled her hand back. He grinned. 'Well, they can't accuse us of rushing things,' he said.

'Oh, I don't know. There's still nobody at your place, is there?'

'Of course not.'

'I do need comforting, Vic. Go separately. Two cars. You first. Me after ten minutes. Write the address down.' She pushed her notebook and a Biro across the table to him, and let her fingers touch his, for longer this time.

He ignored the writing stuff and did not leave. After a while he withdrew his hand. 'No, Kerry,' he said, 'I don't think so. You're stressed – not thinking well. A need for comforting – poor reason to start a love affair. I wouldn't want to be just therapy.'

For a while Kerry mulled this. 'No, you're probably right,' She said.

'For now,' he said.

'Yes, for now. I'll go home. For now.'